John H. Rerick, Hugh B. Reed

The Forty-Fourth Indiana Volunteer Infantry

History of its Services in the War of the Rebellion and a Personal Record of its

Members

John H. Rerick, Hugh B. Reed

The Forty-Fourth Indiana Volunteer Infantry
History of its Services in the War of the Rebellion and a Personal Record of its Members

ISBN/EAN: 9783337118778

Printed in Europe, USA, Canada, Australia, Japan

Cover: Foto ©Andreas Hilbeck / pixelio.de

More available books at **www.hansebooks.com**

THE FORTY-FOURTH

INDIANA

VOLUNTEER INFANTRY

HISTORY OF ITS SERVICES

—IN THE—

WAR OF THE REBELLION

—AND—

A PERSONAL RECORD OF ITS MEMBERS.

BY

JOHN H. RERICK, M. D.,

SURGEON.

LAGRANGE, INDIANA:
PUBLISHED BY THE AUTHOR.
1880.

PRINTED AT

THE COURIER STEAM PRINTING HOUSE,

ANN ARBOR, MICHIGAN.

TO

THE VETERANS,

OTHER SURVIVING MEMBERS,

AND

THE FRIENDS OF THE FALLEN HEROES

OF THE REGIMENT,

WHOSE BRAVE SERVICES ARE

HEREIN RECORDED,

THIS VOLUME

IS

AFFECTIONATELY DEDICATED.

INTRODUCTION.

AT a reunion of Union soldiers at Auburn, Indiana, in September, 1879, a number of the members of the Forty-fourth Indiana Volunteer Infantry met in the public square and formed a preliminary organization for the promotion of future reunions of the Regiment. A motion offered by Lieutenant Nicholas Ensley was unanimously adopted, requesting the undersigned to prepare a history of the Regiment. It was in obedience to that request that this book was undertaken.

It is now more than eighteen years since the organization of this Regiment, and fourteen years since the day of its muster out at the expiration of the Rebellion. Although the writer was with the Regiment during every day of its service except when absent a few weeks on sick furlough, he finds that time has dimmed in his memory many incidents of a personal character, that might be of interest. He has had, therefore, to depend mainly upon his letters written during the war, the official records, and the correspondence of soldiers published at the time, for the material of the following pages.

The Forty-fourth Regiment of Indiana volunteers was but one of tens of thousands, and but one among the one hundred and sixty-two regiments organ-

ized in the State of Indiana, for the immortal work of
suppressing the gigantic and iniquitous rebellion of
1861; yet whatever it accomplished, though no greater
than that performed by many others, is worthy of permanent record, and remembrance by the government
served and saved. Especially should the posterity of
every soldier of that command take patriotic pride in
possessing historic and written proof that in their veins
flows the blood of ancestors who voluntarily left their
homes and loved ones, and upon the most terrible and
bloody battle-fields the world has ever witnessed, fought
to preserve for them the American Union and the freedom of man. If this little book should have the effect
of fostering such pride, and preserving the names and
memory of the brave and patriotic men of this command, it will, I feel assured, accomplish the purpose
for which it was requested. Shelley sang the spirit of
this work:

> "I will teach thine infant tongue
> To call upon those heroes old
> In their own language, and will mould
> Thy growing spirit in the flame
> Of Grecian lore; that by each name
> A patriot's birth-right thou mayst claim."

J. H. RERICK.

CHAPTER I.

THE first gun fired by the Rebellion against Fort Sumter awoke Northern Indiana, as it did the whole North. Before that day the subjects of this record and their friends knew not war, nor the spirit of war. With the exception of a few men scattered here and there, none had seen military service. Thousands of the middle-aged, and those entering upon manhood, had never seen a soldier in line or in uniform. The terrible struggle in the heart of the peace-loving citizen, between love of home, wife, children, and dear friends, and that patriotism aroused by insult to the national flag, was a new and painful experience. But a new day had dawned for the people and the country. Every man, and woman, and the children of discerning age, commenced to live a new life in thought, feeling and action. The hearts of mothers and wives sank in anguish, and then rebounded with patriotism, and sons, husbands and fathers sallied from every hamlet and neighborhood, voluntarily, and offered their services to the imperiled Union. Regiment after regiment was organized at Indianapolis and one or two other places in the State. But these places of rendezvous becoming insufficient, Gov. Morton, in August, 1861, ordered a camp for volunteers at Fort Wayne for the organization of the Thirtieth Regiment, placing Hugh B. Reed, of Fort Wayne, in command of the camp. Before this Regiment was complete, it becoming evident that more men would be needed, the organization of the Forty-fourth Regiment was ordered by the Governor, and the following commissions were issued for the purpose, on September 12th, 1861 : Lieutenant-Colonel, Baldwin J. Crosthwait, of Angola ; Major, Sanford J. Stoughton, of Ligonier ; Assistant Surgeon, John H. Rerick, of La-grange. Hugh B. Reed was to remain in charge of the camp. The organization of the Regiment was now actively commenced, and on October 2d, when the Thirtieth Regiment left camp for the field, the Forty-fourth took possession, with ranks nearly half filled. Before this, however, the following additional field and staff officers had been commissioned : Colonel, Hugh B. Reed, the commander of the camp, September 27th ; Adjutant, Charles Case, Fort Wayne, September 28th ; Quartermaster, George McConnell, Angola, September 28th. The skeletons of all the companies were in camp early in October, but the filling up of the ranks was not finished until in November. An account of the organization of the several companies will be found in connection with the company records. The companies were recruited by patriotic citizens in different localities, who felt it their duty to assist in suppressing the rebellion. These would prepare an enlistment agreement, circulate it among their neighbors for signatures —sometimes canvassing their respective counties—call public meetings, make patriotic speeches, awakening the people to an appreciation of the perils of the Government. When a sufficient number of volunteers had been secured for the nucleus of a company, they were called together at some convenient point in their county, and an election would then be held for company officers. Those so chosen were, we believe, in all cases, commissioned by the Governor. But there was no delay for commissions. The officers selected at once marched their men into camp, and when the ranks were not entirely full, some one or more would obtain leave of absence, to return home and continue the recruiting.

Memory recalls little of interest in camp during the two months the Regiment was recruiting and organizing, though then to soldiers and people almost every day seemed fraught with vital interest. The men in camp were generally healthy. A few cases of measles occurred in October, which infected the command, and afterward disabled many of the men temporarily, and caused the death of a number. Dr. B. S. Woodworth, an honored physician of Fort Wayne, had medical charge of the camp during the organization of the two regiments, the Thirtieth and Forty-fourth, though during the organization of the latter the Assistant Surgeon of the Regiment had immediate charge of the camp hospital, entering upon duty the first day the Regiment went into camp. The citizens of the city took an active interest in providing for the wants of the sick, and when any one became seriously ill, provision would be made for him in town, and kind and generous assistance rendered.

A little incident occurred at this time, which had an important bearing upon the discipline of the camp.

Among soldiers, the first illustration of the metal of their commander, settles many points connected with discipline and respect. A volunteer, while in the city, one day, got intoxicated, and wandering in front of Col. Reed's residence, attracted his attention. The Colonel came out and ordered him to go at once to camp. The would-be soldier replied in an insolent manner and started towards the Colonel with the evident intention of assaulting him. As soon as he came within arm's length, he met a blow from the fist of the Colonel that felled him to the earth, where he remained unconscious a little while. The Colonel ordered out his carriage, and calling Dr. Woodworth, who was near at hand, put the man in his charge and sent him to camp hospital. He was not seriously hurt. Not having, though, as yet been mustered into the service, he was promptly discharged and sent home, and so missed service in the Forty-fourth Regiment. A healthy conclusion was at once formed in the minds of the volunteers, that they had a commander whom it would be well to respect.

On November 22d, 1861, the Regiment was mustered into the United States service by Lt. H. E. Stansbury, U. S. A. The medical examinations were made by Dr. B. S. Woodworth and the assistant surgeon of the Regiment. The appearance of the volunteers, and satisfactory answers to a few general questions, were all that were required at the time, and almost all that the burning patriotism of the people would patiently hear to.

It was thought then that every man who wanted to defend his country, should have the privilege. Several men with black hair and beards, and apparently within the military limit as to age on the day of muster, became quite gray in a short time after, and before they had had an opportunity to be frightened. The young men were not behind the old men in their efforts to get into the service, and a number who had not attained the legal age made a good show of years at the muster in. The service, though, lost little, if anything, through the latter. Among them were afterwards found some of the most enduring and efficient soldiers.

The organization was completed by the appointment of William W. Martin, of Rome City, Surgeon, November 25th, and Rev. G. W. Beeks, of Fort Wayne, Chaplain, November 26th.

The Regiment in line, on dress parade, was much praised by the throngs that visited it on these occasions, and subsequently, as it marched through the city to the field, for the intelligent and splendid physical appearance of its men. Measured by the social standard, all grades of society were represented, as well as nearly all vocations; but the great mass of the Regiment were young men from the farm and shop, and all, with few exceptions, were in possession of a good common school education, whilst numbers had passed through high school grades, and some had "been to college." The officers chosen by the men in line were from their associates at home, and when these donned their shoulder straps, they felt and recognized the fact that in the ranks were left many men just as intelligent, brave and worthy as they. Nearly all were worthy of official rank, and none too good to be privates; but as all could not serve in either position, distinctions had to be made.

The field and staff officers, chosen by the Governor of the State, were also from comrades of the men in line in civil life, though more largely representative of the professions.

THE ORIGINAL ROSTER.

FIELD AND STAFF.

Colonel, Hugh B. Reed.
Lieutenant-Colonel, Baldwin J. Crosthwait.
Major, Sanford J. Stoughton.
Adjutant, Charles Case.
Quartermaster, George W. McConnell.
Chaplain, G. W. Beeks.
Surgeon, W. W. Martin.
Assistant Surgeon, John H. Rerick.

COMPANY OFFICERS.

A.　Captain, Charles F. Kinney.
　　1st Lieutenant, Elias O. Rose.
　　2d Lieutenant, Birge Smith.

B.　Captain, John Murray.
　　1st Lieutenant, John Barton.
　　2d Lieutenant, William C. Ward.

C.　Captain, L. K. Tannehill.
　　1st Lieutenant, William Story.
　　2d Lieutenant, Philip Grund,

D.　Captain, Franklin K. Cosgrove.
　　1st Lieutenant, Charles H. Wayne.
　　2d Lieutenant, J. Delta Kerr.

E.　Captain, William H. Cuppy.
　　1st Lieutenant, Isaac N. Compton.
　　2d Lieutenant, Francis McDonald.

F. Captain, George W. Merrill.
1st Lieutenant, James Colgrove.
2d Lieutenant, Thomas C. Kinmont.

G. Captain, William C. Williams.
1st Lieutenant, Henry J. Shoemaker.
2d Lieutenant, David Cary.

II. Captain, William B. Bingham.
1st Lieutenant, Joseph H. Danseur.
2d Lieutenant, Jacob Newman.

I. Captain, Albert Heath.
1st Lieutenant, Joseph C. Hodges.
2d Lieutenant, James F. Curtiss.

K. Captain, Wesley Park.
1st Lieutenant, Simeon C. Aldrich.
2d Lieutenant, John H. Wilson.

NON-COMMISSIONED STAFF.

Sergeant-Major, Samuel L. Bayless.
Hospital Steward, J. A. Banta.
Principal Musician, John R. Grubb.
Commissary Sergeant, William F. Hinkle.
Quartermaster Sergeant, William Bayless.

CHAPTER II.

THE DEPARTURE.

HARDLY had the muster-in oath of allegiance to the Government and obedience to those in command of her armies, been administered, before orders were received by Col. Reed to report his command for duty. Then came a trying hour for the citizen-soldier. It was to be his first departure from home for the field of war. The toils of march, exposures of camp, scenes of carnage, new and untried duties, the most laborious and perilous that could be presented, were immediately before him. All the endearments of the past, entwined around the home fireside, and the peaceful associations of town and neighborhood, were to be left behind, with the probabilities all against a renewal thereafter. He did not bid parents, wife, children, lovers and friends farewell because he loved war, or sought to follow it as a temporary business, or for gain. His preferences and greatest pleasures were in the peaceful pursuits now abandoned. But a monitor in his heart whispered Duty, save the Union, save it for your children, save it for all posterity, save it for freedom, save it for God. These whisperings decided the internal conflict, and he grasped his musket and knapsack at the bugle's call, fell into line ready for the command, " Forward, march."

That command came the next day, November 23d, 1861. The Regiment never made a better display of the pageantry of war than on that day, as it marched through the city to the depot. Never thereafter were all the men and officers in line at the same time. The uniform and equipment of men and officers were then unsoiled. The imposing scene was witnessed by thousands who thronged the streets. Many hearts among the throng ached to breaking, and groans of anguish were not unfrequently heard to break forth from the burdened souls of fathers, mothers and wives.

Upon reaching the public square, the Regiment was formed in hollow square, to receive a beautiful flag donated by the patriotic women of the city. The flag was presented by Hon. F. P. Randall, the Mayor, who addressed the Regiment as follows:

Address of Mayor Randall.

SOLDIERS OF THE 44TH REGIMENT—OFFICERS AND MEN:

In common with thousands of your fellow citizens, who have so nobly responded to the call of the Government, you have now laid aside for a time the character of civilians and assumed that of soldiers, and now form a part of the grand army of the North.

I congratulate the field officers of the Regiment that they have gathered around them soldiers so fine and intelligent in appearance and so manly in bearing; and I congratulate the Regiment that they have as sagacious, brave and gallant officers.

The history of the world furnishes no example like that we now see occurring around us. Five hundred thousand brave men have voluntarily left the endearments and comforts of home, to sustain the Government

of their choice, and millions will be ready to respond if
their country needs them. This is a Government in
which all participate, in which all have an equal interest, and to the support of which all should be equally
devoted. The humblest citizen, equally with the President himself, can in truth say, this is my government.
And as you are about to leave us to join the armed hosts
which have preceded you, through the kind liberality of
some of our friends residing in this city, I have the
pleasure of presenting to your Regiment these National
Colors. Banners are representatives of Nations. This,
with its thirty-four stars, represents the whole Union as
it was before treason had begun its work of destruction.
To it patriotism now looks with ardent hopes, and upon
it hang the destinies of this Nation. Glorious memories cluster around the Stars and Stripes. For more
than eighty years the people of all the States have been
proud of this emblem of our country's greatness and
power. It has protected the American citizen in all his
wanderings, however distant from home business or
pleasure may have called him ; and the mariner, as he
sailed upon the deep blue sea, bound to the farthest isles
of the ocean, whilst the American flag floated at the
mast, pursued his journey in conscious pride and
security.

But while thus honored at home and respected
abroad, traitors and rebels have banded together, and
with a united effort are now madly striving to strike it
down from its high position, to trample it in the dust
and scatter the fragments over all the land. To pre-
vent this desecration of our flag and the consequent
destruction of the Government it represents, the armies
of the North have been called into existence, and are
now marching to the field of battle.

Seven long years of toil, privation, frequent disaster
and bloody conflicts were spent by the brave men of '76

to give freedom to this land and a nationality to this flag. I believe the spirit of our ancestors still lives among us, and that the loyal and patriotic people of the present generation will nobly protect and defend what cost our fathers so much to establish. In committing this banner to your charge, I have every confidence that you will safely guard and protect it, if necessary, with life itself.

I almost envy you the privilege which you are so soon to have, in fighting in its defense ; and when you meet the enemies of our country in deadly strife,

> "'midst flame and smoke,
> And shout and groan, and saber stroke,
> And death-shots falling thick and fast,"

may some kind angel be sent to accompany this flag, to defend you from the perils incident to the battle-field, and guide you on to victory; and if in that hour anything is required beyond your love of country to stimulate you to deeds of noble daring, remember that your friends and relatives at home will share with you the glory of your victory as in some measure their own, while they will sorrow for any misfortune that may befall you as for a personal calamity.

You are making history for yourselves and for our State. Already have the gallant deeds achieved by the Indiana volunteers made a brilliant record in the history of this war. You, I know, will never dim the lustre of that record. You have cheerfully responded to the call of your country in this her hour of danger, and are now ready to join those who are fighting the battles of Freedom in Freedom's holy land.

You go to suppress this treason and put down this unprovoked rebellion, and save us from the threatened rule of traitors and despots, who in their mad ambition would with ruthless hands pull down and destroy the

2

freest and best government ever vouchsafed to man; and be assured that in this conflict the prayers and blessings of the good and righteous will accompany you, and for your success they will invoke the favor of Heaven. And when far away from friends and home—when in the camp and on the march—may this emblem of your country's honor and the Nation's sovereignty be ever present to remind you of those whose kind regards will follow you wherever duty and patriotism calls you to go.

Blessings brighten as they take their flight; and this national ensign, now that the storm-cloud dark and portentous is rolling up from the South, is dearer to all of our hearts at this moment, yes, a thousand fold dearer, than it ever was before when gilded with the sunshine of prosperity and playing with the zephyrs of peace. It speaks for itself far more eloquently than I can speak for it. Listen to its voice of patriotism. It speaks of earlier and of later struggles in the cause of freedom. It speaks of victories on the sea and on the land. It speaks of statesmen and heroes among the living and among the dead. But before all and above all other associations and memories, whether of glorious men, or of glorious deeds, or of glorious places, it speaks trumpet-tongued for the union of these States, now and forever. Let it tell the story of its birth to these gallant volunteers as they march beneath its folds by day or repose around its sentinel stars by night. Let it recall to their memories the eventful history of its origin, its cost in toil and blood. Let it rehearse to them its trials and its triumphs in peace and in war; and whatever else may happen to it or them, it will never be prostituted to the unholy purpose of revenge or depredation; it will never be surrendered to rebels, or ignominiously struck to treason.

And now, before placing it in your hands, I desire to ask a few questions, to which you will please give audible answers.

Do you solemnly promise to love this flag ?

[Yes.]

Do you promise to honor it ?

[Yes.]

Do you promise to obey it ?

[Yes.]

Do you promise to sustain and defend it, even unto death ?

[Yes.]

I, then, in this presence and before these witnesses, solemnly join you to the American Flag; and what we have now joined together let not Jeff. Davis or his minions put asunder.

" Now bless this Banner, God of Hosts, watch o'er each starry fold :
 'Tis Freedom's Standard, tried and proved, on many a field of old.
 And thou who long hast blessed us, O bless us once again,
 And crown our cause with victory, and keep this Flag from stain."

Adjutant Charles Case responded briefly, on behalf of the Regiment, pledging the Mayor, the patriotic women, and the people, that the flag received should never be dishonored, but if opportunity offered, be made more glorious by the valor of brave men.

CHAPTER III.

IN THE FIELD.—INDIANAPOLIS, EVANSVILLE, AND HENDERSON.

THE Regiment reached Indianapolis about 3 o'clock
A. M., the 24th, the next day after leaving Fort Wayne,
in the midst of a snow-storm, and for the first time went
into tents. The equipage and clothing of the command
were now completed, and on the 26th the Regiment
started, by way of the Terre Haute and Vincennes railroad, for Evansville, where the commanding officer was
ordered to report by letter to Gen. T. J. Crittenden, at
Calhoun, Kentucky.

Upon their arrival at Evansville, the Regiment was
most agreeably surprised to find a dinner in waiting, at
the market-house, an offering of respect and loyal devotion on the part of the citizens of the city. The Regiment went into camp in the eastern suburbs of the city,
and for a few days suffered no little from exposure to
the cold and unusually inclement weather. It was then
thought rather rough soldiering, but many times after
would have been accepted with feelings of much relief.
The sick list now began to increase rapidly, but mainly
as the result of measles, which was becoming prevalent
in all the companies. On the 31st the number of sick
in the Regimental Hospital had run up to thirty, with
many men sick in quarters. The Marine Hospital, a

Government institution for the benefit of the marine service, was opened for the reception of sick soldiers, and all who could not be comfortably cared for in Regimental quarters were sent there for treatment. The first death since leaving Fort Wayne occurred here, in Regimental Hospital, that of David Wert, Co. E. He died with strong confidence in the Christian faith, and was buried with military honors in the city cemetery, all the officers of the Regiment, and nearly all the soldiers, attending.

Pursuant to orders from Gen. Crittenden, the Regiment set out on its first march, December 11th, for Henderson, Kentucky, a point twelve miles distant by land, on the opposite side of the Ohio river. The march was made upon the Indiana side, and the landing opposite Henderson was reached about three o'clock in the afternoon. The Regiment crossed over in ferry boats, and then marching through the city with flying colors, went into camp in a beautiful grove in the suburbs. Kentucky, though it had at first contended for a neutral position between those attempting to sever the Union and those determined to uphold it, and had opposed the entrance upon her soil of the armies of each, had found it impossible to hold to such a silly and unpatriotic position, if such were really the intention of the leaders. Union and Rebel armies were now manœuvring for position and preparing for battle upon her soil, and thousands of her citizens had joined the armies of each side. The State Government had passed under rebel influence, and the Union soldiers felt, when touching the Kentucky shore, that they were in the enemy's country. Such were the feelings of the men of the Forty-fourth Indiana when they crossed the Ohio river at Henderson. Though the place professed loyalty, the coolness with which the command was received, and the expressed sympathy of many for the rebel cause, were so much in contrast with the enthusiastic reception accorded the command on the Indiana side, that the men felt the necessity, and the officers in command the imperative duty, of taking all the precautions obligatory in face of an enemy. Pickets were thrown out, and the Regiment kept in readiness for action.

On November 9th the Military Department of the Ohio had been formed, consisting of the States of Ohio, Michigan, Indiana, and that portion of Kentucky east of the Cumberland River and the State of Tennessee, and General Buell was placed in command on the 3d of December. General Thomas J. Crittenden was appointed commander of the Fifth Division of the Army of the Ohio, comprising the 11th, 13th, and 14th Brigades. The 13th Brigade consisted of the 31st Indiana Infantry, Col. Charles Cruft; 44th Indiana, Col. H. B. Reed; 17th Kentucky, Col. J. H. McHenry; 25th Kentucky, Col. James W. Shackleford. Colonel Cruft was assigned to the command of the Brigade.

General Crittenden's headquarters were at this time at Calhoun, upon Green River, some forty miles distant across the country. All of his regiments except the Forty-fourth were in that vicinity. The enemy had threatened an attack on his lines from Hopkinsville, and had advanced as far as Greenville, late in November, but deflected from there to Bowling Green, near

where was encamped the centre of the Army of the
Ohio, under the command of General A. M. D. McCook.
General Thomas held the left of the line, in Eastern
Kentucky, with the rebel General Zollicoffer in his
front. The Forty-fourth Indiana was alone on the
extreme right of General Buell's forces. Though, as
afterward appeared, no considerable body of the enemy
was near, there were enough rumors and alarms to keep
the command in readiness for battle, and to give to the
needed drill exercises the zest and interest that would
insure most efficiency.

There were rumors to the effect that the enemy was
marauding the country in the vicinity and gathering up
all the live stock possible, for the support of the Confederate forces. These rumors having assumed an
apparently reliable form, the Colonel concluded to send
out a force to investigate the matter, and if possible
capture the parties. On the 16th of December two
detachments of fifty men each, one under command of
Captain Kinney and the other under Captain Merrill,
Co. F, set out on their first march, in search of the
marauders. The Captains were ordered to proceed as
far as Highland Creek, eighteen miles distant, and were
to strike that stream at two points, supposed to be about
five miles apart, at the same time, and then each to
march to a point midway, expecting to find the enemy
between. Captain Kinney's detachment reached the
designated point on time, and then marched down
the stream to the place of union, but neither the
enemy nor the other detachment was found. In the
meantime Captain Heath, Co. I, and a messenger, had

come up on horseback, with orders from camp. These and the Assistant Surgeon volunteered to go in search of Captain Merrill and his detachment, and starting about nine o'clock at night, traveled until break of day, when the command was found fifteen miles distant from the other, the two roads striking the creek that much farther apart than was reported. The two detachments were then brought together, thus consuming the whole of that day. In the meantime the camp had become alarmed, and Lieutenant-Colonel Crosthwait was sent out with another detail of one hundred men to our aid. All returned in two days, without a sight of the enemy or of the hogs he was reported to be stealing.

This little ripple, the first in camp life, was known as the " Hog Expedition." The most serious result was the disability of the Lieutenant·Colonel. The exposure and toil occasioned a recurrence of chronic diarrhœa, contracted during the Mexican war. He was furloughed and went home, where he died February 20th, 1862, greatly to the grief of the command.

The remainder of the month of December was quietly spent in camp. The ravages of the measles kept up a large sick list, but otherwise the command maintained comparatively good health. About one hundred and fifty had been sent to hospital since reaching Evansville. A regimental hospital was established in an old hotel building in Henderson, of which Surgeon Martin took charge. Two patriotic women—Mrs. Burch, wife of Joseph Burch, Co. A, and Sarah Eldridge, wife of Henry Eldridge, Co. K,—under the impression that the Government would allow the employment of hospital

BALDWIN J CROSTHWAIT,
LIEUTENANT-COLONEL.

matrons, accompanied the regimental hospital up to this time, rendering much service to the sick.

The first few weeks in Kentucky were novel, even outside of the new and before untried duties of a soldier. With very few exceptions, not a member of the Regiment had trodden slave soil before. They came to it, many of them, with feelings of extreme hostility to the institution of slavery, many with feelings of indifference, and a few, possibly, with sentiments of approval. But to all, the sight of a slave at daily, unrequited toil was new. Henderson county then ranked second in the State in the number of slaves held. It was reported that there were over 4,000 slaves in the county. The following extract from a private letter, written from the camp, will be of interest in showing the position of the Government, and sentiment of the soldiers, at that time :

" A good negro hires here for from $200 to $300 a year, the hirer bearing all loss by sickness, paying doctor bills, etc. A pretty cosy way of living, that—take one of your fellow men and hire him for $200 a year, and pocket the money yourself! Negro stock, though, is down now—prices one-third lower and few sales. Not a soldier nor officer has attempted to tamper with the institution. They would be severely punished if they should. Even conversation with the slaves is prohibited. The Union men here are very tender upon this point. Should we tamper with the slaves there would soon be an uproar. It is not our mission here to steal 'niggers.' If they want to leave and can follow our trail back, they may, for all of us. We can render them no assistance in getting away, or their masters in holding them. The secessionists here would really like some of the soldiers to run off a few, that they might raise a howl. We will not accommodate them in that line; though, if some of the boys knew it would get up a fight here [for which some were just then spoiling], they would be tempted to try it. We are in the service of our country, intend to obey her laws and fight her battles, and do naught but what we are authorized to do.

"Four or five free negroes living near here were stolen a few nights ago, and taken South ; two of whom were land-holders. The rascally kidnappers went to their houses and presented an order signed, they said, by Colonel Reed, requesting them to come to camp. They started, as they supposed, for the camp, but soon after learned their mistake. One of them, a father, succeeded in making his escape, but one of his sons was taken along. The father came to the camp and offered Colonel Reed his farm and that of his son if he would rescue his boy. The Colonel could not interfere."

Such were the sentiments of even the loyal people then, and such the orders of the Government; that a commander of troops on slave soil, fighting for the union of the States attempted to be overthrown by a rebellion whose corner-stone was acknowledged to be slavery, could fight his whole command to recapture hogs stolen to feed the rebel army, but not to rescue a brother man with a dark face, stolen to serve the men in the rebel army. Is it to be wondered at that a God of Justice deferred a speedy victory to a people so imbued with the evil whose aggressions they were fighting to overcome ? But in a few days, on January 1st, 1862, many of the command witnessed in Henderson the last auction, there, of human slaves. Relief came to the slave before it did to his master.

Upon this day the Colonel received orders to report at Calhoun, with eight companies of his command, and to leave two companies at Henderson until further orders. The companies detailed to remain were Co. G, Captain Williams, and Co. K, Captain Aldrich. The sick—some sixty in all—were left in charge of the Assistant Surgeon. On the 12th of January he was ordered to place the remaining sick in care of a resident physician, and join the command at Calhoun.

The deaths in the command during 1861 were:

Francis Brooks, Co. A, at Camp Allen, Fort Wayne, of apoplexy, October 3d.

Samuel Gilbert, Co. K, at Camp Allen, supposed disease of heart (was found dead in quarters), November 6th.

W. H. Stiver, Co. E, at Recker's Hospital, Fort Wayne, of typhoid fever, December 8th.

James H. Norton, Co. G, at Marine Hospital, Evansville, of typhoid fever, December 19th.

David Werts, Co. E, at Regimental Hospital, Evansville, December 9th.

John L. Shatto, Co. K, December 15th, and William Manier, Co. D, December 23d, at Marine Hospital, Evansville, both of typhoid fever, sequela of measles.

Samuel Endsley, Co. K, December 25th, at Henderson, of pneumonia.

With respect to the services of Companies G and K at Henderson, we copy the following from articles recently published in the De Kalb County *Republican*, entitled "Life in the Ranks of the Forty-fourth Indiana Volunteers," by Sergeant Geo. W. Gordon, Co. K.:

" Following the departure of the Regiment, the battalion moved to the fair ground and guarded all the approaches to the town, and was kept almost constantly on duty until the evening of January 28th, when a courier brought orders from General Crittenden to take immediate possession of the city and secure the strongest buildings for quarters, as a hostile force was approaching. Speedily tents were struck and loaded, and the troops marched in and took possession of the court house, despite strong opposition by the rebel sheriff, who refused the keys until told that the doors would otherwise be broken open. An exciting scene followed. The rebel element swore the soldiers must be driven out, but the Unionists sided with the troops. Meetings were held, irate speeches made, and resolutions passed, but the patrols dispersed the secessionists, and the battalion stood to arms during the ensuing night, fully expecting to fight the coming enemy, aided by the rebels in the city. With morning came the Sixtieth Indiana, and two companies of Home Guards from Evansville. This reinforcement caused the enemy to abandon their design. A hotel across the street, used as rebel headquarters, was occupied, and the stars and stripes hoisted from the roof. During the morning Jacob Fink, Co. K, hearing an insulting remark about Governor Morton by a secessionist, would have shot him had not a sergeant seized his gun, and ordered the rebel to leave, which he did forthwith. The reinforcements returned February 2d to Evansville, leaving the battalion to continue unmolested the round of guard drill and other duties."

These two companies rejoined the Regiment on the Tennessee River, near Fort Henry, on the 10th of March.

The deaths at Henderson, besides those before mentioned, were : Cornelius Hinton, Co. K, January 1st,
1862, of typhoid pneumonia ; Scott Headly, Co. F,
January 4th, of same ; Thomas Parks, Co. D, January
15th, of same ; Deming Barton, Co. I, January 25th, of
consumption ; Andrew J. Hart, Co. H, February 20th,
of typhoid fever ; Phineas Cary, Co. G, February 22d,
of typhoid pneumonia ; Henry Severns, Co. K, February 27th, of diphtheria.

CHAPTER IV.

THE GREEN RIVER CAMPAIGN.

THE Colonel, with eight companies of his Regiment, who had set out on the march overland for Calhoun, after a very unpleasant tramp of four days through mud, rain and slush, reached Calhoun on the 6th of January, and went into camp, which they at once commenced to prepare for winter quarters. But this occupation was very short, as on the 15th of January General Crittenden moved his whole command, except one regiment and the sick, ten miles up Green River, to South Carrolton. Here the Regiment again went into camp. The weather during the stay at Calhoun and South Carrolton was exceedingly inclement, and the sick list was fearfully increased. The Surgeon's monthly report for January showed 86 remaining sick at last report, and 114 taken sick during the month. Of these, 5 had died, 1 had been furloughed, 7 sent to General Hospital, 103 returned to duty, leaving 84 sick on hand. These only included hospital cases. Probably three times as many more were treated in camp, and temporarily exempted from duty.

The troops moved to South Carrolton consisted of the 31st Indiana, Colonel Cruft; 43d Indiana, Colonel Steele; 44th Indiana, Colonel Reed; 42 Indiana, Colonel Jones; 11th Kentucky, Colonel Hawkins; 25th Kentucky, Colonel Shackleford; 26th Kentucky, Colonel Burbridge; —th Kentucky Cavalry, Colonel Jackson, and two battalions of artillery.

An advance of rebel forces from Bowling Green was anticipated here, and on the 25th of January the command was speedily set to work felling trees in front, and throwing up breastworks; but after two or three days of hard toil for the soldiers, the alarm subsided. On the 30th the sick were ordered to be taken to boat to be carried back to Calhoun, preparatory to the movement of the whole command back to that place. The writer went to one of the boats, and found such as were able to walk crowding on by hundreds, but none, however sick, were allowed to enter the cabin. After some words with the captain of the boat, he returned and reported to Surgeon Martin. The Doctor's indignation was aroused, as it was quickly on all occasions when the sick in his charge were heedlessly treated or insulted; and not having, as yet, learned military restraint, he seized his revolver, ordered four or five soldiers with muskets in their hands to accompany him, and the Assistant Surgeon to follow with the sick. The cabin doors opened, upon his demand, though in a somewhat damaged condition, and the floor was soon covered with the sick. The Surgeon's popularity among the soldiers was advanced materially, and he was never disturbed for the act.

The Regiment marched by land to Calhoun, February 1st, and went into camp, but to rest a few days only. Colonel Cruft was ordered to report with all the efficient men of his brigade. to General Grant, on the Tennessee River, and on the 9th boarded boats for that point. The Assistant Surgeon was again detailed to remain behind with the sick, the detail covering the care of the sick of the 25th Kentucky, also. The march to and from South Carrolton, and the inclement weather, had brought very many down, and at that early stage of the war the facilities for caring for the sick were very poor and inadequate. At Calhoun there were probably nearly a thousand sick altogether, and no general hospital provisions whatever. The sick were sheltered from the storms and cared for as well as possible, in bar-rooms, old vacant buildings, a church, a masonic hall, and scattered around in dwelling houses. There were left of the Forty-fourth Indiana, 76 sick in hospital, so called, and 61 in camp quarters. The Twenty-fifth Kentucky left 90 sick, most of them being crowded in the audience room of a church. The care of so many sick, under such circumstances, was an exceedingly hard task for one physician, and was indeed the most toilsome and responsible he had during over four years of service.

The diseases most prevalent were pneumonia and typhoid fever, and the situation and weather as unfavorable as they well could be, for their successful treatment. There died at Calhoun, during the winter of 1861–2 :

Nathan Myers, Co. E, February 7th.
Henry Delater, Co. E, February 8th.
Joseph Cairns, Co. E, February 4th.
Charles Hulbert, Co. D, February 12th.
Thomas Blackburn, Co. D, February 16th.

John Hand, Co. B, February 17th.

John H. Stealey, musician, Co. H, February 21st.

George Fish, sergeant, Co. H, Feb. 24th.

Arthur Haywood, Co. —, died at South Carrolton, January 28th.

The remaining sick were removed to the Marine Hospital at Evansville, on March 1st, and the Assistant Surgeon, with some 80 convalescents, took boat at this point to rejoin the Regiment, then in camp near Fort Henry.

CHAPTER V.

FORT DONELSON.

THE Forty-Fourth Indiana, with the other regiments of the 13th brigade, left Calhoun, Ky., as before stated, February 9th, 1862, and moved down Green River to the Ohio, then down that river to Paducah.

The following lines were soon after published, with the statement that they were composed by a member of the Forty-fourth while floating down the Ohio to join General Grant at Fort Donelson. The name of the member was not given, and is yet unknown to the writer.

Lines by a Hoosier Volunteer.

On Ohio's bright waters I'm floating once more,
As I send forth my greetings to Hoosierdom's shore,
But a sigh is borne with them far over the lee
For my own humble home in that land of the free.

While the curtains of evening are shrouding the day,
Let me turn from the press of our warriors away,
To conceal from the gaze of the strangers a tear
For the land that I love and the home that's so dear.

For the perils of battle my heart may be steel,
But for the home-land and kindred 'tis manly to feel;
Then a moment for grief, as my boat hurries past,
And I look, Indiana, on thee for the last.

Trusting wife of my youth! with a moistening eye,
On my lips is thy name, as I sob my good-bye!
Oh! the field may have terrors, and death may have pain,
But none like the fear, that we meet not again.

And now, while I know thy lone heart is aching,
By the burden that presses mine own to its breaking,
I commit thee and thine to the Father above,
Who has blessed with his smiles all the years of our love.

Thee and thine—THINE AND MINE—Oh, the dear ones who sit
Round the hearth of my home, and in sorrow repeat
The fond name of Father—my children, to you
I breathe forth my last and my saddest adieu.

Oh, pitying God! while to battle I go,
On the idols of home consolation bestow!
And though I may fall, this only I crave;
Be a balm to the hearts that must bleed o'er my grave.

From Paducah the brigade moved up the Tennessee to Fort Henry, on the 11th of February, where it remained but a few hours, being at once attached to General Lew. Wallace's division, which, with Commodore Foote's fleet of gunboats, was just ready to start for Fort Donelson, by way of the Tennessee and Cumberland rivers. This movement down to Paducah and thence up the Cumberland to Fort Donelson, is often referred to, by the old soldiers who were along, as the most orderly and magnificent display of gunboats and transports they saw during the war.

The troops were landed five miles below Fort Donelson, February 14th, and moved at once to the right of the Union line, and bivouacked that night in front of the enemy. The day had been one of the coldest for that part of the country, and without any shelter, or other covering than a blanket apiece, the Regiment sought rest before engaging in its first battle, and what proved the first great, and one of the greatest, victories of the war. A snow-storm blew up during the night, and when the morning light dawned the waking heroes could be seen in all directions creeping out of grave-like hillocks of snow that covered the ground. By the time coffee was made and some hard-tack " munched," the orders came to " fall in" and move forward. I could give no more reliable account of the part performed by the Forty-fourth Indiana, in this battle, than to copy Colonel Reed's official report :

"FORT HENRY, February 18, 1862.

Col. Charles Cruft, commanding First Brigade, Third Division :

SIR:—On the morning of February 15, the Forty-fourth Regiment Indiana Volunteers left their bivouac near the enemy's lines, and marched to the attack on Fort Donelson. By order of General McClernand we first took position near a battery, which was afterward assaulted by the rebels. In this position the enemy's shot flew over our heads. Shortly after, we were ordered forward into line with our brigade. As we marched past the enemy's breastworks we received a heavy fire, wounding some of our men. We took our position on the left wing of the brigade, in front of and within range of the enemy's guns; they were invisible to us, while we were exposed to their view. There was part of a regiment of Union troops (Colonel Logan's) on the slope of the hill between us and the enemy. Colonel Logan came to our line and requested we would not fire, as it would endanger his men. I gave the order to the men to withhold their fire. We remained exposed to the enemy's fire for fifteen or twenty minutes, without being able to return it, or to determine whether our friends were still in danger from our guns. At this time the enemy's fire partly subsiding, the regimental colors were ordered forward, and were planted ten paces in front of the line of battle by First-Lieutenant Story, of Company C. This failing to call forth a fire, Captain

Bingham, Company H, advanced to a point ten or twelve paces farther in front of our line, and waved our colors in the air. This drew his fire, which was most heartily responded to by our men, and was followed up in rapid succession on both sides. Our men behaved most gallantly. In the early part of the action, Captain Cuppy, Company E, was severely wounded, while in advance of his men cheering them on.

By this time the regiment on our left having entirely changed its position, leaving our flank exposed, a movement was made by a well-mounted cavalry regiment, and a body of infantry, to turn our left wing. Captain Murray, Company B, was ordered to open fire upon them, and did so with terrific effect. Companies E and H were ordered to the support of Company B, and poured in a well-directed fire, causing them to fall back in disorder. At this time, finding my regiment entirely alone and unsupported, the regiments on the left having withdrawn and our brigade having changed position to the right, (thus exposing both wings, of which the enemy was about to take advantage,) the order was given to change position to the right, which was done by a right flank in good order; with the exception of a part of the left wing, which, from not having fully understood the order, became separated from the main body, and some confusion ensued. But in a few minutes they rejoined us. Ours was the last regiment engaged with the enemy during the fight in the morning. Having joined the brigade, we took position on an adjoining elevation, and awaited orders.

Major Stoughton, posted during the entire action in the most exposed position, deserves the highest praise for the cool courage and daring displayed. I would gladly mention instances of personal bravery during the entire day. Too much credit cannot be bestowed on our men for their cool and determined courage, and especially during the trying time when exposed to the enemy's bullets, without being permitted to return it—both officers and men, in this our first engagement; but where almost all performed their part so well, it would require too lengthy a list to name them personally, while many, justly deserving, might be unintentionally omitted. The Forty-fourth did its duty. We lost in the engagement 7 killed, 34 wounded, and 2 missing.

From our position on the hill where our column rested we could see the battle-field in the morning, and the enemy again form his line of battle, at about half-past three o'clock P. M. A renewed attack upon his lines was ordered by General Wallace. My regiment advanced to the foot of the hill occupied by the enemy, formed in line of battle in face of a storm of bullets, finding the ground occupied by the Eighth Missouri. I advanced my regiment up the hill at double quick; our men, loudly cheering, advanced rapidly to the summit of the hill, firing at the enemy. The enemy soon retreated inside his entrenchments, closely followed by our troops. A fire was opened on us by their batteries, the shells falling near our lines. Whilst deliberating upon an attack on the fortifications, we received an order from General Grant to fall back to the brow of the hill, which was done. Here we bivouacked for the night. The following morning (Sunday) we were ordered by you to march forward to attack the enemy's works. When just ready to march, the joyful intelligence was brought us that the enemy had surrendered. Our column being in motion, we were the first to march into the town of Dover.

I am, Colonel, your obedient servant,

HUGH B. REED,

Col. commanding 44th Reg't Ind. Vols."

The cool bravery of the commanding officer of the Regiment, in this his first battle, was the admiration and pride of the men. The great chieftain, General Grant, could not more coolly smoke his cigar, and give orders in the midst of the clash of armies, than did Colonel Reed in this conflict. At the moment of making the charge up the hill, so modestly referred to in his report, the Colonel dismounted, gave his horse in charge of an orderly, stepped to the front of his Regiment with a pistol in each hand, and called upon his men to "Come on." They promptly rushed forward, cheering loudly, and in connection with the Eighth Missouri on the right, under Colonel Morgan L Smith, made the most brilliant charge of the battle. It was this charge that broke the line of the enemy, when he fled back to his entrench-ments, and it is believed discovered to him the necessity of immediate and unconditional surrender.

Sergeant Gordon relates, incidental to the second day's action, that some of the over-ranged projectiles from the rebel guns fell in the rear, and among the knapsacks of the Regiments, scattering them generally, and driving the guards to shelter. A cannon ball struck the base drum played by T. B. Totten, Co. F, who became quite excited over this unasked help in playing his drum. At night a detail from the Regiment was sent out to bring in the wounded, who, in the gloom and darkness, could only be found by their moans. Many, in their blood-drenched clothes, were found frozen to the ground. The wearied detail, about eight o'clock in the morning, heard a cry near the rebel picket line, but deemed it unsafe to go to the relief. Alexander Kinmont, Co. F, who had charge of a detail of seven men, decided to attempt the relief of the unknown sufferer, and after some urging pursuaded his comrades to follow him. The wounded man was found almost inside the enemy's line, badly wounded, lying on his back, and his hair frozen to the earth. They cut him loose and brought him safely into hospital.

As illustrative of the valor of the citizens of northern Indiana, it may not be amiss to mention that James R. Devor, then a clerk for the Sutler of the Regiment, borrowed a musket, went into this battle " on his own hook," and fired some forty rounds at the enemy. Two years after he enlisted, and became a member of the Regiment.

Soon after the word came that the enemy had surrendered, General Grant and his staff rode by, and as he passed the head of the Regiment, he said to Colonel Reed, " Come along." The Colonel was not sure whether the order meant himself alone, or his command, but to be on the safe side he passed the word " forward" down the line ; and the Forty-fourth Regiment was the first to enter the town of Dover, and had the honor of receiving and stacking the guns of a number of rebel regiments.

The conduct of the Regiment in this battle elicited much applause at home. A public meeting was called at Fort Wayne, and Colerick's hall was filled to overflowing. Hon. Lot S. Bayliss, who had been on a visit to the Regiment at the time of the battle, gave a description of the part performed by the Forty-fourth,

which was followed by resolutions highly complimentary
of the officers and men engaged, making especial mention of their fellow-citizens, Colonel Reed, Chaplain
Beeks, and Lieutenant Story, and of Major Stoughton
and Surgeon Martin. At this meeting Mrs. Charles
Case, President of the Ladies' Soldiers' Aid Society
of the city, was presented a rebel flag, captured from a
Virginia regiment, bearing upon it the words: " The
Faulkner Guards. In God We Trust."

The killed and wounded of the Regiment in this
battle were:

KILLED.

John C. Dee, Company C; the first to fall.
Daniel Lichtenwalter, Company B.
Marshall Kyle, Company B.
Isaac Graham, Company B.
Andrew J. Stillwell, Company E.
Nelson Parrott, Company E.
David Nelson, Company H.

WOUNDED.

Company A.—Orange Throop, John Ryan, Samuel
Tinsley.

Company B.—John Cagen, Thomas Caldwell, Columbus Crawford, William W. McCourtney, Joseph
Kirkpatrick.

Company C.—Fred Stein, M. Drury, P. Hoban, Wil
liam P. Hedges.

Company D.—D. McCord.

Company E.—Capt. William Cuppy, Henry Rhoades,
Adam Barsh, William Hildebrand, Alexander Goff,
Cary Primlott.

Company F.—Solomon Kinsley, Samuel Jaquès, Thomas O. Sloan.

Company H.—Jacob Deeter, Daniel Bowers, James Longcor, William Starkey, Elias Holsinger, Hiram Pontius, Daniel Spero, William Crow.

Company I.—B. F. Layton, Lewis A. Money, Hiram Missler, Ambrose C. Lamb, A. P. Waterhouse.

CHAPTER VI.

FORT HENRY TO PITTSBURG LANDING.—SHILOH BATTLE.

IMMEDIATELY after the capture of Fort Donelson the Forty-fourth moved with the advance across the country to Fort Henry, and then went into camp. While here, it, with the other regiments which constituted the original 13th brigade, and, in the recent conflict, the 1st brigade, 3d division, was now assigned to the 4th division, General S. A. Hulbert, and numbered the 4th, with Colonel Cruft in temporary command.

On the 10th of March the army again broke camp, and boarding some sixty steamers and transports, proceeded by a number of gunboats, moved up the Tennessee river, making probable the most imposing display of river craft during the war. There was a halt of two or three days at Savannah, during which Companies G and K came up and rejoined the Regiment. The fleet moved forward, to Pittsburg Landing, on the 15th, when the 4th brigade was the first infantry landed. General Hulbert's division went into camp on the Hamburg road, about one mile from the landing, the 4th brigade taking position on the left between the road and the river.

During the voyage up the Tennessee River, and while in camp here, the command suffered severely from diarrhœa, which became so generally prevalent that hardly

a man in the Regiment was known to be entirely exempt
from it.   The praiseworthy ambition of a commander
to make as good a show in numbers as possible, of men
ready for duty, and the duty of the medical officers to
protect the sick and disabled, will not always harmonize.
The morning sick call, the detection of impostors, the
excusing of the unfit from duty, always delicate and
important duties on the part of the surgeons, became
here more than usually embarrassing.   The Colonel
could make but a sorry show of men for duty.   Not
feeling sure that his medical officers were not too lenient
towards the men, he sent one morning for the Assistant
Surgeon who attended the sick call and excused the
men complaining in quarters, to inquire into the matter.
The large number who had just been excused seemed
to him unnecessarily large.   The medical officer suggested that all who had reported at sick call that morning, the excused and non-excused, be called back, and
formed in line in front of the Colonel's quarters, and
that he and the Chaplain, who was formerly a physician, examine the men themselves.   The suggestion was
adopted, and the result was that the heart of the Colonel,
who had a quick sympathy for the really suffering, was
touched, and the excused list was somewhat enlarged,
rather than diminished.   Confidence in the medical
officers was also increased, and never thereafter was
their verdict of fit or unfit for duty called in question.
The sick here were mainly treated in regimental hospital.   A few were taken to the hospital boat, the
Memphis, at the Landing.   There died here, before the
battle of Shiloh :

Andrew Oberlin, Co. F, March 26.

William Bennett, Co. A, March 25.

George Holsinger, Co. H, March 28.

Augustus Coleman, Co. A, March 29.

David McCord, Co. D, April 2.

Alvin Danner, Co. B, April 6.

Richard Swain, Co. —, March 26, on hospital boat *Memphis*, and

William Bender, Co. B, April 6, while being carried to the landing from the hospital, during the battle.

———

Sunday morning, April 6th, 1862, opened as lovely and as beautiful as any sung of by the poets. No minister or priest seemed needed to direct the mind upward from nature to nature's God. The balmy air, the bright new foliage, glimmering in the rising sun, the gentle treble of the blue-birds in the overhanging boughs, seemed all-sufficient to awaken in the soul reverential regard for the Author of all beauty and all good. But the scene soon changed. The demons of war were let loose. The roar of musketry at the front announced the approach of an enemy. The frightened blue-birds ceased their loving twitter; the loveliness of nature around ceased to attract the attention of the soldier as he hurriedly gathered up his implements of war.

The command to "fall in" was speedily obeyed, and in a few minutes the whole effective force of the Regiment was in line with the brigade, marching to the front. While moving to this engagement the Regiment formed its first acquaintance with its new brigade commander, who had been assigned to it only the day before —Brigadier-General Lauman.

For the part performed by the Regiment on this memorable occasion, we will first present the official report of Colonel Reed, made immediately after:

"HEADQUARTERS 44TH INDIANA VOLUNTEERS,
Pittsburg, Tenn., April 9, 1862.

Brigadier-General J. G. Lauman, commanding Third Brigade, Fourth Division Army, West Line:

SIR :—I have the honor to submit the following report of the part taken by the 44th Regiment Indiana Volunteers in the actions of the 6th and 7th, near Pittsburg, Tennessee :

We left our encampment about eight o'clock Sunday morning, with an effective force of 478 men, and marched forward to support General Prentiss' division, which had been attacked by the enemy. We had gone but a short distance when we met his men retreating in much confusion. We proceeded about one mile, and took position in line of battle in rear of a camp lately occupied by him. We formed our line under fire from the enemy's battery,—Colonel Cruft, 31st Indiana, on our right; Lieutenant-Colonel Bristow, 25th Kentucky, and Colonel McHenry, 17th Kentucky, on our left. I sent forward First-Lieutenant Wayne, Co. D, and First Lieutenant Barton, Co. B, each with a part of their respective companies, as skirmishers, in front of our line. They were soon driven in, and the whole line of the 44th and 31st Indiana furiously assaulted by the enemy, and as gallantly met, our men behaving in the coolest manner possible, loading and firing with the utmost rapidity ; and with so much zeal did they enter into it, that the officers had only to watch the fight as a matter of interest rather than of duty. The enemy was driven off with immense loss. They again rallied, and charged up. to within a few rods of our line, and were again repulsed. You, General, were with us, and have since gone over the ground so gallantly contested, and have witnessed how terribly destructive was our fire—the ground being literally strewn with their dead. But again they formed in column, and charged over an open field on our left, and in front of the 17th and 25th Kentucky, the gallant Colonel McHenry commanding, who poured into their ranks a most terrible fire. I immediately wheeled two companies of my left wing to the left, and opened upon his flank; his ranks were mown down at each fire, but he still pressed forward; and as bravely was he received. His front rank went down, leaving a line of dead across his front, when he retreated in good order.

This ending the engagement here, we were ordered to the support of the line on our left, about half a mile distant, which had fallen back. We took position on the left of, and supporting Willard's battery, which soon commenced playing upon the enemy, and we were soon charged upon in large force; and here was the most hotly contested fight of the day, being in an open field, with the exception of a few scattering trees—the enemy far outnumbering us, and fighting with desperate courage. The fire was fearfully severe, but our officers and men behaved with heroic bravery, never for a moment swerving from their position, pouring in their fire with the coolness of veterans, and driving the enemy before them; but again and again, with fresh troops, they advanced to the charge. Our ammunition being expended, a part of a regiment was ordered up by you, to take our place while our boxes were refilled. In a few minutes we again entered the fight, and charged forward far in advance of our former line. Our color-bearer and guard were either killed or wounded, at the same moment, and two other brave men in succession being shot down, and our flag riddled with balls, Lieutenant Newman, in command of Company H, bore it aloft, but soon fell mortally wounded. It was again taken by our brave men, and carried to the front, both officers and men rallying with heroic energy to its support. Captain Murray, Company B, acting Captain George Weamer, and acting Lieutenant Warren Banta, Company E, fell mortally wounded. Lieutenant Kinmont, in command of Company F, and Captain Cosgrove, Company D, were severely wounded. Space will not permit mentioning many instances of personal bravery, nor is it necessary where all acted nobly. By this time our cartridges were again expended. You ordered up the 31st Indiana, which had occupied position as a reserve in our rear, to relieve us. We accordingly moved back in good order, and took position near a battery, by order of General Hulbert. The enemy, in tremendous force, drove back our lines, when we again changed position to the right, by order of General Hulbert. Soon after this you rejoined us, and at your suggestion I drew up in line across the road by which the enemy was advancing, and opened fire upon him. We were here entirely unsupported—our friends passing on. I moved my regiment by the right of companies to the rear, and retired by the flank to the battery on the hill in our·rear, where we again formed in line in support of battery. The enemy made his attack on our left. A fierce contest ensued, in which some of our men were engaged. Night coming on, the enemy withdrew. We advanced our line 150 paces in front of the battery, and rested on our arms during the night.

On Monday morning we were relieved by fresh troops; our men, worn out and drenched to the skin by the pelting storm (as General Hulbert knows, having spent the night with us), and having been twenty-four hours without food or rest, were given a few hours to prepare for the approaching battle. At about ten o'clock you again called us into line, the Forty-fourth on the right wing. Our brigade, sadly reduced in numbers, but still ready for the fight, was put on march for the battle-field, and was led by you to the extreme right, to support General Sherman's division, where we arrived at a very opportune moment. We found the enemy charging upon and driving our forces to our left and front, over cleared ground, and used as drill ground by our troops. I immediately brought my regiment into line, and opened fire on the enemy. Our charge took them by surprise. They immediately retreated to the right and rear. Colonel McHenry, bringing up the left wing of our brigade, charged forward into the thickest of the fight. The enemy slowly retreated, returning our fire. Their battery also opened upon us. We pursued them over half a mile, but not knowing the position of our forces, I called a halt. At this moment, seeing General Sherman at a short distance, I rode to him and reported for orders—(having your horse shot under you, I was unable to find you at the moment). General Sherman ordered me not to advance further, but form our line where we were. Our men had become much scattered in the pursuit of the enemy, leaving us but a small force; and fresh regiments coming up to our support—amongst them the gallant 30th Indiana, Colonel Bass—the enemy were attacked with renewed energy, and after a fierce and bloody contest of half or three-quarters of an hour, were driven from the field.

During the fight of Sunday and Monday my regiment fired over 160 rounds of cartridges at the enemy. No men ever fought more bravely; too high praise can not be given them. Captain Murray and First Lieutenant Barton, Co. B, Lieutenant Newman, commanding Co. H, Captain Tannehill and Lieutenant Grund, Co. C, Captain Williams and Lieutenants Shoemaker and

Carey, Co. G, Captain Cosgrove and Lieutenant Wayne, Co. D, Captain Aldrich and Lieutenants Wilson and Bennett, Co. K, Acting Captain George Weamer, Lieutenant McDonald and Acting Lieutenant Warren Banta, Co. E, Lieutenant Kinmont, commanding Co. F, and Acting Lieutenants Gansenhouser and Kinmont of same company, Lieutenant Hodges, in command of Co. I, and Lieutenant Curtiss, of same company, Lieutenant Burge Smith and Acting Lieutenant Ulum, Co. A, were all in the thickest of the fight, and no men ever fought more heroically, and justly deserve mention. I am greatly indebted to Lieutenant Colonel Stoughton for his valuable aid; there is no braver man. He had his horse shot from under him, and was thrown with much force to the ground, in the fight on Monday; and to Acting Major Heath, Captain of Co. I, to whom too high praise cannot be given for his bravery and devotion to his duties. Adjutant Colgrove had his horse shot under him. Nor ought I to forget the bravery and devotion to their duties of our surgeons, Drs. Martin and Rerick. They were with the regiment at all times during the fight, caring for the wounded, and were exposed to the enemy's shot, and were both hit with balls. Lieutenants Wayne and John Frampton deserve mention for their devotion to our flag in Monday's fight. I cannot refrain from giving expression to my admiration, and bearing testimony to the noble and heroic manner in which General Hulbert and yourself exposed your lives in your constant and unwearied efforts. Each of you was at all times to be seen at your several posts, directing the battle. No General, in my opinion, ever conducted a fight with more ability, or displayed greater bravery.

Our loss in these engagements is 34 killed, 177 wounded, and one taken prisoner.

I am, General, very respectfully,

Your obedient servant,

HUGH B. REED,

Col. commanding 44th Ind. Vols."

We think the part performed by the Forty-fourth on the first day, at Shiloh, was never fully appreciated. The firmness of General Hulbert's division saved the day. General Lauman's brigade, of that division, held all the positions assigned it during the day, and did not retire until ordered, and the Forty-fourth was the last regiment to retire on the left of the army; and the Colonel saw no pressing necessity to retire then, except the want of ammunition and support.

General Lauman, an Iowa man, in his report says:

" When I come to speak of the gallantry and bravery of the officers and men of my command, I find great difficulty in finding language strong enough to express my feelings on the subject, and can only say that they fought from morning until night like veterans. Well may Indiana and Kentucky be proud of them. They have added another bright page to their martial history; and when all behaved so well, I find great difficulty in giving to each one the particular notice they so well earned. * * To Colonel Hugh B. Reed, of the 44th Indiana, I am under many obligations, not only for his gallantry, but also for the valuable assistance he rendered me after my personal staff was disabled, in conveying orders to the different parts of the command."

General Hulbert, in his report, says of General Lauman :

" I saw him hold the right of my line on Sunday with the small body of gallant men, only 1,717 strong, for three hours, and then change over to the left, repel the attack of twice his force for a full hour of terrible fighting, closing by the most gallant and successful charge, which gave him time to draw off his forces in order and comparative safety. His report renders full justice to his officers, among whom Colonel Reed, of the 44th Indiana, was especially distinguished."

The Colonel's conduct on the field richly merited these compliments, and much more. In consideration of his gallantry, President Lincoln sent in his name to the Senate for a Brigadier's commission, but it was accompanied by so many others that the Senate failed to act upon all, his name among others. It would hardly be possible for a mortal to act more bravely in battle than he did. He was in the thickest of the fight on both days, had two horses killed under him, and had his clothing pierced with bullets in several places, but wonderfully escaped serious injury.

One of the immediate chroniclers of the war, a correspondent of the Philadelphia *Press*, after the battle, wrote that it was universally admitted that the Forty-fourth was *the* regiment at Pittsburgh Landing. Once when it made one of the brilliant stands against overwhelming odds, on Sunday, while companions fell back on either hand, a captain of one of the retiring companies of Wisconsin soldiers, said the Forty-fourth "fought like iron men—they wouldn't run." Perhaps that was the origin of the phrase, or it may have been a general thought—but however it came, it stuck, and for a long time the Regiment was known as the "Iron Forty-fourth."

"Early on Sunday morning," the writer continues, "Colonel Reed gave his men an order to 'fall and fire.' Simultaneously the enemy fired, and killed and wounded some of the Indianians. The result of the fire from our side was of the most disastrous nature. The bushes were discovered to be in a blaze, and the groans of the rebel wounded were distressing, as the fact became apparent that they were perishing by fire. It is estimated that the last fire from our men, which consumed the bushes, killed twenty men, and seriously wounded a hundred, who were burned to death. One hundred and twenty of the rebels were buried in one grave in the vicinity. The bodies of nearly all of them were burned to a crisp. Another glorious stand was made by the same regiment, in an open field, against a brigade and a battery of the enemy. They killed nearly all the horses of the battery, and being joined by two more regiments, forced the enemy to retreat. At two o'clock the regiment was fighting a largely superior force. General Hulbert, who had been closely watching the movements and efforts of the men, said to General Lauman : 'General, you will have to retire— you cannot hold your position.' Says General Lauman : 'Did you ever see men fight so calmly and with so much effect before?' The answer was 'No.' 'Do you order me to retire?' 'No, you can do as you please; but you certainly cannot hold your position.' Then said General Lauman : 'I shall fight.' And he did fight, and maintained his position until after four o'clock, and till the last cartridge was fired.'' These points, gathered up by the correspondent at the time, were no exaggerations.

When the brigade to which the Forty-fourth was attached was transferred from General Hulbert's division, he addressed Colonel Reed the following note :

"HEADQUARTERS 4TH DIVISION, April 18, 1862.
Colonel Reed :

COLONEL,—I cannot part with my late 3d Brigade without some expression of good feeling. I have had none but the most pleasant intercourse with the officers, and nothing but the most ready obedience from the men. Your gallantry and good conduct I have officially noticed, and I give up the Brigade with unmingled regret, but with the full assurance that you will keep your well won reputation. I do not think you can add to it.

Very truly,

S. A. HULBERT,

Brig. General comm'd'g 4th Division."

The two medical officers of the Regiment, and the musicians, served both days on the field, dressing the wounded and sending them at once to the boats at the Landing, whence they were transported down the river to Savannah, Paducah, and other points where general hospitals were located. There were several remarkable recoveries. Lieutenant Jacob Newman, mentioned in Colonel Reed's report as mortally wounded, was shot in the abdomen, in front, the ball lodging beneath the skin on the back, from where it was removed by Surgeon Martin, on the field. He was not expected to live to reach the Landing, but he is living to-day, though still a sufferer from the wound. John Nelson, Co. H, was shot through the right lung, and reported dead by his company officers at the time, but recovered, returned to the Regiment, served out his time, and then re-enlisted as a veteran. William Underwood, Co. D, was struck in the head with a minie-ball, which penetrated the skull, and he was left dead, as was supposed, on the field. He was afterwards found alive, and unknown to his company, had been carried to a hospital boat. He finally recovered, though a vacant space in his forehead, like that in an infant's skull, was left. This soldier afterwards re-enlisted in the 129th Indiana, and died of a slight flesh wound received in the Atlanta campaign.

The sick in camp at the opening of the battle were all hastily carried to the Landing by the nurses, as soon as they saw the Union lines were being pressed. The rebels had possession of the camp that night, but we enjoyed all the comfort it could afford the next night.

The number of rounds fired by the different soldiers of the Regiment in this battle could not, of course, be accurately numbered; but William D. Groves, Co. H, a cool and intrepid soldier, and a man of good reputation, claimed that he fired 200 rounds, 30 of which were with deliberate aim. His count for the second day was 77.

The effect of the bravery of the soldiers had quite an inspiring influence on the Assistant Surgeon, judging by a letter to his wife, written a few days after the battle. He said :

" I love the Forty-fourth (the fighting ones), and intend to follow them to the bitter end, if necessary. They richly merit the attention of surgeons, and shall have it as long as I can walk. I am sick, sick, of those puny, long-faced, sniveling, unfortunate mortals who are ever sick when there is a fight on hand. Fortunately we have had precious few of these. The more I study and learn what the Forty-fourth Regiment really did in this great battle, the more do I admire the gallantry and bravery of the men. At one time they charged the enemy alone, and were the last troops to leave the field on the left wing, on Sunday. They marched off in good order, all alone, and far in the rear of the other forces, the enemy following closely behind in overwhelming numbers."

He did serve the Regiment until the day of its muster out; and he is glad to-day, nearly eighteen years after, to make the record in this volume, that from that day on he never saw anything to change his profound regard for the valor and faithfulness of its men.

The following is the report of killed and wounded, made after the battle:

FIELD AND STAFF.

Colonel H. B. Reed, wounded in chest, slight.

Lieutenant-Colonel S. J. Stoughton, wounded in leg, slight.

Acting Major A. Heath, wounded in leg, slight.

Assistant Surgeon J. H. Rerick, wounded in chest, slight.

COMPANY A.

Killed.—Joseph Jackman, Leander Hall.

Wounded.—Lieutenant N. A. Sowers, foot, severely; Lieutenant B. Smith, breast, severe; John Ulam, slightly; N. P. Lewis, hand; Jas. H. Merriman, hip, severe; Wm. Carlin, head, slight; John Ryan, Jr., leg; William Rosser, arm, seriously; Hannibal Scovil, thigh, severely; Henry A. Lords, face; Henry Twitchell, leg; Wm. Yenner, arm, died; John R. Hutchins, face, slight; Wm. McMuire, chin; Joshua West, head, slight; Henry Beard, face, slight; Allen M. Sailor, head, slight.

COMPANY B.

Killed.—Captain John Murray, Sergeant William McNeal, Alva Danner, John Easton, Ralph Goodrich.

Wounded.—Ed. N. Whitney, arm, severe; M. D. Campbell, chest, severe; Benj. Campbell, leg, severe; James Garnett, hand; Basil Hunter, thigh, dangerous; Silas M. Scott, arm; Thomas J. Powers, leg; Clinton Scoby, arm, slight; Albert R. Westfall, arm, severe; Newton Westfall, hand.

COMPANY C.

Killed.—William Woodford, Peter Stall, Robert Stewart.

Wounded.—Lieutenant Grund, leg; John Keefer, foot; George Mayers, arm; John Elzey, arm; Joseph Nicodemus, face; Marion McGinnis, face; Owen Shaw, face; Milton Sites, head; Samuel B. Sweet, leg; Michael Harrison, shoulder; A. P. Waterhouse, arm; Amos French, arm; James M. Flutter, Wm. P. Henderson, shoulder.

COMPANY D.

Killed.—Burke D. Shafer, William H. Casebeer, Jacob H. McClellan, John Poppy, Platt J. Squires, Wm. Underwood.

Wounded.—Captain Cosgrove, arm, severe; Sergeant Geo. W. Shell, Sanford Worden, foot; Randall Simmons, ankle; William M Johnson, arm; Amos T. Britton, arm; Alfred Daugherty, John Farmer, hip; Samuel Hartzell, shoulder; Sylvester Minier, leg; Joseph V. Reed, arm; Robert D. Rhea, arm; Joseph Shook, arm; Stephen P. Waybill, shoulder; Alfred Wilson, severely; Ezra Worden, breast; Samuel Stroman, arm.

COMPANY E.

Killed.—Acting Captain George Weamer, Warren Banta.

Wounded.—Samuel W. Hovens, hip; Henry Rupley, arm; O. P. Kountz, neck; Michael Sickafoose, elbow; John T. Howard, thigh; Henry Brenneman, arm; Joseph Anderson, leg; Elam Robbins, arm; Adam Borsh, thigh; Francis A. Grable, arm; George Holloway, shoulder; Ezra Buschnell, hand; Jacob Brandeburg, knee; John M. Collins, hand; Joseph W. Compton, hand; Simon Oberbatzer, hip; Theodore F. Nave, groin.

Henry Rupley, Joseph Anderson, Michael Sickafoose and Henry M. Engle were discharged because of their wounds.

COMPANY F.

Killed.—William Collier, William Bender.

Wounded.—Lieutenant Thomas C. Kinmont, thigh, severely; Alexander Kinmont, hand; I. N. Thomas, knee; J. M. Milliman, arm; Geo. W. Cosper, face; Isaac Firestone, face; Peter Countryman, finger off; Robert R. Dirrim, arm; Isaac Detmer, abdomen; Hiram Goff, knee, died; Henry C. Pryer, face; Alfred Rose, thigh; Thos. O. Sloan, arm; Nathan Stockwell, shoulder; John H. Webster, arm; Hiram B. Williams, arm; George W. Wallace, chest.

COMPANY G.

Killed.—Jacob Mohn, Andrew P. Botzell.

Wounded.—Chauncey Wright, thigh; John Goff, thigh; Samuel Wertsbaugher, thigh; Martin Minard, elbow; Paul Bean, arm; William McKee, arm; Henry O'Grady, arm; Sergeant O. Z. Rawson, leg; James C. Riddle, shoulder; Edwin W. Matthews, shoulder; John Y. Johnson, arm; Henry Eley, foot, died; Milton Edsall, breast; John Minkey, breast; Henry Aumsbaugh, leg; George Adams, arm.

COMPANY H.

Killed.—John V. Curtis, Augustus A. S. Galloway, Jerome Wright, Orwin Page.

Wounded.—Lieutenant Jacob Newman, bowels; William Crow, wrist and side; John B. Rowe, knee; Geo. Gregory, back; Daniel P. Strecker, foot; Victor Ketcham, foot; George Ray, thigh; David Randall, arm;

John Burridge, leg; Daniel Spearow, leg; George Benham, thigh.

COMPANY I.

Killed.—Frank Lammers, John Declute.

Wounded.— Frank Baldwin, head; Nelson Mansfield, neck, mortally; Alexander Devor, arm; Jacob Cordie, hand; Daniel Brooks, neck; Peter Harney, shoulder; Wentworth Irwin, shoulder; Frederick Johnson, George Maybee, thigh; Irvin Robinson, arm; John Tavener, hand; Joseph Benedict, leg.

COMPANY K.

Wounded.—Captain S. C. Aldrich, slight; Sergeant Moses B. Willis, hand; John G. Long, hand; Oscar Knapp, side; Thomas O. Leslie, lower jaw; George Sanderson, shoulder, died; Andrew Hollopeter, arm; Elias Baylor, head; Benjamin F. Cornell, hand; Jacob Casebeer, hand; Nicholas Endsley, abdomen, slight; J. F. Housel, thigh; John H. C. Hoffman, arm; Henry H. Hawley, neck; Jacob Link, leg; Lemuel Richey, foot; Charles M. Thomas, breast; Joseph Thompson, arm; Norman C. Shank, arm; Samuel Fair, arm; Hiram M. Fanning, shoulder; Robert Hall, hand; Joseph P. Sisson, shoulder; Madison Rodgers, shoulder; James E. Pence, knee.

The preceding is the official report of killed and wounded, as made to the Surgeon of the Regiment immediately after the battle, by the company officers. Several then reported killed were found afterward not to have been killed. In the company records will be found the killed as they appear in the Adjutant General's report. Joseph Jackman, M. J. Culp, Wm. H. Underwood, though reported killed, were severely wounded only, and recovered, and were discharged; whilst Henry Brenneman, Co. F, and Henry Ely, Co.

G, not reported killed, died a few days after the battle, of their wounds.

Indiana soldiers, at this time, came to appreciate the care and devotion of Governor Morton as they never had before. As speedily as the boats could carry them he had extra physicians on the field, to help care for the sick and wounded; and by obtaining a special permit from the Secretary of War, hundreds of Indiana soldiers gained an opportunity to return home to recover from wounds and disease, who otherwise could not have had the privilege. Dr. George W. Carr, of Ligonier, and Dr. B. C. Rowan, of Fort Wayne, were sent by him to the Forty-fourth, to assist in the care of the sick and wounded. The latter remained a few days. Dr. Carr was detained until authority was given to appoint two assistant surgeons for each regiment, when he was regularly commissioned Second Assistant Surgeon of the Forty-fourth, and served it faithfully and efficiently until promoted Surgeon of the 129th Indiana.

The conduct and merits of the battle were almost the exclusive topics of discussion for weeks. While resting up, officers and men of different commands visited each other, and compared their views and experiences. In the Forty-fourth there was but one opinion, apparently, and that was, that the troops in the front were surprised on the morning of the 6th, and that the surprise was the result of gross carelessness and an insufficient system of picketing. This view was confirmed by the new duties imposed upon the Regiment. Before the battle there had been no details for picket duty, but now they came frequently, and occasionally

the whole command was required to go out for that
purpose. While out with the Regiment on picket duty,
one day, we visited a rebel hospital within our lines,
and conversed with a Captain of the 11th Mississippi,
who claimed that his regiment lost 298 men out of 400.
In answer to the inquiry, "At what distance from our
camp did you strike our pickets?" he answered, about
150 yards. He said they were greatly surprised at the
easy and unmolested approach they made upon the
Union lines.

Those who witnessed the bravery of the Union soldiers on the first day at Shiloh, will ever remain confident that they could have whipped General Beauregard
then and there had the front lines been protected as
they were afterward, when in face of an enemy. These
feelings on the part of the troops made the assumption
of personal command by General Halleck quite agree-
able. The enthusiasm for Grant subsided for a while,
but only to be revived again, after Halleck had a brief
day of favor, which closed with the siege of Corinth.

CHAPTER VII.

TO CORINTH AND BATTLE CREEK.

GENERAL HALLECK arrived at Pittsburgh Landing April 11th, and at once commenced reorganizing the army, and adding to its numbers, preparatory to a movement upon Corinth, twenty miles distant. The army was divided into five grand parts: the right, center, and left wings, the reserves, and the cavalry. General Thomas was assigned to the command of the right wing; General Buell, the center; General Pope, the left; General McClernand to the reserve, and General A. J. Smith to the cavalry. General Grant was assigned a nominal position as second in command. Each of the wings was composed of four divisions. To General Buell was assigned the divisions of Generals McCook, Nelson, Crittenden, and Wood. The Forty-fourth was assigned to General Crittenden's division, and to the brigade commanded by General Vancleve.

On the 29th of April the order came to strike tents, and the great movement on Corinth commenced. For the next thirty days, we thought we were being handled with great care and skill, though towards the last it became apparent, with excessive caution. We were marched out the first day one mile and a quarter, the next day one mile and a half, and thus we moved every few days, to the right, or left, or forward, occasionally skirmishing with the enemy, until we reached Farmington, near Corinth. Here we halted long enough to form camp, but with continuous picket firing along the line in our immediate front, which broke out occasionally into sharp skirmishes. Early on the morning of the 30th of May, the brigade was called out, as though for battle, when terrific sounds, as of explosions, were heard in the direction of Corinth. The division advanced, and without opposition marched directly into Corinth, finding it evacuated, and a large amount of army stores on fire. The thundering sounds heard before starting were the explosions of a large pile of shells the enemy had fired, being unable to get them away. Thus ended the siege of Corinth. The Forty fourth lost no men in the movement, except such as died of disease on the march. These were:

Jacob Coldren, Co. H, May 8th; James A. Dirrim, Co. F, May 21st; Elijah Locke, Co. K. June —; Henry Crafts, Co. H, June 9th, and John T. Johnson, Co. —, June 11th,—the two latter at the general field hospital.

General Crittenden's division pursued the enemy south as far as Booneville, Mississippi, some twenty miles, when further pursuit was abandoned, and the great combination of armies under General Halleck was broken up. The army of the Ohio, with General Buell in command, was ordered to face to the east, and move on Chattanooga, two hundred miles distant, while the army of the Tennessee, under General Grant, was to operate west of Corinth.

General Crittenden's division started eastward from Booneville, June 4th. When the Regiment reached Iuka, the writer, who had fallen sick, was left, and John R. Grubb, musician, also in ill health, was detailed to care for him. A furlough was sent in a few days, and they managed to get to the river, and thence home. I am therefore without personal knowledge of the march from this point to Florence, Tuscumbia, Athens, Huntsville, Stevenson, and finally to Battle Creek, Tennessee, which the command reached about the middle of July. The march was much complained of by the soldiers on account of the lack of full rations, and of insufficient clothing. The last part of the journey was performed by many barefooted. There was no action with the enemy on the march. Two soldiers who fell sick on the route and were left at general hospital at Huntsville, Alabama, died, viz.: John Monkey, Co. G, July 5th, and Joseph Eckles, Co. D, July 12th.

The writer reached the command again, July 26th, and found it very pleasantly encamped about five miles above Bridgeport, in a narrow valley, with the Tennessee River in front, the Cumberland range in the rear, and Battle Creek on the left. Generals Crittenden's and McCook's divisions were scattered along the line from Stevenson, Alabama, to this point. We were now at the extreme front, with the enemy's pickets in full view across the river. Chattanooga, about thirty miles distant, was the objective point of General Buell, but he now found his forces scattered all along the railroad lines in Northern Alabama and Middle Tennessee, trying to keep communication open to Bridgeport, and yet was unable to keep these two divisions in full rations or forage.

Soon after reaching Battle Creek, the Colonel and Lieutenant Colonel each being absent, the command of the Regiment devolved upon Major Bingham. August 18th, 1862, was grand muster day, under the noted Order No. 14, according to which the muster rolls were to be revised, and all found absent without leave were to be stricken off. The order was the occasion of much trouble, and in many instances of great injustice. Many who had no thought of deserting, nor in the least proving recreant to their duty, were unavoidably detained away longer than their leaves allowed. It was only through the decision of a court martial that any could be restored to their positions in the army. And the subsequent movements of the army prevented the convening of these courts for several months. Several officers and a number of men of the Regiment had trouble under the order. At this muster there were 437 men and 26 commissioned officers present, and 200 men and four officers absent. The loss by death, discharge and desertion up to this date was 272. The deaths had been 80. The killed and wounded numbered 250.

It was now apparent that another movement was approaching. The sick were all ordered back to Stevenson, and the command put in readiness for motion. What the movement would be was a matter of much speculation in regimental quarters, but without knowledge. Subsequent history reveals the fact that General Buell and General Thomas differed as to the intent of the rebel General Bragg, then at Chattanooga. Buell thought it was his intention to strike for Nashville, whilst Thomas believed that his objective point was Kentucky and Louisville. Thomas was right, but the movements of the army of the Ohio were conducted for some thirty days upon Buell's theory.

Before we depart, let us count the little mounds that cover the remains of the heroes who have departed this life in camp here. They were:

Sergeant Charles Beverly, Co. F, July 20.

James Murray, Co. D, July 23.

Simon C. Cutter, Co. K, July 30.

Charles Danks, Co. F, August 1.

William Slade, Co. I, died August 14, between Bridgeport and Stevenson, on the way to general hospital.

Quartermaster William Bayliss died at Fort Wayne, August —, 1862.

CHAPTER VIII.

THE GREAT FOOT RACE.

As soon as darkness had enshrouded the valley, on the evening of August 20th, 1862, Generals McCook's and Crittenden's divisions, in light marching order, with ten days' rations in haversack, silently broke camp, marched up the valley, crossed Battle Creek, and marching until midnight, bivouacked at Jasper. The next day they moved some four miles up the Sequachia valley, and the day after, back again to within two miles of the old camp.

August 23, marched westward about two miles, and bivouacked in Gizzard Cove.

August 24, moved slowly westward five miles, to foot of Cumberland mountains. General McCook's division in the advance, moved up the mountain.

August 25, moved up the mountain, on a very rough road. Were nearly all day making two miles to the summit, then marched seven miles on the mountain and went into bivouac at midnight.

August 26, marched five miles, crossed the Tracy City railroad, and descended the mountain on the north side, and camped near a large spring flowing from the mountain side.

August 27, no movement; men rest and wash up.

August 28, aroused at 1½ A. M. to march, but after getting ready the order was countermanded, and General Crittenden's division remained in camp all day.

August 29, marched northward through Pelham and camped on Hillsborough road, seven miles.

August 30, marched to Hillsborough.

August 31, marched to Manchester.

September 1, marched at 4 A. M., on Murfreesboro road, twelve miles. Began now to understand that we were falling back, and really on a foot race with Bragg's army, which was moving nearly on a parallel, though shorter line, for Kentucky.

September 2, marched fourteen miles, and camped within three miles of Murfreesboro.

September 3, marched to Murfreesboro, and thence out on Lebanon pike eight miles.

September 4 and 5, in bivouac.

September 6, marched to and through Lavergne, and camped six miles south of Nashville.

September 7, marched to and through Nashville, and went into bivouac six miles north of the city.

September 8, marched four miles.

September 9, marched twelve miles.

September 10, marched fourteen miles, and camped near Mitchellville.

September 11, marched at 4 o'clock A. M., crossed the State line into Kentucky, and camped at noon near Tyne Springs, making fourteen miles.

September 12, a large detail sent back to Mitchellville to protect the trains.

September 13, marched to within three and a half miles of Bowling Green.

September 14 and 15, in bivouac.

September 16, marched through Bowling Green and went into camp one mile north of the town.

September 17, marched eighteen miles.

September 18, marched to Cave City, and a few miles out towards Munfordsville.

September 19, skirmishing with the enemy. Troops posted as if for battle. Some 4,200 Union troops, surrendered to Bragg at Munfordsville, a few days before, came into General Buell's lines on parole.

September 20, held in readiness for action all day. The soldiers were very anxious for a contest with the enemy here, believing from what they could learn that the enemy could be severely punished, if not completely routed. A General probably never had an army so anxious to grapple with the enemy as General Buell this day. His failure to show any energetic disposition to engage his foe here, lost him the confidence of the rank and file of his army.

September 21, marched at 4 o'clock A. M. to and through Munfordsville, General Bragg having marched out.

September 22, marched twelve miles.

September 23, marched thirty miles, through Elizabethtown.

September 24, marched to West Point, on the Ohio River, and thence out toward Louisville three miles, making fifteen miles.

September 25, marched to Louisville, some fifteen miles.

We beat Bragg to Louisville. The race was a three hundred mile heat, and was walked in light marching order, without shelter at night, and most of the time on half rations. The men went into bivouac at Louisville, foot-sore, ragged and weary, though really in better health than when they left camp at Battle Creek. But they felt that their loyalty to the commanding General had been very severely tested, and, with a few, their loyalty to the Government. The whole retrograde movement, it seemed to them, could have been avoided; and that engagements with the enemy which would have cut the movement short had been purposely avoided by General Buell, was the firm belief of thousands of men in the army of the Ohio, and throughout the country.

CHAPTER IX.

THE PERRYVILLE CAMPAIGN.

A few days' rest only was given at Louisville, but in these few days General Buell's army was reorganized, partially re-clothed, and a large number of new regiments added. General Crittenden was now assigned to the command of one of the three corps newly formed, and General Vancleve to the command of a division. The second brigade, under the latter, consisted of the 11th Kentucky, 13th Ohio, 44th Indiana, and 86th Indiana, a new regiment; Colonel Hawkins, of the 11th Kentucky, in command.

General Bragg was reported at Bardstown, some twenty-five miles southeast, and on October 1st, Buell's army moved again to meet him, but hardly a soldier in the ranks believed a hostile meeting at all probable. On the second day out, the Regiment was greeted with the presence of a paymaster, for the first time since June. That night two Lieutenants and some ten men deserted. Their dishonored names can be found in the report of the Adjutant General of the State. We omit them here.

Vancleve's division reached the vicinity of Bardstown on the 4th. There was more or less skirmishing at the front every day, but only with the rear-guard of

the enemy, who had fallen back to Springfield. and then
to Perryville.   General Crittenden reached the vicinity
of Perryville about noon, October 8th, and formed his
corps in line of battle on the right.   The roar of battle
was distinctly heard to the left, and riderless horses
rushed through the lines of the Forty-fourth ; but there
were no orders to advance until the 9th, when the corps
moved in fine line of battle, through wood and field,
on Perryville.   The Surgeons of the Regiment, getting
weary of the slow pace, and the whole farce, rode ahead
into Perryville, which had been abandoned by the enemy the night before, and was then occupied by troops
from the left.   To the men in line it seemed a crime
that General Crittenden was not ordered forward on
the 8th.   Such a movement would have resulted in a
most crushing defeat of Bragg's army, if not in its
capture.

General Crittenden's corps manœuvred around in
the triangle between Perryville, Harrodsburg and Danville, a portion of the time in line of battle, until the
13th, when pursuit of Bragg was commenced, and we
were marched to Danville, Stanford, Crab Orchard,
Mt. Vernon, and thence into a mountainous section to
Wild Cat, where we lay in bivouac from the 20th until
the 23d, when we were marched back to Mt. Vernon,
and thence southward to Somerset, where we arrived
on the 25th, in the midst of a snow-storm.   Snow fell
that night to the depth of some four or five inches.
The command was wholly without shelter, and the
men had only a blanket apiece.   Large fires were built,
and taunting jibes, and the current army slang, " Here's

your mule," resounded from the camp fires all night long. After a halt of a day or two here, we marched on, moving through the Mill Spring battle-field to the vicinity of Glasgow, which was reached October 3d. Here the command was gladdened with the news that General Buell had been relieved and General Rosencrans placed in command of the army of the Ohio, which name he soon had changed to that of the army of the Cumberland. .

As the Regiment went into bivouac one evening while on the march from Somerset, the attention of the medical officers was called to Paul Bean, Co. G, who was found lying prostrate on the ground, but presenting no indications whatever of any disease. To all appearance he was utterly exhausted, and this alone. Stimulants and tonics were administered, but being still unable to be carried the next morning, he was left in the care of a friendly family, where he died a day or two after. He fell a martyr to his abhorrence of the shirk, and of that class who for every trivial ailment sought medical aid, excuse from duty, or a ride in the ambulances or wagons. He would ask no favors, and literally fell in the ranks before his disability was known by the company officers.

CHAPTER X.

NASHVILLE.

THE Army of the Cumberland was now faced toward Nashville, and General Crittenden, with two of his divisions—Vancleve's and Wood's—started on the 5th, marched through Scottville, reaching Gallatin, Tennessee, where they drove the rebel cavalry, on the 9th, making a distance of sixty-three miles in four days. The next day the command marched out on the Lebanon road, to the crossing of the Nashville and Lebanon pike, when it turned eastward toward Nashville three miles, and went into camp six miles from General Jackson's Hermitage. Here the great marches of 1862 ended. The Regiment had marched, since leaving Louisville, about three hundred and sixty miles, in foity days, and with only six days' rest by the way. Since leaving Battle Creek, August 20, the distance traveled was nearly seven hundred miles. All this time the men were without shelter of any kind, carried but one blanket apiece, and were nearly all the time on half rations, and very poorly shod.

There was a rest here until the 15th, when Colonel Hawkins's brigade was ordered to move south about eight miles, to Rural Hill. The enemy was reported in the vicinity, but the camp was not disturbed until early dawn on the 18th, when a dash was made upon the camp. But the men were quickly in line, and the rebels withdrew, leaving six dead on the field. No losses resulted in the Regiment, and we believe there were none in the brigade. The next day the brigade moved back to the Lebanon pike, and went into camp on Mill Creek, near the Hermitage. On the 30th of November the division was moved up to Nashville, and across on to the Nashville and Murfreesboro pike, and went into camp near the Tennessee Insane Asylum. Here the Regiment prepared for winter quarters.

Important changes occurred in the Regiment on the first of December. Colonel Reed's resignation, tendered a few days previous, was accepted. The Regiment was called into line, just before his departure ; the flag carried up to this time, and which had been presented the command on the day it set out for the field, by Mayor Randall, on behalf of the ladies of Fort Wayne, was planted in front. Sadly torn and tattered by shot and shell at Donelson and Shiloh, it attested the fidelity of the Colonel and his brave men in maintaining the pledge given when it was first presented, " to honor, sustain, and defend it unto death." At Shiloh, when all its brave bearers were stricken down, he gathered it up with his own hands and carried it unfurled and unsullied from the field. The old flag was held as a precious emblem by the men, but as he who had led them in its honor and defense was now about to depart, to be associated again with its donors, the Regiment thought it appropriate, as a token of their appreciation of his gallant services, to present him the flag. A more significant and touching testimonial could hardly be given a brave man. The Colonel, deeply moved, responded in a few remarks, highly complimenting the men and officers for their bravery and fidelity. He then presented the Regiment a new flag, purchased at his own expense, trusting it would be honored as the old one had been. And it was. The old flag is yet sacredly preserved by the Colonel, at his home in New Jersey. The Colonel also carried with him testimonials of regard from all the officers of the brigade.

Lieutenant-Colonel Stoughton, who had been promoted to Colonel of the 100th Indiana Infantry, and Chaplain Beeks, resigned, also departed about the same time.

After these officers left, the commissioned company officers met and held an informal election for Lieutenant-Colonel and Major, choosing Captain William C. Williams, Co. G, Lieutenant-Colonel, and Captain Charles F. Kinney, Co. A, Major. The companies also met and made recommendations for all official vacancies in their respective companies. Captain Kinney being the senior captain of the Regiment, and feeling aggrieved at the choice that had been made, tendered his resignation, and obtaining leave of absence, departed for home.

On the 2d, General Rosecrans reviewed his army, making a very favorable impression on the minds of the men. As he passed along the line of the Forty-fourth, he made some quite flattering comments upon the healthy and hearty appearance of the men. Noticing a man not completely equipped, he chided him pleasantly, remarking, " that when men are soldiers they must act as soldiers, and when they keep grocery, tend the grocery."

While in camp here, forage for the army was mainly obtained by foraging expeditions, and the Regiment was out on several occasions, some of which were attended with skirmishes with the enemy. On the 11th the brigade camp was moved back two miles, to within five miles of Nashville.

Commissions were received on the 13th, making Captain Williams, Co. G, Colonel; Captain S. C. Aldrich, Co. K, Lieutenant-Colonel, and Captain Kinney, Co. A, Major. The latter declined to muster, and his resignation was accepted. The brigade was also reorganized on the 15th, and was made to include, besides the Forty-fourth, Colonel W. C. Williams, the 86th Indiana, Colonel A. S. Hamilton; 13th Ohio, Colonel J. G. Hawkins; 59th Ohio, Colonel J. P. Fyffe; 7th Indiana Battery, Captain G. R. Swallow. Colonel Fyffe was assigned to the command of the brigade.

The sick were now ordered to Nashville, and the command held in readiness for momentary orders to move on Murfreesboro.

CHAPTER XI.

STONE RIVER.

GENERAL CRITTENDEN moved his corps, consisting of Wood's, Palmer's, and Vancleve's divisions, on the 26th, advancing on the Murfreesboro pike, Palmer's division in the advance. There was considerable skirmishing during the day, and General Vancleve went into bivouac in the vicinity of Lavergne that evening, with the enemy apparently in force in the town. The next morning there was a sharp skirmish in the village, during which it was almost wholly consumed by fire. General Vancleve moved through the place and then filed off to the left, some three miles, and bivouacked on Stuart's Creek, where we remained over Sunday.

On Monday, the 29th, we advanced again towards Murfreesboro, and went into bivouac in the rear of Generals Wood's and Palmer's divisions, who were in line of battle in front of the enemy. General Rosecrans came up the next day, the 30th, and established his headquarters a few paces in front of our brigade. During the day other divisions came up and took position. General Crittenden's corps was formed on the left of the Murfreesboro and Nashville pike, with orders to cross Stone River the next morning, and move into Murfreesboro. General Vancleve's division was to cross

at the lower ford and advance against the rebel General
Breckenridge. General Wood was to support him on
the right, crossing at the upper ford, and General Palmer
was to engage the enemy in his front. Next, in the
centre, was Thomas's corps, and on the right was
McCook's corps. General Rosecrans' plan of battle
was to open on the left, and extend the engagement
from left to right.

Early on the morning of the 31st, General Vancleve
initiated the execution of this plan by moving his division towards the left. The advance brigade was crossing the river, and Colonel Fyffe had just reached the
banks of the river, when the movement was arrested by
an order for Fyffe to face his brigade about, and march
with all possible speed to resist an attack of the enemy's
cavalry on the trains in the rear, on the Nashville pike,
and about one mile in the rear of the point left in the
morning. The enemy had wholly disconcerted the
plans of General Rosecrans by a furious onslaught on
the extreme right about sunrise, driving back the whole
right wing to a right-angle with the centre. Colonel
Fyffe reached the point of attack on the trains, but the
Union cavalry had already succeeded in repulsing the
attack, and in recapturing the trains. The brigade was
then ordered to the support of the right, and returning
on the pike about half a mile, marched through a cedar
wood to an open field. The enemy filled the wood
beyond, and also a wood on the right of the field. The
brigade advanced across the field, and by some blunder
moved far beyond the supporting columns on the right
and left. As soon as the men were across the field, the

enemy opened a terrific fire from the front and right. The place was too hot, and the brigade would have been annihilated in a few minutes had it not fallen back, which it did speedily but in order. The lines were again formed near the Nashville pike, and held during the remainder of the day and night. The day was a terrible one. Many brigades and regiments on the right were broken up and scattered, and wandered from place to place, officers in search of their men, and men in search of their officers, until they were gathered up without regard to former organization, and placed in line of action. There was no place of safety within the Union lines. The Surgeons of the Forty-fourth dressed the wounded at times during the day when the balls whizzed about from the four points of the compass.

General Rosecrans re-formed his lines in the darkness of the night of the 31st, and the next morning Vancleve moved his division across Stone River to the point started for the morning before. Colonel Fyffe's brigade was placed some forty rods in front of the river, in face of the enemy, where the Forty-fourth remained all the day of January 1st, 1863, without engagement except picket firing. The morning of the second was opened with a lively artillery duel of about an hour's duration, and sharp skirmishing was continued along the whole line until about 2 o'clock P. M., when the enemy under General Breckenridge advanced in heavy storming columns. The two brigades in front, General Beatty's and Colonel Fyffe's, were forced back to the river, where they were met by supporting columns. A massed battery of some fifty-eight pieces, that had been collected in anticipation of such a movement, now opened on the enemy. A battle scene ensued that hardly had a parallel during the war. More musketry and artillery firing, probably, occurred in a like number of minutes on longer lines, but not so much on so short a line. The earth trembled under the shock, and it was reported that window-glass was broken by the concussion of the air two miles distant. The noise could hardly have been exceeded by the concentration of several thunder storms. General Breckenridge's columns melted away, and he fled back with their remnants, and the Forty-fourth planted its colors on the enemy's breastworks, and slept that night on the field of battle.

The enemy evacuated Murfreesboro that night and the next day, and General Rosecrans entered the day after.

I have been unable to find any official report of the part performed by the Forty-fourth at the battle of Stone River, and owing to the capture of Colonel Williams, in command, during the furious charge of the enemy, it is probable that none was made. Having been an eye-witness of nearly all its movements, I can testify as to its honorable conduct. Though the brigade was twice repulsed, it was under circumstances that reflected no discredit. An attempt to hold its position in either case would have been utter annihilation. The columns were in each case readily rallied, with the loss of very few stragglers. Lieutenant Dancer, of Co. H, Inspector General on Colonel Fyffe's staff, conducted himself bravely, and was severely wounded. Sergeant

Gordon relates that during the repulse on the left, Captain Cosper, Co. F, was closely pursued by a rebel, who repeatedly ordered him to halt and surrender, or he would shoot. Not heeding the demand, the rebel fired, wounding Cosper in the hand. At that he turned upon his adversary and thrust him through with his bayonet, killing him on the spot. He then continued his retreat.

The Regiment went into action with about 300 men, and lost 8 killed, 52 wounded, and 25 missing. Following are the names, as given in the official report of Surgeon Martin :

KILLED.

Thomas Helsper, Co. B.
John Webster, Co. F.
Jacob Parker, Co. F.
George W. Wallace, Co. F.
Jefferson Shannon, Co. G.
Childs Drake, Co. I.
First Sergeant Franklin Baldwin, Co. I.
Harrison Harwood, Co. K.

WOUNDED.

COMPANY A.

Corporal George W. Pervis, severe flesh wound in leg.
Frederic Swambaugh, in back, dangerously.
Joseph Willius, in leg, slight.

COMPANY B.

Sergeant Albert Ritz, slight flesh wound in foot.
Sergeant William Cartwright, slight flesh wound in leg.
John Cogan, slight flesh wound in head.
William Clark, in finger; amputated.
Scott Eddy, severe flesh wound in hip.
George Scott, in finger; amputated.

Gable Scott, severe flesh wound in thigh.
Samuel Widner, severe flesh wound in thigh.

COMPANY C.

First Sergeant Sidney Livingston, in leg, slight.
Samuel Sweet, in finger; amputated.
Owen Shaw, in arm, slight.
Jackson Hyser, in nose, slight.
Jacob Smith, fracture of thigh; amputated.

COMPANY D.

John Haller, in chest, mortal.
William Opie, in arm, slight.
Amos Britton, severe flesh wound in leg.
William Routson, in hand, severe.

COMPANY E.

Sergeant Andrew Reed, in thigh, flesh, severe.
Hiram Biddle, in back, flesh, severe,
F. A. Grable, in shoulder, severe.
Frederic Banta, in shoulder, slight.
John Spurgeon, in leg, severe.

COMPANY F.

David Robison, wounded, and probably prisoner.
P. Robbins, in arm, flesh, severe.
David Greenawalt, in leg, fracture.
Jacob Hicks, in wrist, slightly.
Francis A. Johnson, in back and elbow, slight.
George Casper, in finger; amputated.
Bennett Robe, in arm, flesh.
Lewis Tiffany, hip, severe.
Asa Harwood, arm, severe.
Chester Grimmerman, in foot.
Robin E. Ford, in thigh, flesh, slight.

COMPANY G.

Lucius McGowan, in thigh, flesh, slight.

COMPANY H.

Lieutenant J. H. Dancer, Brigade Inspector, in thigh, flesh, severe.

Peter Alspaugh, wounded, and probably prisoner.
Victor Ketchum, in thigh, flesh, severe.
Van Buren Ketchum, in leg, severe.
John J. Crist, in foot, severe.

COMPANY I.

Frederick Lavenir, in side and arm, severe.
Frederick Stroup, in arm, slight.
John Robinson, in wrist, slight.
Martin Damer, in shoulder, severe.
James A. Smith.
Martin G. Hurd, in head; missing.
John Lesher, character unknown.

COMPANY K.

Sergeant Frank Willis, in foot, slight.
Samuel Squires, in hand, severe.
Orlando Wright, in knee, serious.

CHAPTER XII.

MURFREESBORO.

THE Army of the Cumberland moved into Murfrees-boro, and went into camp in the vicinity, January 5th, 1863, General Crittenden's corps taking position on the left along the Lebanon pike. The Forty-fourth was located about one mile out, in the vicinity of the Spence mansion, which was assigned to Surgeon Martin for hospital purposes. The house was a commodious brick residence, richly furnished when abandoned by the owner during the evacuation. The Regiment passed the beautiful place in its northward march in September previous, and the lady of the house tauntingly asked some of the boys who called, "Why are you going north?" The sick boys, as they came in, were now glad she had gone south. The proprietor, we believe, was a rebel General.

Assistant Surgeons Rerick and Carr were detailed for work in the general field hospital in the rear of the battle-field. The former worked there about two weeks, when he was taken severely sick, and was brought to the Spence house, where he lay until about the middle of February, when he was granted leave of absence and sent home in charge of a nurse, with little expectation of ever being able to return. But he did return, in

April. Dr. Carr remained at the field hospital several weeks, and then returned and took medical charge of the Regiment in camp.

During the six months' encampment at Murfreesboro the Regiment was comfortably located. It had excellent hospital quarters, and the men no harder duties than work on the fortifications being erected. This period, though, was in one respect the darkest of the war, especially to Indiana soldiers. The results in the field were far from being satisfactory, and at home there was much opposition to all the vigorous measures proposed for the prosecution of the contest. The formation of secret organizations to oppose the prosecution of the war were reported, and desertions from the army were encouraged. A formidable conspiracy, known as the Knights of the Golden Circle, with headquarters in Indiana, created much alarm, not only in the public mind of the North, but in the army at the front. The Legislature that convened on the first of January, 1863, was believed to be largely under its control, an open and startling effort being made to deprive Governor Morton of his constitutional right of Commander-in-Chief of the State Militia. The Emancipation Proclamation of President Lincoln had just gone into effect, and the prejudices of the people, both at home and in the army, against the colored race, were being actively aroused. The great theme of the real sympathizers with the rebellion was, that the war was being prosecuted, not to restore the Union, but to liberate the slaves. The soldiers had all enlisted to maintain the integrity of the Union, and any deviation of the Administration from this purpose would be productive of great if not fatal disaffection in the ranks. The enemy and his sympathizers at the North well understood this, and hence the strenuous efforts, secretly and openly, to make such a deviation apparent. The soldiers, though, had no sympathy for the rebel. They were anxious for his overthrow by the most speedy and efficient means. Though they had enlisted only to restore the Union, and not to liberate a race, they were not unwilling to deprive the enemy in their front of the assistance of that race. The mass of them looked upon the Proclamation in its true light, as a military necessity, a measure needful for the overthrow of the rebellion. Thousands, though, while recognizing it as a military necessity, saw in that necessity an overruling Providence leading men who attempted one good act, to do another and possibly a greater than they had originally intended. Good begets good, and evil begets evil. The sin of slavery begot rebellion. The love of Union begot opposition to rebellion, and the liberation of an oppressed race. Slavery did not intend rebellion at first, neither did the love of Union, emancipation. The sequences in both cases were natural, and probably inevitable.

During the first months of 1863 these questions were much discussed in army circles, as well as throughout the North. The Indiana soldiers were generally indignant at the hostility to Governor Morton, and at the manifest sympathy in many parts of the State for the enemy. Memorials and resolutions were considered and adopted by regiments, and sent to the State authorities, expressing the sentiments of the soldiers. A memorial to the Legislature was read to the Forty-fourth, as well as to a number of other regiments, and by a vote of the Regiment was unanimously adopted. This memorial closed with a proposal that the Legislature adopt the following resolutions as a basis of all their acts :

1.   " *Resolved :* That we are unconditionally and determinedly in favor of the preservation of the Union.

2.   *Resolved :* That in order to the preservation of the Union, we are in favor of a vigorous prosecution of the war.

3.   *Resolved :* That we will sustain our State and Federal authorities with money and supplies, in all their efforts to sustain the Union and prosecute the war.

4.   *Resolved :* That we will discountenance every faction and influence tending to create animosities at home, or to afford consolation and aid to our enemies in arms, and that we will coöperate only with those who will stand by the Union, and with those fighting the battles of the Union.

5.   *Resolved :* That we tender to His Excellency Governor O. P. Morton, the thanks of his grateful friends in the army for his extraordinary efforts in their behalf, and assure him that neither time nor the corrupting influence of party shall ever estrange the soldier from the soldier's friend."

These resolutions fairly expressed the sentiments of the soldiers. They were presented to the Indiana Senate, February 12th, 1863, when they were assailed and finally referred to the committee on federal relations. Resolutions from the Sixty-sixth and Ninety-third Indiana Regiments, in much stronger terms, presented immediately after, caused still greater commotion. A motion was made " to reject them," " to reject the whole batch," "they were an insult to all who favored an armistice." The memorial, with the resolutions, were rejected by a vote of 28 to 18; but a petition from rebel-sympathizing citizens, denouncing the war as an "infernal abolition war," and asking "that not one man nor one dollar be voted to prosecute it," was deemed sufficiently appropriate to refer kindly to a committee.

Such was the contrast between the sentiments of the soldiers in the field, the Indiana Legislature of 1862–3, and a large body of the citizens of the State.

CHAPTER XIII.

THE CHICKAMAUGA CAMPAIGN.

THE Army of the Cumberland commenced another movement against General Bragg, June 23d, 1862, and by the next day all the divisions, except General Vancleve's, were under motion. The latter was moved into the fortifications for a few days, but set out for the front on the 4th of July, moving on the McMinnville road by way of Woodbury. The division reached McMinnville on the 7th, and went into camp. The Forty-fourth was pleasantly camped near the residence of a Mrs. Stubblefield.

On the night of the 10th, after the men had retired, the news came of the fall of Vicksburg and of the defeat of General Lee at Gettysburg. As the word passed around from tent to tent, the men jumped up and rushed out, and gave cheer after cheer. They thought surely the war was then nearly at an end.

Colonel Williams, who, after his capture at Stone River, had been carried to Libby prison, and after some months' confinement there, had been exchanged, reached his command again on the evening of the 16th, and some ten days thereafter resigned. Surgeon Martin also resigned at the same time, on account of disability.

The only commissioned officer now left of the original Field and Staff, was the writer.

While in camp here, details from the Regiment went out on several raids in the vicinity in pursuit of bush-whackers, escorted trains over the mountains to Dunlap, guarded railroad trains to Tullahoma, and worked on fortifications which were commenced near the depot.

On September 3d the division broke camp and started for the front, crossed the Cumberland Mountains to Dunlap, thence down the Sequatcha Valley to Jasper and Battle Creek, passing by the old camp left about a year before, to Bridgeport, where we crossed the Tennessee River, moved up the river road to Shell Mound, thence around the Point of Lookout Mountain in full view of Chattanooga, which had been evacuated a day or two before. We bivouacked that night at Rossville, and here rejoined the rest of General Crittenden's corps.

The march from McMinnville to this point, a distance of one hundred and thirty miles, had been made in eight days, which, considering the passage over the mountains, was considered pretty hard service. The next day, the 11th, Crittenden moved to Ringgold, and Vancleve's division was advanced some two miles south of this place. That night the body of the rebel army lay between General Crittenden and the remainder of the Army of the Cumberland, slumbering in the mountains twenty and forty miles distant. It was a golden opportunity for General Bragg, but he appeared not to know it. The next morning the division was withdrawn to Ringgold, and the whole corps marched westward twelve miles to Lee and Gordon's Mills, reaching out towards Thomas. On the 13th, Vancleve's division crossed the Chickamauga at the Mills and advanced on the Lafayette road to John Henderson's plantation, where a sharp skirmish ensued, the rebels shelling the whole line. The division was withdrawn about four o'clock P. M., and bivouacked near the Mills that night. Crittenden was here still exposed to the whole rebel army. The danger evidently becoming apparent, he moved the next day further to the west and in the direction of General Thomas, and that night rested in the Chattanooga valley on the east side of the Lookout range. Here connection was made with Thomas's corps, or a part of it, and Crittenden moved back the next day, the 15th, to Crawfish Springs, in the vicinity of Lee and Gordon's Mills. The command was held here, on the 16th and 17th, in momentary readiness for action. The great clouds of dust that could be seen across the Chickamauga to the east, and which were veering around to the north, showed the enemy in motion for our rear and for Chattanooga. With the exception of the cavalry, our division was then at the extreme left. McCook's corps was still in the mountains somewhere, struggling through. Late in the afternoon of the 18th, two regiments of Colonel Fyffe's brigade were hastily ordered to the support of General Wilder, who faced the enemy at a crossing of the Chickamauga, a mile or two north of Lee and Gordon's Mills.

For the part performed by the Forty-fourth on the bloody field of Chickamauga, we subjoin the official report of Lieutenant-Colonel Aldrich, the brave and intrepid officer in command.

"Camp of the 44th Indiana Volunteers,
Chattanooga, Sept. 27, 1863.

Colonel Dick, comd'g 2d Brig., 3d Div., 21st Army Corps:

In compliance with orders, I herewith submit a report of the part my Regiment took in the series of battles near this point. On the 18th my Regiment and the 59th Ohio were ordered three miles to the left of our camp at Crawfish Springs, to the support of Colonel Wilder. We reached the point and formed line of battle, in the after part of the day, in a wood in front of an open field. Here our cavalry were driven in a little after dark. I kept my line, expecting to see the enemy's cavalry approach, but not showing themselves, and being left alone (the 59th having fallen back), you ordered me to fall back to a new line that was forming in the field. Here we remained until near daylight the next morning. When our division came up, we were, with them, ordered still further to the left in line of battle, when we engaged the enemy, in large force, my Regiment and the 59th Ohio in front, 86th Indiana and 13th Ohio in second line. We had a very severe fight, contesting the ground inch by inch. The 59th, on our right, gave way, also the second line behind, leaving us alone to contend with a powerful force of the enemy without any support on our right. In this condition we fought the enemy as best we could for some time, until discovering that the left had also fallen back. I then ordered a slow retreat, fighting our way back to a small hollow, where I rallied my Regiment again, brought it about face and advanced a short distance and poured a destructive fire into the enemy. Again we were driven back to the ravine, again rallied, and again obliged to leave the field. This we did in tolerably good order, joining the remainder of our brigade on the hill in rear of the battle ground. These are the main points of the part performed by the Regiment in the engagement on Saturday, the 19th.

Sunday morning, after drawing rations (which part of the Regiment did not have time to do), we were ordered to the front again, to double column on the centre, and proceed by flank and forward movements until we reached a point near where the battle was raging. We advanced along a low piece of ground, making a distance to the left, where we made a short halt, deployed column, and waited the enemy's approach. A regiment engaged in the front fell back suddenly in a shattered condition, and caused a panic with most of our brigade. I succeeded in holding most of my men, and fought the enemy against great odds. At this point my horse was shot. We held them in check some time, but on their breaking around our left, I ordered a retreat, and in good order went in search of our brigade. On our march to the rear, we heard, to our then left, quite heavy firing, and directed our march to that point. Found it to be General Wood's command contesting the holding of a hill, a very important point. We arrived very opportunely, and took position with Colonel Harker's brigade, placing our flag on the brow of the hill. Our men nobly rallied and fought like veterans indeed, and assisted in repulsing the enemy three times and effectually, the enemy abandoning the ground. Here Captain Gunsenhouser and George Wilson fell. I must say I never saw troops handled better, and fight more desperately, than did Colonel Harker's brigade. We remained here until after dark, some time after the firing ceased, until the army fell back, when we proceeded to the rear, reaching Rossville about ten or eleven o'clock at night. On hearing that General Vancleve was near the forks of the roads, we moved in the morning of the 21st to find him and our brigade. I had found some of the 13th Ohio, of whom I took command the night before, and also collected from different regiments a considerable number by the time we reached the spring near the Chattanooga road, where we received orders from Captain Otis, General Vancleve's adjutant, to march to town. This we did, being the last of any amount of our brigade to take that place. Soon after reaching town I was ordered by you to take my Regiment and the 13th Ohio and proceed to Missionary Ridge. This I did, and threw up a breastwork to the right of the road across the top of the ridge. I also placed the 13th Ohio in a very commanding position one half mile to the right. We were supported by Colonel Harrison's mounted infantry. On the 22d, about 10 o'clock A. M., our videttes exchanged shots with the enemy's advance, who were driven back by Colonel Harrison's men. Between 11 and 12 o'clock the enemy advanced again, drove in the pickets and appeared in force. I reserved my fire until two lines appeared, and, being completely covered, took them by surprise when I ordered my men to rise and fire. The distance being short, and the enemy in fair view, we made terrible havoc among them. They fell back, came up again, and were met again by another volley. At this juncture they sent a force to our left to try to dislodge us, but we met them with such a shower of bullets, they did not succeed. In this way we fought them until Colonel Harrison informed me by one of his aids that they were coming down the Ridge upon our right and left, with the probability of cutting us off. I then ordered a retreat, and threw out skirmishers in my rear, and fell back in perfect order to the railroad. This ended the most important events. It would take a volume to give full particulars.

I must say for my men and officers that I never saw men fight better or more bravely, or keep together so well. Captain Gunsenhouser, Co. F, fell nobly and bravely fighting. No braver man ever fought. His life has been laid on the altar of his country. His example in the Regiment has ever been one worthy of imitation. Adjutant Hodges nobly assisted me in the management of the Regiment. Captain Curtiss deserves especial notice. He fought like a hero. Captains Wilson, Burch, King, Hildebrand, Grund and Getty did nobly. Lieutenants of the several companies did exceedingly well, with but few exceptions. The ever faithful Surgeon Rerick followed us from point to point, assisted by Dr. Carr; and I am pleased to say that no regiment has had better care for their wounded than the 44th Indiana, in this army. He succeeded also in getting all of our wounded from the hospital which was captured on Sunday evening by the enemy. All my men, with very few exceptions, deserve great praise, and earned additional honor and glory. Our casualties are as follows: Killed, 3; wounded, 59; missing, 10. Those missing I think are wounded. Attached you will find a list of killed and wounded, with name, rank, and company, nature of wound, etc. All honor to the noble dead and wounded. I cannot restrain my feelings in view of their sufferings and noble deeds.

I have the honor to be

Your obedient servant,

S. C. ALDRICH,

Lieut.-Col. Commanding."

Colonel Harker, in his official report, made honorable mention of the Regiment for its gallant aid of his command in the critical moment referred to by Lieutenant-Colonel Aldrich. Also did Generals Crittenden, Vancleve, and Wood. We regret that we have not their official reports at hand. General Thomas also compli-

SIMEON C. ALDRICH,
LIEUT. COLONEL.

mented the Lieutenant-Colonel in person. Van Horne, in his history of the Army of the Cumberland, in describing the battle after the enemy had broken through the Union lines (Vol. I, page 343), says: "For a time after the disaster on the right, there were but few divisions in line against the whole rebel army. These divisions were all firm, but the enemy was concentrating on both flanks of the line which lay across the Lafayette and Chattanooga roads. And as soon, under the inspiration of partial victory and the hope of complete triumph, most vigorous and persistent assaults were made, whose successful resistance under the circumstances makes the closing struggle of this great battle one of the most remarkable which has occurred in modern times—one of the grandest which has ever been made for the existence of army or country. From noon till night the five divisions which had previously constituted 'Thomas's line,' and such other troops as reached him from the right, under orders, or drifted to him after the disaster, and two brigades from the reserve corps, successfully resisted the whole confederate army. * * * The 44th Indiana from Dick's brigade, and the 17th Kentucky from Beatty's brigade, of Vancleve's division, were the only regiments that, without orders, diverged from the line of retreat, and reached General Thomas in time to participate in the final conflict."

And again, describing more particularly the struggle on the hill when the Forty-fourth assisted Harker's brigade of Wood's division, Van Horne says (Vol. I, page 352), after referring to the posting of the troops by General Thomas in person: "There was scarcely time'

7

for the execution of these movements before the left wing of the confederate army fell upon Wood and Brannan. It is impossible to compute with accuracy the number of troops with these Generals. Portions of their respective divisions had been previously severed and lost, and there were troops with them representing at least two divisions. General Beatty, of Negley's division, was acting as a fragmentary force, and a large portion of Stanley's brigade, Colonel Stoughton commanding, Colonel Stanley having been wounded, the 21st Ohio regiment from Sirwell's brigade, of the same division, and the 17th Kentucky, Colonel Stout, and the 44th Indiana, Lieutenant-Colonel Aldrich, from Vancleve's division. But this isolated line composed of fragments of brigades and regiments, about four thousand men in all, repeatedly repulsed the most furious attacks of Longstreet's massive lines."

The report of Lieutenant-Colonel Aldrich might seem somewhat colored to some, but the above facts obtained by Chaplain Van Horne from official reports of his superior officers, fully vindicate the Colonel's plain statement of the part performed by the Forty-fourth Indiana.

The Forty-fourth had the first fight on Missionary Ridge, and commenced it near the spot where General Bragg, a few days after, established his headquarters, and it fought over the same hill-side that General Wood's column charged up, two months later, in the great battle of Missionary Ridge. Sergeant Gordon, Co. K, who was in the fight, relates that after the Regiment had fallen back to the railroad, volunteer skirmishers were called for, and that Nicholas Ensly, Co. K, one of the number who responded, had a single-handed contest with a rebel. After firing four or five rounds at each other, " Nick " wounded his antagonist, drove him from under cover, captured his knapsack, finding it full of fresh meat, and meat only.

The two regiments were sent out to the Ridge only to retard the approach of the enemy at that point, and were not expected to enter into a regular engagement. They executed their orders satisfactorily, and during the night were withdrawn, and went into bivouac in line of battle in a cemetery on the left of a spot where, in a few days afterward, Fort Wood was built. The enemy came over the Ridge, camped along the valley at its base, extending his line from the Tennessee River around to and including Lookout Point.

The new flag was carried through the battle of Chickamauga and the engagement on Mission Ridge by Sergeant Owen Shaw, Co. C. Though slightly wounded several times, he clung to it all through, except for a few moments at one time when it was knocked out of his hands by a ball, which also struck his hand. He gathered it up immediately, and afterward planted it on the hill in front of Colonel Harker's line, in the crisis of the battle at that part of the line. He and three other sergeants, whose names we cannot recall, were subsequently examined and recommended for commissions in the colored regiments, for their gallantry in this battle.

CHAPTER XIV.

THE SIEGE OF CHATTANOOGA.

AFTER a few days in bivouac on the left of Fort
Wood, tents were brought, and we went into camp.
The location was a splendid one for scenery, and an
exciting one for peril. On our left ran the Tennessee,
and beyond it Waldron's Ridge majestically stood
frowning upon Lookout, Missionary Ridge, and all the
surrounding country; in front and east, two miles distant, lay Mission Ridge, extending from the Tennessee
southward. General Bragg's headquarters on the Ridge
were in full view, and a large part of his army lay in the
valley about midway; on the right extended the Chattanooga Valley southward, between Missionary Ridge
and Lookout Mountain, and further to the west and the
rear, as our line ran, towered Lookout Point, overlook-
ing the town and the lines of both armies, where the
enemy erected a battery and threw shells toward us
day after day for a month. Around still further to the
rear, a glimpse of Lookout Valley and Raccoon Mountains was presented, when the Waldron Ridge, footing
up to the Tennessee as it wound around Moccasin Point,
closed up the view. The railroad came up from Bridgeport, our base of supplies, through Lookout Valley and

around Lookout Point. But a few days after the battle of Chickamauga, the enemy took possession of Lookout Mountain, cut off our supplies by rail, and in a few days more sent detachments across Raccoon Mountain and cut off the approach of supplies by boat. Wagon trains were at once started to carry supplies from Bridgeport, twenty-five miles distant—air line—by way of the Sequatchie Valley and across Waldron's Ridge, making a circuitous route of sixty miles. The enemy crossed a large body of cavalry, under Wheeler, and captured and burned one train of three hundred wagons, but were finally repulsed, and this line of communication reopened after a manner, and the Union army thus, in connection with foraging expeditions up the little valleys on the north side of the river, kept from death by starvation. The road to Bridgeport became so lined with dead mules that died from starvation and exhaustion, that it became almost impassable for the stench. In camp the rations were reduced to one-half, one-third and then one-fourth, and some days none were issued at all. Sergeant Gordon, who dealt out the rations to his company, relates that on one occasion when the Regiment had drawn no rations for several days, and the men had become wild with hunger, he drew three and one-half Government crackers and three table-spoonfuls of coffee for his sixteen men. In order to give satisfaction, he broke the crackers up and formed the pieces into sixteen little piles of equal size, and thus distributed them ; then the coffee he divided out by the grain. The boys of the Forty-fourth had gained some reputation, long before this, for skill in maintaining full haversacks. Some General, none too dull of imagination, started the story that the men of the Forty-fourth Indiana could pick up a sheep grazing in the fields by the wayside, skin, dress, and divide it up among them without missing step in the march. Whatever their ability to provide for their haversacks, it did not forsake them in this trying emergency. The officers' horses, though, maintained only at the point of starvation, lost their rations of corn. Sacks of corn, black with must and rot, were found and then washed and dried, ground with coffee-mills, and made into bread. It was reported, though no one at the time would acknowledge it, that some of the boys on guard one night where a herd of cattle were crossed over the river for the army, managed to get up a stampede, and two or three of the cattle ran near the line of the Forty-fourth, where their flight was intercepted by the polls of axes in the hands of sturdy men on the lookout. There was no hoof, horn, or blood visible in the proximity of the camp the next morning, but the boys for several days appeared very contented to do without beef rations. Levi Wallack, Co. K, an eccentric and well-known character, was noted for the size of his haversack, it being about three times as large as others' and always well filled. But he was not partial, and balanced it by carrying on the other side a triple supply of ammunition, which he dealt out fearlessly to the enemy whenever opportunity offered. He did not know fear, and as little of discipline, unless he was inclined that way at the time. In the skirmish on Missionary Ridge he fired thirty-one rounds, and at every shot was heard to mutter, " There, dem you, take that." One night, while on the picket, he ascertained that there were some cattle within the rebel picket lines. The old haversack was sadly depleted just then, so down he dropped on the ground and stealthily stole his way to the cattle, faced them for the Union lines, and started them on the run. The rebels sent the bullets whizzing after him, but when they ascertained that he had escaped, and come out with fifteen head of cattle, they joined the Union boys in a cheer over the exploit. Wallack was granted the privilege of killing three of the cattle for the benefit of himself and his regiment.

None of these deprivations dampened the ardor of the men. They were heard to remark that they would prefer, after the mules and horses gave out, to go by detail to Bridgeport and carry up supplies on their backs, than abandon the position at Chattanooga. So far as suffering was concerned, there was little choice in the alternatives. These were, to starve until communications could be opened, surrender, or re-cross the Tennessee and flee for the Ohio River, three hundred miles distant, on the same roads marched over a year before from Battle Creek, only twenty miles distant. The lines of fortifications very soon became apparently impregnable. The enemy's guns on Lookout Point neither intimidated nor did any injury. An assault by the enemy was earnestly desired by the men, and the occasional threatenings of such an assault did much to reconcile the men to the situation ; as also did the news from the North of the result of the elections of this month, which were received along the whole line with immense cheering.

General Rosecrans was relieved of the command of the Army of the Cumberland, October 19th, by an order of the President, which established the military division of the Mississippi, General Grant in command and General Thomas in immediate command of the Army of the Cumberland. General Grant, instantly, upon receiving the order, telegraphed Thomas, "Hold Chattanooga at all hazards; I will be there as soon as possible." General Thomas as promptly replied, "We will hold the town until we starve." It was held. General Thomas had movements already in progress for breaking the blockade in the Tennessee River below. General Grant arrived on the 23d, and inspected and sanctioned the movements in hand. Hooker moved up from Bridgeport, where he had been concentrating, and a skillful movement down the Tennessee from Chattanooga on the night of the 26th, to Brown's Ferry, opened the river from Bridgeport to that point, only five miles distant. The two little boats in readiness commenced to bring up supplies, the size of the rations began to increase, and very soon the men began to change their speculations upon the possible duration of starvation to conjectures as to the time for advancing upon the enemy.

In the reorganization of the army after the arrival of General Grant, Lieutenant-Colonel Aldrich was appointed Provost-Marshal of Chattanooga by General Thomas, and the Forty-fourth was assigned to Post duty, with Major Hodges in command. The Regiment broke camp on the front line November 8th, and moved into town, went into camp, and entered upon the discharge of their new duty. This change deprived the Regiment from participating in the great battles on Lookout Mountain and Missionary Ridge, November 23d, 24th, and 25th. The booming cannon, and the rattling musketry on the left, center, and right, were distinctly heard, and the men standing in camp and at post witnessed, as the clouds lifted their vail from the mountain side, the grand battle of Hooker on Lookout Point, saw the rebel flag carried in retreat across the open field, near the white house under the cliff, and the stars and stripes of the Union, moistened by the heaven-kissed clouds, following close after the treacherous banner ; and when the darkness of night enveloped the mountain, saw it lighted up from base to cliff by the flashes of musketry. From more elevated points were witnessed the advance of General Wood's division, in the center, and the capture of the first line of rifle-pits at the base of Missionary Ridge, the furious charge of General Sherman on the summits on the left, and the grand charge of General Thomas's corps in the center, up Missionary Ridge, and the capture of General Bragg's headquarters.

The Forty-fourth boys, though they had before thought they had seen enough of battle at Fort Donelson, Shiloh, Stone River, and Chickamauga, were reinspired by the magnificent scene, and chafed under their new duties, and especially when they learned that their old brigade was one of the very first to scale the Ridge. Had they been with it, the banner of the Forty-fourth would undoubtedly have been planted once more on or near the very summit where it was two months before waved defiantly in the face of the enemy.

CHAPTER XV.

VETERAN ORGANIZATION.

IN December, 1863, the regiments of 1861 were offered extraordinary inducements to re-enlist. Each company and regiment was to be entitled a Veteran Organization, if three-fourths of their number should re-enlist, and the men re-enlisting were to receive four hundred dollars bounty and thirty days furlough. The matter was thoroughly discussed, and early in January, 1864, each company commander reported that the requisite number of men had re-enlisted, and on the 9th of January they were mustered in as veterans, and the Regiment became a veteran organization. The re enlisted men numbered two hundred and twenty. Nearly all the officers promised to remain with their men, but a number were mustered out at the expiration of their original enlistment in the ensuing November.

The officers at the time of re-enlistment were:

Lieutenant-Colonel, S. C. Aldrich.
Major, Joseph C. Hodges.
Adjutant, Samuel E. Smith.
Quartermaster, Samuel P. Bradford.
Surgeon, John H. Rerick.
Assistant Surgeon, George W. Carr.

Co. A.—Captain, Joseph W. Burch.
First Lieutenant, Lewis W. Griffith.
Second Lieutenant, Onius D. Scoville.

Co. B.—Captain, James S. Getty.
　　First Lieutenant, George R. Murray.
Co. C.—Captain, Philip Grund.
　　First Lieutenant, Sedgwick Livingston.
Co. D.—Captain, George W. Schell.
　　Second Lieutenant, David K. Stopher.
Co. E.—Captain, William Hildebrand.
　　First Lieutenant, Andrew J. Reed.
Co. F.—First Lieutenant, George H. Cosper.
Co. G.—Captain, Edwin W. Matthews.
　　First Lieutenant, James C. Biddle.
　　Second Lieutenant, William H. Murray.
Co. H.—Captain, Hiram F. King.
　　First Lieutenant, Daniel P. Strecker.
Co. I.—Captain, James F. Curtiss.
　　First Lieutenant, David S. Belknap.
　　Second Lieutenant, Cullen W. Green.
Co. K.—Captain, John H. Wilson.
　　First Lieutenant, Eugene S. Aldrich.
　　Second Lieutenant, Moses B. Willis.

NON-COMMISSIONED STAFF.

Hospital Steward, Charles A. Pardee.
Sergeant Major, Willis P. Andrews.
Quartermaster Sergeant, Samuel Havens.
Commissary Sergeant, Bastian Shoup.

Of the commissioned officers, Adjutant Smith, Captains Getty, Schell, Hildebrand, Matthews and Wilson, First Lieutenants Reed, Biddle, Strecker, Belknap, Aldrich, and Second Lieutenant McMurray, were mustered out at the expiration of their original enlistment, and did not properly become veterans.

As soon as transportation could be furnished, the veteran portion of the Regiment and the officers started for home, reaching Fort Wayne without accident on the last of January. Here, with orders to obtain as many recruits as possible, and to rendezvous at Kendallville March 10th, all dispersed for their homes.

They met with a hearty reception from friends and neighbors. "Ah, ha, old worn-out soldier, is it you?" was realized to be more than a poetic fancy. In a number of places public receptions were given, and the veterans treated with feasting and music.

At the date for return, the veterans promptly met at Kendallville, bringing with them some one hundred and fifty recruits, and on the next day started for Indianapolis by way of Toledo. Upon reaching Toledo, the Regiment was very agreeably surprised to find a splendid supper for them in waiting at the Island House. The Regiment was detained at Indianapolis from the 12th to the 18th, when it again set out for the front, reaching Nashville, Tennessee, on the 20th. Here the railroad to Chattanooga was found overburdened with troops being pushed to the front, and by returning veterans. A large number were required to move on on foot, the Forty-fourth being of the number. The line of march was taken up on the 23d of April, by way of Murfreesboro, Tullahoma, Deckard, Manchester, Stevenson, to Bridgeport, which was reached in twelve days. Here transportation was provided, and the Regiment was, in a few hours, in Chattanooga again, ready for whatever duty might be assigned. The non-veterans had remained here on detail duty during the absence of the veterans.

CHAPTER XVI.

POST SERVICE.

In the reorganization of the Army of the Cumberland under General Thomas, in April, 1864, General James B. Steedman was placed in command of the garrison of Chattanooga, and had assigned to him the first separate brigade, consisting of the 8th Kentucky Infantry, the 15th, 29th, 44th, 51st, 68th Indiana Infantry, and the 3d and 24th Ohio Infantry, an engineer brigade, a pioneer brigade, eight colored regiments, and numerous batteries.

Chattanooga was now the most important war center in the west, and was the point of concentration for the armies making ready to move southward under General Sherman, and was to be the base of supplies for all the movements then in hand. Whether it was more important and glorious to march on Atlanta or guard the base of operations and keep the communications open, was not for the Regiment to discuss, but that the services required were of grave importance and peril could readily be inferred from the assignment of one of the best fighting generals to the command of the garrison, and a number of the old and best fighting regiments to him. The Forty-fourth, on the 10th of April, relieved the 15th, regulars, and took their camp on the hillside facing the town from the east, and resumed general guard duty. A number of the officers were detailed on courts-martial. In this capacity the officers and men served during the summer of 1864.

Assistant-Surgeon Carr was in March promoted Surgeon of the 129th Indiana, and moved with his new command to the front. Dr. Edward B. Speed, of Lagrange, Indiana, a good physician and an estimable man, was appointed to the vacancy in July, but fell sick soon after his arrival, a misfortune which was due, in part, to a railroad accident on his way. He was taken to the officers' hospital on Lookout Mountain, where the best care and treatment possible in the army was provided, but he died September 15th. He never had an opportunity to get acquainted with many of the Regiment, but in his sickness had the sympathy of all, and the officers, upon his death, had his body embalmed at their expense and sent home.

Lieutenant-Colonel Aldrich was in poor health all summer. Early in August he obtained a furlough and went home for the benefit of his health, but in a few days after reaching there he was suddenly taken worse, and died August 15th. His death was much lamented. He was a brave man, a good disciplinarian, and took great pride in the good appearance and discipline of his men. He had commanded the Regiment from Stone River to the day of his leave, except when temporarily absent on some other duty. He was commissioned Colonel in July, 1863, but could never be mustered as such owing to the reduced number of men in the Regiment.

The command now fell upon Major Joseph C. Hodges, who in a few days was mustered in as Lieutenant-Colonel. Early in September, when rebel General Hood turned his army northward, the whole line of communication from Atlanta to Nashville was roused into great activity. General Forrest crossed the Tennessee in the vicinity of Decatur, Alabama, September 20th, and at once advanced on Athens and the railroad communications with Nashville. General Steedman was ordered to send out troops to protect the line, and on the 28th the Forty-fourth, with other regiments, started northward on the railroad. The Regiment was carried on a train of freight cars, and moving slowly, reached Tullahoma about midnight. When within about three miles of this place, Lieutenant-Colonel Hodges, while walking on the cars looking after his command, by some accidental misstep fell between the cars and was run over by part of the train. His right knee and thigh were crushed into shreds. The train was stopped, he was taken up, put in a car, and carried to the hospital at Tullahoma, where his thigh was amputated near the hip joint. He never rallied from the operation, and died before morning. His sudden and untimely death was a severe shock to his command, by whom he was much respected for his bravery and devotion to the best interests of his men. The Regiment had now lost two Lieutenant Colonels and an assistant surgeon within less than forty days.

The command now fell upon Major James F. Curtiss, who was soon after promoted Lieutenant-Colonel. The

Regiment lay at Tullahoma until October 2d, when it, with a number of other regiments, was ordered to report at once to General Rousseau, at Nashville, where it arrived that night, and before morning was mounted. Day dawned upon an inspiring scene, which, though, possessed some ridiculous and amusing features. General Rousseau, with some eight thousand cavalry, light artillery and mounted infantry, was moving rapidly southward on the Franklin pike, presenting, at first sight, a grand line. A little closer view, though, along the line of mounted infantry, revealed a fountain of material for the comic artist and humorist. The streets of the city and the corrals in the vicinity had been stripped of everything in the shape of a horse; the lame, the halt, and the blind had been gathered up for the expedition, and the Forty-fourth was especially unfortunate in the lot assigned it, being among the last to arrive. Men were mounted who had not been in the saddle for years, and some never. Many were on horses that could not be forced into a trot, and some not even into a walk. A number of horses were abandoned at the start, and the others as fast as the boys could find somebody to trade with. The trading was decidedly one-sided, but so poor was the country in horses at that time that no advantage could be obtained even in that way. Before starting on this trip, it may be remarked that after arrival at Chattanooga, while on duty in the dark—and it was very dark—Lieutenant Strecker, Company H, fell into a deep cut in the railroad, and was severely injured; and that just at this time, the State election in Indiana was pending, in which every soldier was deeply interested, as upon its decision depended the re-election of their best friend in the State, Governor Morton. It was also a time General Thomas had good reason for being relieved of all disabled men. The opportunity was a rarely good one for the soldier to get home to vote, and Lieutenant Strecker and several others of the Regiment unfit for mounted service, who were left behind, were soon being whirled northward. Strecker reached his home about an hour before the closing of the polls, and did his duty.

The Forty-fourth was assigned to Colonel Grosvenor's brigade of the expedition, with the surgeon of the Regiment as brigade surgeon. The first day, October 3d, the expedition marched to Franklin, twenty-one miles; October 4th, to Stone House, four miles south of Columbia; October 5th, to the vicinity of Lawrenceburg, twenty-six miles; October 6th, to Blue Creek, twenty-eight miles; October 7th, to Florence, Alabama, and thence down the river four miles to Cypress Mills. Here we came upon some of the rear guard of Forrest's command. Had a slight skirmish, killing one rebel. October 8th, marched out seven miles on the Savannah road; returned and marched four miles out on the Waterloo road; October 9th, marched about ten miles on the Waterloo road, and then countermarched to Cypress Mills. The enemy had safely escaped across the Tennessee River. October 10th, 11th, and 12th, in bivouac and foraging. In this expedition General Rousseau had to depend wholly upon the country for forage, and in part for rations for the men. The rebel forces had just advanced and then retreated over the same country, living in like manner off of it. There were some most distressing scenes of poverty and misery seen. The people were literally stripped of all the provender and provisions they had in the world, and were, in many cases, apparently not left with enough to maintain life until they could flee to sections of the country not passed over by the two armies.

October 13, marched on the return to within three miles of Athens, Alabama, making a distance of forty-eight miles. Went in bivouac at midnight, and arose at four o'clock in the morning, marched to Athens, turned over the horses, and at midnight took train for Chattanooga, arriving there in the afternoon, October 15th. The Regiment had been out nineteen days, and had traveled two hundred and eighty miles by railroad and two hundred miles on horseback. The men were satisfied with mounted service.

Chattanooga was now again the scene of much activity. Rebel General Hood had flanked General Sherman at Atlanta, and was now striking his line of communication at various points, and advancing towards Chattanooga. General Thomas was concentrating all his forces as fast as possible at Chattanooga and points along the line. But Hood, when he reached La Fayette, turned westward, indicating his intention of invading Tennessee west of the Cumberland Range. General Sherman quickly reopened his lines, received his final equipments, and set out from Atlanta on his march to the sea. Thomas moved all the troops that could possibly be spared from East Tennessee, around to Bridgeport, Stevenson, Tullahoma, and finally to Nashville, where he made his final stand against Hood.

During November, the non-veterans of the Regiment having served three years, the term of enlistment, were mustered out, and early in December eleven commissioned officers also. The latter had entered the service as enlisted men for three years, and had since been promoted, and could not be held longer than their original enlistment, unless they had chosen to be so under the veteran enlistments. Only three of the original officers now remained : Lieutenant-Colonel Curtiss, Captain Grund, and Surgeon Rerick ; and only about two hundred of the original men. On the 17th of November the Regiment was recruited by two hundred drafted men, and on the 20th by two hundred more, nearly all from the southern part of Indiana. These, with the previous volunteer recruits, gave the Regiment a numerical strength of some eight hundred.

During the last days of November, General Steedman was ordered to hasten to Nashville with all available forces that could be spared. Chattanooga was so shorn of troops that all the citizens and sojourners were ordered to be enrolled as "Civic Guards," to assist in the protection of the post, should their services be needed. The front was now changed from the South to the North, from Atlanta to Nashville, and communications with the new front were cut about the first of December, and for about three weeks we were without news from the North, or from Nashville, even. They were wearisome and somewhat anxious days. Disaster at Nashville would have been disaster at Chattanooga, and the loss of all that had been achieved in Kentucky, Tennessee, and of nearly all in the South-west. The new line would again have been the Ohio River, as at the beginning of the war. There was, probably, no more critical day in the whole war than the day General Thomas moved out from Nashville to attack Hood. General Grant's telegrams to Thomas show that he felt keenly the immense issues at stake. He had even started to Nashville to superintend the battle himself, but upon reaching Washington he was intercepted by a telegram announcing the great victory—great not only in valor, but in saving what had been attained in the South-west, and virtually ending the war in that part of the Union. There was no engagement of any magnitude after this, west of the Alleghany Mountains. Communications were opened on the 24th of December, and the soldiers at Chattanooga made glad by the receipt of a month's accumulated mail, and the "Civic Guards" pleased by a release from military restraints and prospective service.

CHAPTER XVII.

1865 AND HOME.

EARLY in January, 1865, the troops at Chattanooga were re-brigaded, the Forty-fourth being assigned to the 2d Brigade, 1st Separate Division of the Army of the Cumberland. The Regiment had now to assist in picket duty, as well as post duty. On the 29th of January the Forty-fourth was hastily moved by railroad to Athens, Tennessee, to repel a raid on that place, but upon reaching there found the raiders had already been repelled, and the Regiment returned the next day. On the way back, two cars of the train were thrown off the track by the spreading of the rails, killing Samuel A. Baker, Co. E, and severely wounding five others.

And again, at midnight, February 4th, the Regiment was aroused, rushed to the depot, and put on board a train for Altowah, fifteen miles distant, to repel a raid of guerrillas, but returned the next day without having a sight at them. This was the last call on the Regiment to face the enemy during the rebellion.

The news of the fall of Fort Sumter and capture of Charleston, reached Chattanooga February 22d, and was the occasion of great rejoicing. The heavy guns in the forts, and the field guns were fired, a score of engines at the depot blew their whistles, and the men screamed until hoarse or exhausted. The improvised

windows in the soldiers' "shanties," and many even
in the more solid structures, were shattered by the concussion of the air. The best things in the soldiers'
larders, and some things that had not got there before,
were prepared for supper, and feasting and joy were
unbounded.

On March 17th, Lieutenant-Colonel Curtiss was promoted and mustered in as Colonel, Captain Grund as
Lieutenant-Colonel, Captain Burch, Co. A, as Major,
and Isaac N. Plummer, a regularly educated physician
who had been drafted into the service at Evansville,
Indiana, and was among the four hundred drafted men
received in November before, and who had been recommended by the Surgeon, with the approval of the
Colonel, for promotion to Assistant Surgeon, and commissioned by the Governor, was also mustered in, April
8th.

The rejoicings of the Regiment over the surrender of
Lee, and the grief over the assassination of President Lincoln, the writer did not witness, being at the time absent
on leave. The men became quite anxious for a muster
out after the surrender of the great rebel armies, but
had to await the result of the predictions of guerrilla
warfare, the adjustment of many war questions, and the
disposition of the immense amount of army property
accumulated. During the month of May thousands of
rebels came into the post, surrendered, and returned to
their homes. They brought with them a considerable
amount of silver coin, which they largely spent in pur-
chases, putting in circulation a currency that had not
been seen before by Union soldiers since the opening of

the war. An exchange of greenbacks at the rate of $1.25 for a silver dollar was made, until almost every Union soldier had a silver piece which was claimed to be one of the identical dollars the Confederates had stolen from the United States mint at New Orleans.

In June, one hundred and fifty of the drafted men were mustered out. General Steedman was relieved of command at Chattanooga about the first of July, and assigned to the command of the department of Georgia, with headquarters at Augusta. Captain Bradford, Co. H, who had served on his staff since the first assignment of the General to the Post, went with him, accompanied by his wife, who had come to her husband when the Regiment lay at McMinnville, in July, 1863, and had accompanied him on horseback in the march to Chickamauga, sharing the soldier's fare of her husband nearly all the time since.

The Forty-fourth, under the new arrangements, was assigned to the District of East Tennessee, and required to report by letter to General A. C. Gillam, commanding at Knoxville. About the middle of July the troops left in East Tennessee were formed into two brigades, composed each of white and colored regiments. The second brigade consisted of the 44th Indiana Infantry, the 11th Michigan Infantry, and the 16th, 18th, 42d and 44th United States Colored Infantry, with Colonel Johnson, of the 44th U. S. C. I., in command. The Surgeon of the 44th Indiana was detailed on his staff as Brigade Surgeon, and Captain M. B. Willis, Co. K, as Inspector General.

The "spotted brigade" arrangement was the occasion of much joking and amusement, but much of it

not so merry as to hide the deep-seated prejudice of the
white soldiers to such close relations with the colored
race.   This prejudice was fully developed in a few days,
when the guard detail was required to form in line with
guard details from the colored regiments, at guard
mounting.   Men who had passed through nearly four
years' service, and readily obeyed every order in battle,
on march, and in camp, now hesitated to form in line
with colored men, and obey the orders of white officers
of colored regiments   They actually stacked arms, voluntarily surrendered themselves, and with their Lieutenant in charge, who surrendered his sword, submitted
to be marched off to the guard-house under a colored
guard, and there be guarded by colored soldiers.   The
citizens took side with the white soldiers, and many
seemed ready to fan up a general disturbance.   But this
was readily averted.   Colonel Curtiss at once called
upon the brigade commander, and they upon the Pro-
vost Commandant, and all visited the men.   They were
released after a few hours' detention, and the next day
guard mounting was gone through in regular form, the
white details being formed under their own officer, on
the same line with the colored detail, though at a
" respectable distance."

This event, though showing considerable inconsis-
tency and prejudice, nevertheless marked much progress
on the part of white soldiers in their regard for the
colored race.   When they first entered the service they
would not have accorded freedom to the slave; now
they respected their freedom, and their right and privilege of serving the same country as soldiers, but had

not yet advanced to the point where they would not feel that there would be an odious equality in forming in line with them in peaceful guard mounting. Had they been forming a line of battle, there would have been no objection. Patriots can, in the face of peril and death, forget the prejudices that may rule them on fancy parade in times of peace.

During the month of July, one hundred and fifty more of the drafted men were mustered out. In August the "grape vine" dispatches began to thicken fast of a probable early muster-out, and the officers began to prepare their papers for the earnestly hoped-for event. The Surgeon, after an examination of all his medical reports since the Regiment entered the service, made, at the time, a summary as follows :

Died of disease,	212
Died of wounds,	26
Killed on the field,	39
Whole number of deaths,	277
Whole number killed and wounded,	350

Of these, twelve were commissioned officers, and two hundred and sixty-five enlisted men. Two officers were killed on the field, two died of wounds, one from railroad injury, and five of disease.

Died with the command in camp or in Regimental Hospital,	58
Died in General Hospital, or at home,	180
Killed in the field as above,	39
Total;	277

There was but one death from disease in Regimental Hospital or camp quarters after August 1st, 1863. There were some one thousand five hundred and fifty men altogether in the command, exclusive of about three hundred from the 68th and 72d Indiana, assigned to it a few weeks before muster out. The recruits received were: Fifty in the fall of 1862; one hundred and forty in the spring of 1864; four hundred drafted men and substitutes in November, 1864; three hundred and sixty men, detachments of the 68th and 72d Indiana Regiments. Of the recruits, one was killed, and forty died of disease. This leaves the casualties of the original officers and men at two hundred and thirty-five, or about twenty-four per centum.

The distance traveled by the Regiment during its service, on foot, on horse, by boat, and by railroad, including return home on veteran furlough, was about five thousand miles. About fifteen hundred miles of the distance was marched on foot.

Adjutant General Terrell's report shows the total number belonging to the Regiment to have been twenty-two hundred and three. But in this he counts the veterans twice, as original enlisted men and again as enlisted veterans, and also a large number of unassigned recruits.

The welcome order of relief from further duty as soldiers came September 3d, and on the 6th the Regiment boarded a train for Nashville, reaching there on the 7th. The Chattanooga *Gazette*, in noticing the departure of the Regiment, said:

" The officers and men of the 44th Indiana V. V. I. have, during their stay in this city, won the respect and admirat on of the citizens as a brave and well disciplined regiment. They will take with them to their homes in Indiana the hearty wishes of the citizens and residents of Chattanooga."

The muster-out rolls were prepared at Nashville, and the Regiment was mustered out September 14th, 1865, and then sent on to Indianapolis for payment and final discharge. There were six hundred and seventy men and thirty five officers mustered out at this time. Of these, one hundred and ninety-three were original enlisted men and three original officers. Thirty two of the officers mustered out entered the service as enlisted men, and the three original officers, Colonel Curtiss and Lieutenant-Colonel Grund, as Second Lieutenants, and Surgeon Kerick as Assistant Surgeon. Eighty-nine of the original men were mustered out as non-commissioned officers, and seventy-one as privates.

Original commissioned officers	39
Mustered out September 14th, 1865,	3
Original enlisted men	950
Mustered out September 14th, 1865,	193

The earliest date of the commissions to the company officers at the organization of the Regiment was September 20th, 1861, and this, we judge, was the earliest date of enlistment by the men. Three commissions for field and staff officers for the organization of the Regiment were issued September 12th, 1861. The Surgeon mustered out bore one of these three commissions, and had therefore served four years and two days, the longest service shown on the record of any member of the Regiment. And an examination of Adjutant General Terrell's reports shows this to have been the longest service in the field of any medical officer from the State, with possibly one exception.

As soon as payment was made at Indianapolis, the Regiment disbanded, every man returning to his home, where he at once donned the garb and assumed the duties of the private citizen.

The farewell address of General Grant in June, 1865, to the Armies of the United States, being as largely applicable to the Forty-fourth Indiana as any other regiment in the service of the Union, and being a tribute worthy the remembrance of every ex-soldier and loyal citizen, will summarize and close our record:

"SOLDIERS OF THE ARMIES OF THE UNITED STATES:

By your patriotic devotion to your country in the hour of danger and alarm, your magnificent fighting, bravery and endurance, you have maintained the supremacy of the Union and the Constitution, over-thrown all armed opposition to the enforcement of the laws, and of the proclamation forever abolishing slavery —the cause and pretext of the rebellion—and opened the way to the rightful authorities to restore order and inaugurate peace on a permanent and enduring basis on every foot of American soil.

Your marches, sieges and battles, in distance, duration, resolution and brilliancy of result dim the lustre of the world's past military achievements, and will be the patriotic precedent in defense of liberty and right in all time to come.

In obedience to your country's call, you left your homes and families, and volunteered in its defense. Victory has crowned your valor and secured the purpose of your patriot hearts; and with the gratitude of your countrymen and the highest honors a great and free nation can accord, you will soon be permitted to return to your homes and families, conscious of having discharged the highest duty of American citizens. To achieve these glorious triumphs and secure to yourselves, your fellow-countrymen and posterity the blessings of free institutions, tens of thousands of your gallant comrades have fallen, and sealed the priceless legacy of their lives. The graves of these a grateful nation bedews with tears, honors their memories, and will ever cherish and support their stricken families."

PERSONAL MENTION.

PERSONAL MENTION.

FIELD AND STAFF OFFICERS.

THE COLONELS.

Colonel Hugh B. Reed is a native of Ohio, and studied for the medical profession in Cincinnati, where he afterward engaged in the drug business. In 1845 he moved to Fort Wayne, and at the breaking out of the war was conducting an extensive wholesale and retail business as a druggist. He answered the first call of the Government for troops by aiding in raising and organizing the 12th Regiment of Indiana Volunteers, and when a camp was ordered at Fort Wayne for the organization of the 30th and 44th Regiments, he was placed in command of the camp by Governor Morton; and as soon as the first was organized, and enough for the second regiment was assured, was commissioned Colonel of the 44th. He led it as coolly and bravely as a troop was ever led, in the battles of Fort Donelson and Shiloh, to which reference is more fully made in the description of those battles. He commanded the Regiment in the advance on Corinth, and in the march from there to Booneville, Miss., and thence to Tuscumbia, Athens, Stevenson, Ala., and to Battle Creek, Tenn. Up to this time he had not been absent a day from his command.

Here he was granted a short leave of absence, but rejoined the Regiment soon after it had crossed the Cumberland Mountains upon the Buell and Bragg foot-race, and was with it, most of the time, in the tiresome march to Nashville, Louisville, Perrysville, Wild Cat, and back to Nashville. His health was much impaired in the service, and he resigned, November 26, 1862, and at the close of the war, to promote his health, moved to the East, and now resides at Somerville, N. J., in the vicinity of New York.

COLONEL WILLIAM C. WILLIAMS is a native of Pennsylvania; received a classical and medical education, and was, at the breaking out of the war, a practicing physician at Albion, Noble county, Indiana. He entered the service as Captain of Company G, which he helped to recruit. With Companies G and K he was in command of the Post at Henderson, Ky., from January to the middle of March, 1862, rejoined the Regiment with his command on its way up the Tennessee River to Pittsburg Landing, led his company in the battle of Shiloh, and thence in all the marches until promoted Colonel to fill the vacancy occasioned by the resignation of Colonel Reed, November 27, 1862. He led the Regiment in the battle of Stone River, where, on the third day, in the furious charge of General Breckenridge on the left, he was captured, and afterwards sent to Libby Prison. After several months' detention there he was exchanged, and returned to the Regiment at McMinnville, Tenn., where he was received with much joy by the Regiment. Resigned July 27, 1863. Since the war he has filled the office of Clerk of his county two terms, and now resides at Albion, Indiana.

COLONEL SIMEON C. ALDRICH was a native of Vermont; went to California in 1860, and returned to his home at Pleasant Lake, Steuben county, Indiana, September 1st, 1861, and in a few days commenced to assist in recruiting Company K; was elected First Lieutenant, but was soon promoted to Captain, and led the Company in the battle of Shiloh. Was promoted to Lieutenant-Colonel, November 27, 1862, commanded the Regiment from January 2, 1862, and led it through the battle of Chickamauga. In this battle, after the lines were broken, and the brigade and division scattered, he led the Forty-fourth, without orders, except the sound of artillery showing where heroes were needed, to the left, coming to the aid of General Harker's line, in General Thomas's command, at a most critical moment, and rendered a service that won for him and the Regiment flattering comments from Generals Thomas, Wood, and Harker, who were eye-witnesses. He found his brigade and division after the battle. As soon as the army fell back to Chattanooga, he was sent out with the 44th and the 13th Ohio Volunteers to Missionary Ridge, to observe and retard the approach of the enemy, and here had a brisk skirmish. November 8th, 1863, he was appointed Provost-Marshal of Chattanooga, and the Regiment placed on Post duty. He filled the duties of Provost-Marshal until the Regiment re-enlisted, when he accompanied the veterans home, and returned with them to Chattanooga, and was in command of the Regiment until early in August, 1863, when he was granted leave of absence on account of ill-health. A few days after he reached home he was suddenly taken worse, and died, August 15, 1863. He was commissioned as Colonel, July 27, 1863, but owing to the reduced number of men in the Regiment, could never be mustered in as such.

COLONEL JAMES F. CURTISS was a jeweler by trade; resided at Elkhart; entered the service as Second Lieutenant of Company I; was promoted First Lieutenant January 18, 1862; Captain, March 21, 1863; commissioned

Major, August 23, 1863, but was not mustered as such;
promoted Lieutenant-Colonel, September 28, 1864, and
Colonel, March 12, 1865, and was mustered out with the
Regiment. He was with the Regiment in all its
marches and battles, from the first to the last day of its
service. His bravery was noted in all the battles, and
especially complimented by his commander at Chickamauga. He returned after the war to Elkhart, and a
few years after went from there to Northern Michigan
and entered a soldier's homestead, but while working
on it, one day, suddenly died.

THE LIEUTENANT-COLONELS.

LIEUTENANT-COLONEL SANFORD J. STOUGHTON was
at the opening of the war an attorney-at-law, in active
practice at Ligonier, Noble County. He was commissioned Major, September 12, 1861, for the organization of
the Forty-fourth Regiment, and rendered active and
efficient aid in recruiting its ranks. He served bravely
in the battles of Fort Donelson and Shiloh, and was
with the Regiment in the advance on Corinth and in
the march to Battle Creek, Louisville, and back to
Nashville. He was promoted to Lieutenant-Colonel,
March 10, 1862, and to Colonel of the 100th Indiana
Volunteer Infantry, November 12, 1862, where he
served until January 7th, 1864, when he resigned. He
is now a resident of Ottowa, Kansas.

LIEUTENANT-COLONEL SIMEON C. ALDRICH. See
"COLONELS."

LIEUTENANT-COLONEL JOSEPH C. HODGES was a
resident of Elkhart, assisted in the organization of
Company I, and was elected First Lieutenant, which
position he held until May, 1862, when he was promoted Adjutant. He was promoted Major, October 24,

1863, and Lieutenant-Colonel, August 15, 1864. He died from the effects of a railroad accident near Tullahoma, Tenn., September 28, 1864, as more fully noted in the preceding pages. He participated in all the movements and battles of the Regiment from the first day of its entrance into the service until the hour of his death. He was brave as a lion, and too impulsive to witness cowardice without burning indignation. An instance of the latter occurred when the Regiment was marching out to engage the enemy at Shiloh, on the morning of April 6th. General Prentiss' division had been surprised and routed, and detachments of it were fleeing back as the Regiment marched out. A stampeded Colonel came dashing along to the rear, exclaiming, "We're whipped, we're whipped; we're all cut to pieces!" Lieutenant Hodges was marching along with his company, but his wrath boiling over, he rushed from the line, caught the cowardly Colonel's horse by the bridle, at the same time drawing his revolver, and exclaimed: "You —— cowardly wretch, utter those words again and you are a dead man! You infernal coward, have you no more sense than to try and demoralize troops going into action? Go to the rear, you coward, but don't open your head on the way." The trembling coward did not resent, but it was noticed he rode at a more moderate gait, and it is supposed was somewhat more reflective.

LIEUTENANT-COLONEL JAMES F. CURTISS. See under "COLONELS."

LIEUTENANT-COLONEL PHILIP GRUND was a foreman in the railroad shops at Fort Wayne; assisted in recruiting Company C, entering the service as Second Lieutenant of that Company; was promoted to First Lieutenant, January 20, 1863; Captain, June 11, 1863, and Lieutenant-Colonel, March 12, 1865, and was mustered out with the Regiment, serving with it during its entire service, participating in all its marches and battles. After the war he returned to Fort Wayne, and resumed his old position in the shops, which he yet holds.

THE MAJORS.

MAJOR SANFORD J. STOUGHTON. See "LIEUTENANT COLONELS."

MAJOR WILLIAM B. BINGHAM is a native of Ohio; served with an Ohio regiment in the war with Mexico; was a resident of Lagrange; assisted in recruiting Company H, and several companies in Lagrange county; entered the service as Captain of Company H, and for gallantry at Fort Donelson was promoted Major, April 15, 1862. Was in command of the Regiment at Battle Creek, and on the march from that point to near Bowling Green, Ky., when he resigned, September 7, 1862, on account of recurrence of chronic diarrhœa, contracted in the Mexican war. He returned to his home at Lagrange, where he now resides.

MAJOR CHARLES F. KINNEY resided near Metz, Steuben county; assisted in organizing Company A, of which company he was chosen Captain. He was as ranking Captain in command of the Regiment while in the vicinity of Nashville, and was commissioned Major November 27, 1862, but declined to muster as such, and resigned. He was a worthy, exemplary man and good officer, and by seniority entitled to promotion to the Colonelcy at the time. After his return home he moved to Angola, where he died a few years after.

MAJOR WILLIAM M. MILES was a resident of Indianapolis, and was promoted to Major from a lieutenancy in the 22d Indiana Volunteers, to give him rank on

WILLIAM B. BINGHAM,

MAJOR.

General Rosecrans' staff, where he was serving. He never served with the Regiment, and was soon changed from the roster of the Forty-fourth, being promoted again, in his own regiment. He died at Indianapolis in April, 1880.

MAJOR JOSEPH C. HODGES. See "LIEUTENANT-COLONELS."

MAJOR JAMES F. CURTISS. See "COLONELS."

MAJOR JOSEPH W. BURCH was a resident of Steuben county; entered the service as a private of Company A; served some time as Hospital Steward; was promoted to Second Lieutenant. March 1, 1863, Captain, June 11, 1863, and Major, March 12, 1865, and was mustered out with the Regiment. He now resides in Minnesota.

THE ADJUTANTS.

ADJUTANT CHARLES CASE was a resident of Fort Wayne, and prominent as a lawyer and politician. Had served the Tenth Congressional District one term in Congress, his term expiring March 4, 1861. He felt it his duty to serve the country in the field, and was willing to accept any position at the time open. Not only his, but the heart of the whole command, responded to the sentiment of the poet:

> "To fight
> In a just cause, and for our country's glory,
> Is the best office of the best men;
> And to decline, when these motives urge,
> Is infamy beneath a coward's baseness."

He was commissioned Adjutant, September 28, 1861; was promoted Major of the 3d Cavalry, April 15, 1862; resigned in June, 1862; was appointed Colonel of the 129th Indiana Volunteers, March 1, 1864. Resigned in June, 1864, to accept appointment as Paymaster in the army. When last heard from, he was practicing law in the United States Supreme Court, at Washington.

ADJUTANT JAMES COLGROVE entered the service from DeKalb county, as Second Lieutenant of Company F. Was promoted Adjutant, January 10, 1862, and resigned May 27, 1862. He now resides in Chicago.

ADJUTANT JOSEPH C. HODGES. See "LIEUTENANT-COLONELS."

ADJUTANT SAMUEL E. SMITH was a resident of Elkhart; had been a student in the Michigan University; entered the service as a private of Company I; served some time as Sergeant-Major; was promoted Adjutant, November 14, 1863, and was mustered out at the expiration of his three years' enlistment. He is now a resident of California.

ADJUTANT WILLIS P. ANDREWS entered the service as a private of Company F; succeeded Smith as Sergeant-Major; re-enlisted as a veteran, and was promoted Adjutant, April 11, 1865, and was mustered out with the Regiment, September 14, 1865. He is now practicing medicine in Michigan.

THE QUARTERMASTERS.

GEORGE W. McCONNELL was a merchant and land dealer at Angola; took an active interest in the organization of the Regiment; was commissioned Quartermaster September 28, 1862; resigned January 3, 1863, on account of disability. He returned to his business at Angola, where he still resides.

MARQUIS L. BAYLISS was a resident of Fort Wayne; was appointed Quartermaster, February 4, 1862; was with the Regiment at Fort Donelson, Shiloh, and Corinth. At the latter point he was taken sick, was given leave of absence, and died at his home in Fort Wayne, July, 1862.

SAMUEL P. BRADFORD was a resident of Lagrange county; entered the service as a private of Company H; served some time as Wagon-Master, and then as Commissary-Sergeant, and after the illness of Quartermaster Bayliss, performed the labor of Quartermaster, although commissioned officers who only could officially act as such, nominally held the place. Was commissioned Quartermaster, February 21, 1863, and Captain of Company H, January 16, 1865. He was detailed as Chief Quartermaster on the staff of General Steedman in the spring of 1864, and went with that General as a member of his staff to Augusta, Georgia, in July, 1865, and was not present at the muster-out of the Regiment. He was not finally discharged until by special order of General Grant, November, 1868, though only in pay from the Government some fifty days after the muster-out of the Regiment. He is now a resident of Lagrange, filling the office of Clerk of the Lagrange Circuit Court, to which he was elected in 1876.

LIEUTENANT ALEXANDER KINMONT was a resident of DeKalb county; entered the service as a private of Company F; was promoted Sergeant; re-enlisted as a veteran; was promoted First Lieutenant June 3, 1864, and Quartermaster January 17, 1865, and was mustered out with the Regiment September 14, 1865, serving with and sharing all the marches and battles of the Regiment.

THE CHAPLAINS.

REV. GEORGE W. BEEKS was educated for the profession of medicine, which he practiced some years, and then entered the Methodist ministry. At the breaking

out of the war he was pastor of one of the Methodist
Episcopal churches at Fort Wayne, and held in high
esteem by that denomination. He was commissioned
Chaplain November 25, 1861, went to the front with the
Regiment, and rendered some valuable service for the
wounded at Fort Donelson. Resigned December 1st,
1862. He died in 1879.

REV. ISAAC F. ROBERTS was an Episcopalian clergy-
man, resident in the southern part of the State, and
was commissioned Chaplain January 10, 1863, and resigned November 7, 1863. While with the command he
took creditable interest in the moral welfare of the men.

THE SURGEONS.

DR. WILLIAM W. MARTIN was a native of Balti-
more, Indiana, received a medical education, and at the
breaking out of the war was in active practice at Rome
City, Noble county. Recruited about one-third of Company D. Was commissioned Surgeon November 25,
1861, served the Regiment on the field at Fort Donelson,
Shiloh, and Stone River, and was with it in all the
marches until August 1st, 1863, when he resigned on
account of ill health. Died at Kendallville, about the
close of the war. The ardent devotion with which he
served the sick under his care, and the determination
with which he sought the best advantages possible for
them, is a memory warmly cherished by many survivors of the command.

DR. JOHN H. RERICK was born in Tippecanoe
county, Indiana; graduated in the Medical Department
of the University of Michigan in 1853; was in practice
at Lagrange at the breaking out of the war; assisted in
recruiting the first volunteers from Lagrange county;
was appointed Assistant Surgeon for the organization

of the Regiment, September 12, 1861. Was promoted Surgeon, October 28, 1863. Served on the field at the battles of Shiloh, Stone River, Chickamauga, and Mission Ridge. At the close of the war he returned to Lagrange, and resumed the practice of his profession. Entered the newspaper business in 1867, was elected Clerk of the Lagrange Circuit Court in 1868, and in 1872, serving eight years in that capacity. Is now editor and proprietor of the Lagrange *Standard*.

THE ASSISTANT SURGEONS.

DR. JOHN H. RERICK. See "SURGEONS."

DR. GEORGE W. CARR was a regular practicing physician at Ligonier. Immediately after the battle of Shiloh he volunteered his services to the Governor, temporarily, in the field, and was appointed Additional Assistant Surgeon *pro tem.* for the Regiment. A law afterward being enacted allowing two assistant surgeons for each regiment, he was commissioned Second Assistant Surgeon of the 44th Indiana, which he served until March 1st, 1864, when he was promoted Surgeon of the 129th Indiana Volunteers. He served this regiment until May, 1865, when he resigned. He is now a resident of Ligonier, and in the practice of his profession.

DR. EDWARD B. SPEED was a regular physician, in practice at Lagrange. Was commissioned Assistant Surgeon June 24, 1864, and at once started for the Regiment at Chattanooga, but soon after reaching there was taken down sick. Was removed to Officers' Hospital, on Lookout Mountain, for treatment, where he died September 14, 1864. His death is more fully noticed in the preceding pages.

DR. ISAAC N. PLUMMER was a regular physician; was drafted into the service from Evansville, Indiana, in the fall of 1864, and assigned to the 44th Regiment. Upon reaching the command, his qualifications as a physician becoming known, he was put on service in the Regimental Hospital, and afterward recommended for appointment as Assistant Surgeon, and was so commissioned, and was mustered in April 8, 1865. He was mustered out with the Regiment, September 14, 1865.

———

THE NON-COMMISSIONED STAFF.

All mention of the non-commissioned staff of the Regiment having been omitted in Adjutant-General Terrell's Military Report of the State, I find it impossible to give full statements in respect to these.

SERGEANT MAJORS.

The first Seargeant-Major was Samuel L. Bayliss. His name does not appear on the Adjutant-General's report at all. He was discharged on account of disability in 1862, and is now a resident of Minneapolis, Minn.

Bayliss was succeeded by Samuel C. Smith, Company I, who served until promoted Adjutant, November 14, 1863. He was succeeded by Willis P. Andrews, Sergeant, Company F, who served until promoted Adjutant, April 11, 1865. The position was filled from this date until muster-out of the Regiment by William Ulrey, Company B.

HOSPITAL STEWARDS.

The first Hospital Steward was Jacob A. Banta, of Co. B, who served until disabled by sickness. He died at home, March 21, 1862. He was succeeded by Joseph W. Burch, Co. A, and he by Charles A. Pardee, Co. D, who was promoted to the position in 1863, re-enlisted, and held it until the muster-out of the Regiment.

QUARTERMASTER SERGEANTS.

Marquis L. Bayliss was the first Quartermaster-Sergeant, but his name does not appear in the Adjutant General's report. He was succeeded by Samuel P. Bradford, Co. H, and he by Adam Clark, and he by Samuel R. Havens, Co. E, who served from July, 1862, to November, 1864, when he was mustered out at the expiration of enlistment. He was succeeded by Sebastian Shoup, Co. H, who served until promoted Second Lieutenant, May 1, 1865. Jeremiah J. Shatto, Co. K, filled the position from this time until muster-out.

COMMISSARY SERGEANTS.

The Commissary-Sergeants were William F. Hinckley, Co. K, Samuel P. Bradford, Co. H, Sebastian Shoup, Co. H, and James Tuck, Co. H, serving in the order named.

LEADERS OF THE BAND.

The first leader of the Band was John R. Grubb, of Lagrange. His name also does not appear on the Adjutant General's report. He was noted as an excellent tenor drummer. He was discharged in November, 1863, on account of disability. After the war he was stricken with paralysis, and is still living in a helpless condition under the care of a guardian appointed by the Court, who so economizes his pension money as to provide comfortably for him.

William T. Kimsey, I believe, succeeded Grubb, as leader of the Band. He re-enlisted, and was mustered out with the Regiment as Principal Musician.

PERSONAL MENTION

OF

MEMBERS OF COMPANIES.

NOTE.—In the record of the Companies, all mention of dishonorable discharge of the officers, and the names of the men who deserted the service, are omitted. The names of all such can be found in Adjutant-General Terrell's report, in every county officer's office in the State. This is, we think, a sufficient reminder of these unpleasant things, at this late date. The record of the original enlisted men is first given—those who entered the service at the organization of the Regiment, and were mustered in November 22, 1861, for three years. These are classified as "Veterans": those who re-enlisted for another three years' service, and were mustered in as veterans, January 9, 1861, and were mustered out with the Regiment, September 14, 1865. 2d. "Three Years Men": those who were mustered out at the end of three years' enlistment, November, 1861. 3d. The original men killed on the field, discharged on account of disability from wounds or disease, and those transferred, will be found under the heads, "Killed," "Discharged," and "Transferred." 4th. All who enlisted after the Regiment entered the service will be found under the head of "Recruits," except substitutes and drafted men. These came mostly from the southern part of the State, and were with the Regiment but a few months. The word "dead" is attached to the names of those who are known to have died since discharge or muster-out, and the present residence of the survivors given when known. The rank following a name indicates the rank when mustered out.

COMPANY A.

Company A was recruited and organized in Steuben County, the volunteers mostly residing in the vicinity of Orland, Metz, and Hamilton. The enlistments were mostly in September, 1861, but the Company was not mustered in until November 22, 1861, the date of the muster of all the companies. The officers chosen by the election of the men, were: Captain, Charles F. Kinney; 1st Lieutenant, Elias O. Rose; 2d Lieutenant, Burge Smith.

CAPTAINS.

Charles F. Kinney. See "MAJORS."

Nelson A. Sowers was mustered in as a private, but having served in the regular army, he was enabled to render much useful service in drilling, not only this Company, but others, and was promoted 1st Lieutenant May 22, 1862, and Captain, January 20, 1863. He is reported as residing in Illinois now.

Joseph W. Burch. See "MAJORS."

Lewis W. Griffith entered the service as a private; was promoted 1st Lieutenant, June 10, 1863; Captain, April 8, 1865; and was mustered out with the Regiment September 14, 1865. Resides now at Hamilton, Ind.

FIRST LIEUTENANTS.

Elias O. Rose entered the service with the Company, was elected 1st Lieutenant, and was mustered in as such September 25, 1861. Resigned July 22, 1862; disability. Now editor of *The Magnet*, Big Rapids, Mich.

Nelson A. Sowers. See "CAPTAINS."

Marion B. Butler was mustered in as 1st Sergeant; promoted 2d Lieutenant September 13, 1862; 1st Lieutenant January 20, 1863; resigned May 20, 1863, after a disabling sickness. Resides at Salem Center, Steuben County, Ind.

Lewis W. Griffith. See "CAPTAINS."

George W. Twitchell was mustered in as a Corporal; re-enlisted as a veteran; promoted 2d Lieutenant April

24, 1865, and was mustered out with the Regiment.
Resides at Orland, Ind.

SECOND LIEUTENANTS.

Birge Smith was elected 2d Lieutenant by the Company, was mustered in September 25, 1861, and resigned September 11, 1862. He was honorably mentioned in Colonel Reed's report of Shiloh. Dead.

Onius D. Scovill. See "COMPANY I."

George W. Twitchell. See "FIRST LIEUTENANTS."

Newell P. Lewis entered the service as a private; re-enlisted as a veteran; was promoted 2d Lieutenant April 24, 1865, and was mustered out with the Regiment. Residence, Brushy Prairie, Lagrange Co., Ind.

VETERANS.

Sergeant John Ulam. Michigan.

Sergeant Joseph Milnes. Dead.

Corporal George W. Twitchell. See "FIRST LIEUTENANTS."

Musician Alonzo B. Sage. Dead.

James A. Aumend.

Charles H. Barr. Gone west.

Thomas D. Butler. Michigan.

Henry W. Beard. Angola, Ind.

Charles Clink, Sergeant. Pleasant Lake, Ind.

William C. Carlin.

John T. Crow.

John Carlin.

Solomon M. Cox, Corporal. Alvarado, Ind.

Adolphus Ewers. Angola, Ind.

John Gilbert. Bettsville, Seneca county, Ohio.

David O. Goodrich, Corporal.

Emanuel Heller. Alvarado, Ind.

John B. Hutchins, Sergeant. Angola, Ind.

Newell P. Lewis.   See " SECOND LIEUTENANTS."

Henry A. Lords, Corporal.

Charles Miller, Corporal.   East Gilead, Branch Co., Michigan.

Jasper Munday, Corporal.   Michigan.

John Ryan, Jr.   Angola, Ind.

Michael Ryan.   Angola, Ind.

James Ryan, Corporal.   Angola, Ind.

Benson K. Robbins, Corporal.   Reading, Mich.

Seymour P. Snyder.   Michigan.

David Sowle.   Angola, Ind.

Joshua Showalter.   Angola, Ind.

Simon M. Sines.

Oscar B. Thrasher, Corporal.   Pleasant Lake, Ind.

John Thompson.   Dead.

David J. Tiffany.   Transferred to U. S. Engineers August 26, 1864.   Gone west.

Thomas C. Hyatt.   Transferred to U. S. Engineers August 26, 1864.   Orland, Ind.

THREE YEARS MEN.

Nicholas Arnold.   Flint, Ind.

Caleb J. Bates.   Michigan.

Jacob Dotts.

Christopher Oberst.   Clear Lake, Ind.

William Rosser.   Orland, Ind.

Frederick Swambaugh.   Angola, Ind.

Henry West.   Flint, Ind.

Robert Wilkes.   Hamilton, Ind.

DISCHARGED.

Sergeant James H. Merriman, June 14, 1863; wounded at Shiloh.   Dead.

Corporal John Ryan, Sr., March, 1863.   Dead.

Corporal John M. Benedict, May 13, 1862.   Dead.

Musician Christian Stealey, July, 1862. Angola, Ind.

Wagoner John M. Kinnear, January 1, 1862.

John Burgett, October 22, 1863.

Miles T. Culp, June 28, 1862; wounded at Shiloh. Ohio.

William H. Dotts, August 5, 1862. Angola, Ind.

Harrison Grant, Feb. 15, 1863.

Marcenas Green, January 25, 1863. Dead.

John Hall, August 29, 1863. Metz, Ind.

John Lutz.

Thomas R. Moffett. Amydes, Ind.

William McMuire, March 22, 1863. Dead.

Stephen A. Powers, March 1, 1862.

Stephen Ryan, September 13, 1862. Dead.

William Scoles, May 6, 1863. Dead.

George W. Strong, November 8, 1863.

Hannibal Scoville, January 12, 1863; wounded at Shiloh. Pleasant Lake, Ind.

Samuel Tinsley, June 17, 1862. Michigan.

Henry Twitchell, July 26, 1862; wounded at Shiloh. Orland, Ind.

James Van Auken, October 21, 1862. Pleasant Lake, Indiana.

KILLED.

Leander Hall, at Shiloh, April 6, 1862.

DIED.

Joseph Jackman, mortally wounded at Shiloh, April 6, 1862. Died April 10, 1862.

Sergeant William W. Wright, at St. Louis, March 2, 1862.

William Bennett, at Pittsburg Landing, March 26, 1862.

Giba Belcher, McMinnville, Tenn., Sept. 9, 1863.

Francis Brooks, Fort Wayne, October 4, 1861.

Cleveland J. Spencer, Huntsville, Ala., August 25, 1862.

John Eckhart, in Steuben Co., Ind., April 20, 1862.

James B. Ewing, in Steuben Co., Ind., May 14, 1862.

Henry Field, Cairo, Ill., April 5, 1862.

Marion Grant, Evansville, Ind., January 26, 1862.

William Humblebough, New Albany, Ind, January 11, 1863.

Charles F. Hulbert, Calhoun, Ky., February 17, 1862.

Joseph F. Lords, Nashville, Tenn., October 22, 1862.

John Stealey, Calhoun, Ky., February 21, 1862.

Richard P. Swain, March 21, 1862.

Orange Throop, April 1, 1863; wounded at Fort Donelson.

George W. Vancleve, Evansville, Ind., March 15, 1862.

Joshua West, Keokuk, Iowa, July 21, 1862.

William Yenner, Mound City, Ill., April 17, 1862; wounded at Shiloh.

TRANSFERRED.

Corporal John Imhof, to 15th U. S. Infantry, December 15, 1862.

Daniel Heller, to 15th U. S. Infantry, Dec. 15, 1862.

Robert Raisen, to 15th U. S. Infantry, Dec. 15, 1862.

DISCHARGED FOR PROMOTION IN OTHER REGIMENTS.

John M. Parrett, August 6, 1862, and Albert H. Ewing, August 16, 1862.

ENLISTED MEN PROMOTED TO COMMISSIONS IN THE REGIMENT.

Marion B. Butler, Joseph W. Burch, Lewis Griffith, Nelson A. Sowers, Onias D. Scoville.

Deserted, 5; names omitted.

VOLUNTEER RECRUITS.

[The date of muster-in on the left; muster-out on the right.]

1862.

Sept. 20.   George W. Purvis, died of wound at Camp Denison, Ohio, August, 1863.

Sept. 20.   Russell C. Taylor.

Aug.   9.   Joseph M. Wilson, m. o. Sept. 14, 1865.

1863.

Jan.   3.   Adam Clark, discharged Feb. 15, 1863.

Dec. 29.   Elias Cranshon,   m. o. Sept. 14, 1865.

 "   26.   Samuel Faust,   "   "   "   "

 "   26.   Jacob Malott,   "   "   "   "

 "   29.   Henry H. Herron,   "   "   "   "

 "   24.   Francis P. McCutcheon,   "   "   "   "

 "   26.   John F. Nyce,   "   "   "   "

 "   "   Christopher O'Brien,   "   "   "   "

 "   "   Robert B. Thompson,   "   "   "   "

 "   "   Henry Wilson,   "   "   "   "

 "   23.   Isaac Winchell,   "   "   "   "

 "   26.   John H. Yaugst,   "   "   "   "

1864.

Jan. 11.   Albert Felterhoof, disch'd dis. Sept. 17, 1864.

April 18.   Julius H. Chappel,   m. o. Sept. 14, 1865.

 "   "   Silas L. Crandle,   "   "   "   "

 "   "   Edwin Gillespie,   "   "   "   "

 "   28.   William Gillespie,   "   "   "   "

May   5.   Jerome C. Gannon,   "   "   "   "

Mar. 11.   Anderson Henderson,   "   "   "   "

Sept. 22.   Daniel Haggerty, m. o. June 13, 1865.

Oct.   6.   Andrew J. Hamilton, m. o. Sept. 14, 1865.

 "   6.   Curtis B. Haywood,   "   "   "   "

Mar.   7.   Emanuel Krotzer,   "   "   "   "

Oct.   6.   William H. Kesterson,   "   "   "   "

April 18.   George Kerr,   "   "   "   "

Oct.   6.   George Kesterson,   "   "   "   "

Jan. 12.   Henry Lonbarger, m. o. Sept. 14, 1865.

Mar. 27.   Thomas L. Larue, died at Chattanooga March 10, 1865.

April 18.   Frank B. Lewis, m. o. Sept. 14, 1865.

"   "   Leland Morrison, died at Chattanooga June 26, 1864.

Mar. 27.   Willard A. Miller,   m. o. Sept. 14, 1865.

Oct. 16.   William B. Pointsett,   "   "   "   "

April 18.   Daniel S. Parker,   "   "   "   "

Mar. 9.   James Richardson,   "   "   "   "

"   7.   James Stewart,   "   "   "   "

"   7.   Robert Sowle,   "   "   "   "

"   3.   Joseph L. Stump,   "   "   "   "

Sept. 22.   David P. Stewart,   "   May   "   "

April 19.   Jacob A. Truby,   "   "   "   "

"   21.   Walter Vanalstine,   "   "   "   "

"   18.   Lewis West,   "   April 28,   "

Mar. 21.   Newell A. Wilson, died at home, July 20, '64.

"   11.   David J. Wilburn,   m. o. Sept. 14, 1865.

Feb. 2.   William Wilburn,   "   "   "   "

Jan. 16.   George G. Wickham,   "   "   "   "

"   16.   James Woods,   "   "   "   "

Mar. 7.   Isaac Beil,   "   "   "   "

1865.

Mar. 3.   Frederick H. Aldrich,   "   "   "   "

"   3.   John L. Aldrich,   "   "   "   "

"   3.   Nehemiah Andrews,   "   "   "   "

Feb. 15.   Alonzo Jordan,   "   "   "   "

"   15.   Lockwood L. Black,   "   "   "   "

Mar. 3.   Elias Martin,   "   July 26,   "

Feb. 20.   Mark A. Newman,   "   Sept. 14,   "

"   22.   Daniel Sinks,   "   "   "   "

"   22.   John D. Thomas,   "   "   18,   "

Mar. 3.   George W. Wagoner,   "   "   14,   "

Twenty-nine substitutes and drafted men were added to the Company in September and October, 1864, and were mustered out in June and July, 1865, except John Smith, Jr., who died at Chattanooga, June 2, 1865.

COMPANY B.

Company B was recruited and organized by volunteers from Pierceton and vicinity, Kosciusko County, who elected for their first officers: John Murray, Captain; John Barton, 1st Lieutenant; William C. Ward, 2d Lieutenant. The men enlisted early in September; mustered November 22, 1861. The officers were commissioned September 20, and mustered September 25.

CAPTAINS.

John Murray, the first choice of the Company for Captain, was mustered as above stated. He led his Company in the battle of Fort Donelson, receiving honorable mention, and again led the Company at Shiloh until he fell mortally wounded, on the first day of the battle. He was carried to a log house previously occupied by General Hulbert as headquarters, and then to a boat, where he died.

John Barton was elected 1st Lieutenant at the organization of the Company. Promoted Captain April 10, 1862.

James S. Getty was mustered in as 1st Sergeant; was promoted 1st Lieutenant May 15, 1862; Captain, March 21, 1863, and was mustered out at the end of original enlistment, December 5, 1864. Resides at Pierceton, Indiana.

John S. Deardoff entered the service as a recruit, was mustered in as a private, October 5, 1862, and was promoted Captain February 15, 1865, and was mustered out with the Regiment. Residence, Denver, Colorado.

FIRST LIEUTENANTS.

John Barton. See "CAPTAINS."

James S. Getty. See "

George R. Murray was mustered in with the Company as Sergeant, promoted 2d Lieutenant May 15, 1862, and 1st Lieutenant, March 21, 1863. Resides at Pierceton.

Thompson Doke was mustered in as a Corporal, re-enlisted, and was promoted 1st Lieutenant February 17, 1865, and was mustered out with the Regiment. Residence, Red Oak, Iowa.

SECOND LIEUTENANTS.

William C. Ward was chosen 2d Lieutenant at the organization of the Company, was mustered in September 25, 1861, and resigned April 8, 1862.

George R. Murray. See "FIRST LIEUTENANTS."

William Sherburne was mustered in as a wagoner, was promoted 2d Lieutenant March 21, 1863, and resigned September 3, 1863. Resides at Pierceton, Ind.

James S. Wheeler entered the service as a recruit; was mustered in as a private, October 3, 1862; was promoted 2d Lieutenant April 8, 1865, and was mustered out with the Regiment.

VETERANS.

Corporal Thomas Doke. See "FIRST LIEUTENANTS."
Musician John G. Waldo. Pierceton, Ind.
Musician David F. Goodrich. Falk's Store, I. T.
Marshall Bagden, 1st Sergeant.
David Brawlier. Dysart, Fama county, Iowa.
James P. Bills, Corporal. Pierceton, Ind.
Benjamin B. Campbell.
John Fluke, Corporal. Galleon, Ohio.
Andrew J. Fluke.
James Garnett.

John A. Griffith, Corporal. Nora Springs, Iowa.
Isaac Harrison, Corporal. Larwell, Ind.
George R. Hughes. Warsaw.
Francis Phillips. Newaygo, Mich.
Valentine Phillips, Sergeant.
John H. Smith, Sergeant.
Joseph Stafford, Corporal.
Clinton Scobey, Sergeant.
Jacob Schoof, Corporal. Pierceton, Ind.
Daniel W. Thompson, Sergeant. Silver Lake, Ind.
William Ulrey, Sergeant-Major.

THREE YEARS MEN.

Henry Craig. Pierceton, Ind.
Jonathan Hand.
Benjamin McIntyre. Pierceton, Ind.
Frank Phillips.
Thomas J. Powers. Warsaw, Ind.

DISCHARGED.

Sergeant Charles H. Ward, June 5, 1862. Warsaw, Indiana.

Sergeant William T. Eddy, April 8, 1863. Pierceton, Ind.

Corporal Thomas Caldwell, May 10, 1862. Wounded at Fort Donelson.

Corporal Edward N. Whitney. Warsaw.

Corporal Henry B. Lamb, December 30, 1862.

Mccaslin Campbell, July 25, 1862; w. at Shiloh.

John B. Cole, June 23, 1862. Pierceton.

Columbus Crawford, July 26, 1862. Pierceton.

John Cogen, May 28, 1863.

Abraham Dille, August 23, 1863. Pierceton.

Scott Eddy, 1863. Pierceton.

William Fenton, January 1, 1863. Pierceton.

Thomas W. Griffith, 1863. Dysart, Iowa.

William Gobal.

Basil Hunter, November 5, 1862.

Thomas Hancher, October 28, 1862.

Peter Huffman, July 1, 1862.

Robert Jack, January 5, 1862.

Jacob Kyle, May 10, 1862. Oswego, Ind.

Levi Lightfoot, wounds at Shiloh.

Joseph Mosier, September 19, 1862.

William W. McCourtney, 1862; wounds at Fort Donelson. Dead.

George Pringle, July 9, 1862; wounds at Shiloh.
Warsaw, Ind.

Thomas Powers, April 28, 1862.

Andrew Stafford, June 30, 1862. Bourbon, Ind.

George W. Scott, May 30, 1863.

Silas M. Scott, September 10, 1862. Pierceton.

Gabriel M. Scott, May 12, 1862; w. at Stone River.

Albert R. Westfall, September 30, 1862; wounds at
Shiloh. Pierceton.

Newton Westfall, May 22, 1862; wounds at Shiloh.
Pierceton.

William Widner, May 16, 1864.

James Wells, July 2, 1862.

KILLED.

Captain John Murray, at Shiloh, April 6, 1862.

John Easton, at Shiloh, April 6, 1862.

David Lichtenwalter, at Fort Donelson, Feb. 15, '62.

Sergeant William McNeal, at Shiloh, April 6, 1862.

Corporal George Shurber, at Stone River, Dec. 31, '62.

DIED OF WOUNDS.

Samuel Firestone, November 11, 1863; received at
Chickamauga.

William D. Grose, March 6, 1862; received at Fort
Donelson.

Ralph Goodrich, April 9, 1862; received at Shiloh.

Thomas Helper, March 7, 1863; received at Stone River.

Joseph Kirkpatrick, February 22, 1862; received at Fort Donelson.

Samuel Widner, January 29, 1863; received at Stone River.

DIED OF DISEASE.

George W. Slate, died at Andersonville, Oct. 10, 1864.
Jacob A. Banta, at home, March 21, 1862.
Henry Bares, in hospital, December 13, 1863.
Alvin Danner, April 6, 1862.
Isaac Graham, February 17, 1862.
Henry Goldsmith, April 3, 1862.
John Hand, February 17, 1862.
Stephen W. Moore, March 5, 1862.
Henry Slack, February 12, 1862.

TRANSFERRED.

Corporal William Graves, to Veteran Reserve Corps, November 26, 1863. Pierceton, Ind.

Corporal Albert Reitz, to same, April 3, 1863.

William W. Johnson, to Engineer Corps, August 8, 1864.

Thomas J. Vaughn, discharged January 20, 1863, to enter the Mississippi Marine Brigade, which he did the same date, and was mustered out with that command January 18, 1865. Is now Deputy Collector of Internal Revenue at Fond du Lac, Wisconsin.

ENTERED MEN PROMOTED TO COMMISSIONS.

James S. Getty, George R. Murray, Thompson Doke, William Sherbur.

Deserted, 4; names omitted.

VOLUNTEER RECRUITS.

1862.

Nov. 11. Abram Archer, discharged May 2, 1863.

Oct. 3. Amos Bryant, died April 24, 1863.

" 3. Michael Bankhart, died December 9, 1862.

Nov. 11. William A. Brown, died December 18, 1862.

Oct. 3. Martin Brother, discharged Oct. 9, 1863 ; dis.

" 3. William Cartwright, transferred to V. R. C. November 23, 1863.

Nov. 11. Elisha Craizan, died at Chattanooga, February 6, 1864.

Sept. 25. Isaac Clark, discharged Oct. 27, 1864, dis. Warsaw, Ind.

Oct. 3. Jasper N. Corder, " May 2, 1863, "

" 3. Bennett F. Clevenger, " " " "

" 3. James L. Cowgill, m. o. Sept. 14, 1865.

" 3. George S. Cowgill, " " "

" 3. Mathias Clay, " " "

" 3. William E. Davis, m. o. Sept. 18, 1865. Warsaw, Indiana.

" 3. John Deardoff. See " CAPTAINS."

Nov. 11. Jonathan P. Eddy, m. o. September 14, 1865. Pierceton, Ind.

" 11. Presly G. Frary, disch'ged May 6, 1863. Warsaw, Ind.

" 11. James P. Phillips, died at Nashville, December 31, 1862.

Oct. 3. Edward Lightfoot, died March 22, 1863.

Sept. 3. Jacob Ream, m. o. September 18, 1865. Larwell, Ind.

" 3. Egbert M. Rogers, discharged Aug. 21, 1863.

" 3. Josiah A. Redman, transferred to V. R. C., November 26, 1863.

" 3. James W. Rouse, died January 29, 1863.

" 3. Henry Strunk, died February 14, 1863.

Oct.	3.	David Stauffer, died March 29, 1865.
"	3.	Lafayette Sherburne, m. o. Sept. 14, 1865. Corporal. Pierceton, Ind.
"	3.	Alonzo Sherburne, discharged May 16, 1863. Pierceton, Ind.
"	3.	Ira C. Solis, discharged April 28, 1865. Pierceton, Ind.
Nov.	11.	William W. Smith, discharged April 30, 1865. Pierceton, Ind.
Oct.	3.	Albert Vanness, discharged April 23, 1863. Wooster, Ind.
"	3.	James S. Wheeler. See "SECOND LIEUTENANTS."
Nov.	12.	John W. Groves, unaccounted for.

1863.

Dec.	23.	Joseph W. Syant,	m. o. Sept. 14, 1865.		
"	17.	John Todd,	"	"	"
May	1.	Henry A. Winter,	"	"	"
July	1.	William Ward,	"	"	"

1864.

Nov.	7.	Oliver Brady,	"	"	"
Mar.	19.	Asa Bills,	"	"	"
"	9.	John H. Barnes,	"	"	"
Sept.	25.	John Cisley,	"	July 13,	"
Mar.	11.	John L. Douglas, Pierceton, Ind.	"	Sept. 18,	"
"	1.	William Fisher,	"	Sept. 14,	"
Oct.	19.	James Fulwiler,	"	"	"
Nov.	12.	John W. Groves, Larwell, Ind.	"	"	"
"	12.	Jacob F. Gooding,	"	"	"
Mar.	9.	Isaac C. Havens,	"	"	"
"	11.	Stephen Harter,	"	"	"
Nov.	17.	William Henry,	"	"	"
"	29.	James Ireland,	"	"	"

Oct. 28. Abraham J. Jenkins, m. o. Sept. 14, 1865.
Mar. 11. David C. Lambertson,   "   "   "
Feb. 24. William Littleton,   "   "   "
Oct.   6. William Losiers,   "   "   "
Nov. 12. Hugh H. Myers,   "   "   "
Mar. 10. Lewis C. Sink,   "   Sept. 18,   "
Nov. 19. Solomon Sullers,   "   "   "
 "   11. Nathan Small,   "   Sept. 14,   "
Sept. 25. George W. Slote.
 "   25. William Sprinkle,   "   June 13,   "
Oct. 29. Daniel Smith,   "   "   "
 "   15. Kifer Thomas,   "   Sept. 14,   "
 "   5. William Tiffany,   "   "   "
Nov. 30. Henry Thrasher,   "   "   "
 "   12. Thornton VanBuskirk,   "   Aug. 29,   "
Mar. 11. Joel Underwood, died at Chattanooga, Sep-
              tember 15, 1864.
Mar.   9. William Werts,   m. o. Sept. 14, 1865.
Sept. 27. William Williams,   "   July 13,   "

1865.

Feb.   6. Joseph H. Corder,   "   Sept. 18,   "
 "   6. Francis M. Cox,   "   Sept. 15,   "
 "   6. Isaac R. Cary,   "   "   "
April 30. Lemuel Pincher,   "   Sept. 14,   "
Feb. 17. Jonathan B. Fox,   "   "   "
April 5. Alexander Johns,   "   "   "
              Pierceton, Ind.
Feb. 22. Peter M. Jamison,   "   "   "
 "   17. John Keyton,   "   "   "
April 5. Charles Linn,   "   "   "

Thirty drafted men and substitutes from the southern part of the State were added to the Company in the
fall of 1864, and mustered out in June and July, 1865,
except—

Albert James, died at Nashville, June 12, 1865.
Samuel E. Spear, died at Chattanooga, June 15, 1865.

Deserted, 11 ; names omitted.

COMPANY C.

Company C was recruited at Fort Wayne, Indiana, in September and October, 1861, and was mustered in November 22, 1861. The officers first chosen were commissioned September 20, 1861, and mustered in Sept. 22.

CAPTAINS.

L. R. Tannehill was the first Captain commissioned and mustered in as above. He led his Company in the battles of Fort Donelson and Shiloh, and was honorably mentioned by Colonel Reed in his report of the battle of Shiloh. Died since the war.

William Storey entered the service as 1st Lieutenant at the organization of the Company. Promoted Captain January 20, 1863. He received honorable mention for gallantry at Fort Donelson, for planting the regimental colors in advance of the line and under fire of the enemy. Residence, Deadwood, D. T.

Philip Grund. See "LIEUTENANT-COLONELS."

Adam Hull was mustered in as a private, re-enlisted as a veteran, promoted 2d Lieutenant March 24, 1865, 1st Lieutenant June 1, 1865, and Captain June 12, 1865, and was mustered out with the Regiment. Resides at Cherubusco, Whitley County, Ind.

FIRST LIEUTENANTS.

William Story. See "CAPTAINS."
Philip Grund. See "LIEUTENANT-COLONELS."
Sedgwick Livingston was mustered in as Sergeant with the Company, promoted 2d Lieutenant January

SAMUEL B. SWEET,

COMPANY C.

20, 1863, 1st Lieutenant June 11, 1863, and died January 26, 1864.

Owen L. Shaw was mustered in as a private, promoted 1st Lieutenant March 11, 1864, and resigned March 27, 1865. Resides in Nebraska.

Adam Hull. See "CAPTAINS."

James S. Eldridge was mustered in as a private, re-enlisted as a veteran, was promoted 2d Lieutenant June 1, 1865, and 1st Lieutenant July 11, 1865, and was mustered out with the Regiment. Died since the war.

SECOND LIEUTENANTS.

Philip Grund. See "LIEUTENANT-COLONELS."

Sedgwick Livingston. See "FIRST LIEUTENANTS."

John H. Strong was mustered in as Sergeant. Was promoted 2d Lieutenant June 11, 1863. Resigned October 18, 1863. Residence, Pleasant Lake, Steuben Co., Indiana.

James S. Eldridge. See "FIRST LIEUTENANTS."

Joseph Smith was mustered as a private; re-enlisted as a veteran. Was promoted 2d Lieutenant July 12, '65.

The records of the Company as published by the Adjutant-General of the State, are very imperfect as to the original men, not showing, with few exceptions, when they were mustered out, who were killed, wounded, and who died. For what information I have in respect to the following, I am indebted to Samuel B. Sweet, of Fort Wayne. Mr. Sweet was but a few months past sixteen years of age when he entered the service. He was at first set aside by the mustering officer, as too young, but his importunity and tears finally prevailed, and he was duly mustered in. His record as a soldier was an excellent one. He was in all marches and battles of the Regiment, was slightly wounded at Shiloh, Stone River, and Chickamauga, but was never

in hospital on account of sickness. After a service of
four years and one month, he was mustered out with
the Regiment. In 1866 he entered the employ of the
Wabash railway company as bill clerk at Fort Wayne,
and was promoted freight and ticket agent in 1874, which
position he still holds. In honor to the privates of the
Regiment and the patriotic boys of that day, we present
elsewhere a picture of this model citizen-soldier.

VETERANS.

Corporal Jacob Kress.
Sergeant Joseph Bay.
William H. Arney, died at Nashville, July 5, 1865.
John Elzey, Corporal. Decatur, Ind.
James Eldridge. See "SECOND LIEUTENANTS."
Christian Earman. Decatur, Ind.
Henry Fry. Fort Wayne, Ind.
Amos French. Dead.
Jackson Heyser. Fort Wayne, Ind.
Adam Hull. See "SECOND LIEUTENANTS."
Patrick Hoban, Sergeant.
Alexander Humbert. Fort Wayne, Ind.
William N. Logan. "
Leander McGinnis, Corporal. "
Joseph Merica.
Isaiah McDowell, Sergeant. Maples, Allen County.
William Nodding, Sergeant.
Alexander Runel, Corporal.
Emri Sites. Fort Wayne, Ind.
Milton Sites, Corporal. Fort Wayne, Ind.
Samuel B. Sweet, 1st Sergeant.
Joseph Smyth. See "SECOND LIEUTENANTS."
James Taylor.
Alonzo Woodworth, Corporal.
William Weaver, Corporal. Fort Wayne, Ind.

NON-VETERANS.

Sergeant Caleb Carman, disch'ged 1862. Ft. Wayne.
Sergeant William Riley, discharged 1862.
Sergeant J. R. McCool.
Corporal Benton McCool.
Corporal Joseph Kennan, discharged, wounds at Shiloh. Dead.
Corporal E. B. Slocum, died 1862, at Battle Creek.
Corporal William Keefer.
Corporal Fred Stine, discharged. Kalamazoo, Mich.
Corporal Robert Stewart, discharged.
Corporal Thaddeus Helm, discharged.
Musician Royal Dean, discharged.
Wagoner William Henderson, discharged.
Sebastian Albright, discharged.
Joseph Bay, m. o. Sept. 14, 1865.
James Berry, discharged.
William Crawford, discharged 1862.
John Crawford, discharged of wounds at Shiloh.
L. B. Carr, died 1862.
Patrick Coney, discharged.
Michael Carl.
Hugh Dennis, discharged.
John C. Dee, killed at Fort Donelson.
Charles Divine, discharged Nov. 4, 1864.
Michael Drury, discharged.
George S. Decay, m. o. Nov. 25, 1864.
John Engle, discharged, wounds at Shiloh. Dead.
Jacob Fogwell, died 1862.
J. M. Flutter, discharged 1862 ; wounds at Shiloh.
William Hyser, discharged 1862. Fort Wayne, Ind.
Michael Harrison, discharged 1862 ; wounds at Shiloh. Maples, Allen County, Ind.
William P. Henderson, discharged 1862.
William Hedges.

John Higgs, died 1862.

William Higgs, died ; wounds at Stone River.

Charles Johnston.

John Knox.

John Keefer, discharged 1862 ; wounds at Shiloh. Fort Wayne.

Jacob Luly.

William McDermitt, discharged 1862.

Marion McGinnis, m. o. Nov. 25, 1864.

James McDonald, discharged.

George Myers, discharged.

Joseph Nicodemus, died ; wounds at Shiloh.

Michael O'Conner.

George Parrin, discharged.

A. L. Robinson, discharged.

Thomas Russell, discharged.

James Shaw.

Willard Story, discharge l.

Owen T. Shaw. See " First Lieutenants."

Peter Stahl, killed at Shiloh.

Christian Smith, died 1862.

Jacob Smith, killed at Stone River.

Jacob Stalkolfe, discharged.

Joseph Sedgwick, discharged.

William Woodford, killed at Shiloh.

Henry Wilkison, discharged. Died 1880.

James Wilkison. Fort Wayne, Ind.

VOLUNTEER RECRUITS.

1862.

Aug. 19. Thompson P. Burch, m. o. Sept. 14, 1865.

"   19. Stephen Bounger,   "   "   "

Oct. 5. Bronson H. Bell,   "   "   "

Jan. 9. Joseph W. Hersh, vet., "   "   "

Oct. 11. John W. Cress, transferred to Pioneer Corps, Aug. 15, 1864.

1863.

Dec. 11. Joseph Bates,   m. o. Sept. 14, 1865.
 "   9. Corbin Murray,   "   "   "
Sept. 22. Otho Reese,   "   "   "

1864.

Mar. 8. Peter T. Bolger,   "   "   "
 "   6. George W. Countryman, "   "   "
Oct. 19. Thomas Comer,   "   "   "
Mar. 10. James M. Clark,   "   "   "
Dec. 5. William Coulter,   "   "   "
Sept. 29. Joseph Daniel, at died Chattanooga, April
            10, 1865.
Feb. 26. William Engle, m. o. Sept. 14, 1865.
 " 13. George Earl, m. o. Sept. 14, 1865.
 " 26. Nicholi Gobert, died, Nashville, June 29, '64.
Jan. 13. Raphael Gall,   m., o. Sept. 14, 1865.
Sept. 29. Andrew Hoffmire,   "   "   "
Oct. 28. Wiley C. Hooper,   "   July 17,   "
Feb. 26. Robert Hamilton,   "   Sept. 14,   "
Mar. 14. Joseph Humbert,   "   "   "
Jan. 13. George W. Higgs,   "   "   "
Oct. 13. James A. Halstead,   "   "   "
Jan. 12. James A. Hines,   "   "   "
Apr. 10. Wesley A. Logan,   "   "   "
Mar. 8. Noah S. Long,   "   "   "
Feb. 6. George A. Lewis,   "   "   "
Jan. 12. Napoleon P. Lyon,   "   "   "
Feb. 6. Harmer L. Mayor,   "   "   "
Mar. 8. Eli Miser, m. o. Sept. 14, 1865. Mace, Ind.
 "   8. Joseph Manor,   "   "   Fort Wayne.
Feb. 28. Alex. Ormiston,   "   "   "
 "   6. August Perot,   "   "   Dead.
 "   6. Joseph Parisot,   "   "   Fort Wayne.
 "   6. Francis Provert,   "   "   "
 " 23. John Slocum, Corp'l,   "   "

" 26.   John W. Smith, m. o. Sept. 14, 1865.
Jan. 13.   James Smith,   "   "   "
Dec. 5.   James A. Smith,   "   "   "
"   5.   John Swanson,   "   "   "
Feb. 13.   William H. Snellbaker, m. o. May 16, 1865.
Oct. 6.   Caleb Thair,   "   "   "
Feb. 26.   George W. Valentine,   " Sept. 14,   "
"   26.   Martin H. Wright,   "   "   "
1865.
Mar. 23.   John Cavanaugh,   "   "   "
"   14.   James L. Miller,   "   "   "
"   8.   James W. Berry,   " June 5,   "
Mar. 23.   William Lyon,   " Sept. 14,   "
Jan. 27.   James S. Potts,   "   "   "

There were thirty substitutes and drafted men added in the fall of 1864, who were mustered out in June and July, 1865, except Isaac N. Plummer, promoted Assistant Surgeon.

Deserters, 12; names omitted.

COMPANY D.

Company D was organized by volunteers principally from Allen County, from the vicinity of Maysville, and from the vicinity of Rome City, Noble County. The first officers were commissioned September 20, 1861, and mustered in with the men November 22, 1861.

CAPTAINS.

Franklin K. Cosgrove was a resident of Maysville, Allen County, conducting an extensive practice as a physician and surgeon. He had served in the Mexican war as a volunteer in an Ohio regiment, and at the breaking out of the war of the rebellion was early seized

with the war fever, and at once commenced assisting in
the enlistment of men for the different regiments called
for. He concluded to enter the Forty-fourth, which he
also helped organize. Was chosen Captain of Co. D,
which he led through the battles of Fort Donelson and
Shiloh. In the latter he was severely wounded, on
account of which he was honorably discharged, by special order of the Secretary of War, September 3, 1862.
Residence, Harlan, Allen County, Ind.

Charles H. Wayne entered the service as 1st Lieutenant, at the organization of the Company; had seen
military service in the regular army; was honorably
mentioned by Colonel Reed in his Shiloh battle report.
Resigned after the battle; was re-commissioned April
15, 1862, and resigned January 13, 1863.

George W. Schell was mustered in as Sergeant; was
promoted 2d Lieutenant April 16, 1862, for gallantry at
Shiloh; promoted 1st Lieutenant March 21, 1863, and
Captain July 4, 1863, and was mustered out at the expiration of original enlistment, January 28, 1865. Died at
his home near Hall's Corners, Indiana, from the effects
of wounds received in the battle of Shiloh.

George W. Squier was mustered in as a Corporal, re-
enlisted as a veteran, was promoted 1st Lieutenant May
18, 1864, and Captain February 17, 1865, and was mustered out with the Regiment. Post-office address, South
Haven, Van Buren County, Michigan.

FIRST LIEUTENANTS.

Charles H. Wayne. See "CAPTAINS."

George W. Schell. See "CAPTAINS."

James Collier was mustered in as a private, was promoted 2d Lieutenant March 21, 1863, and 1st Lieutenant
July 4, 1863.

George W. Squier. See "CAPTAINS."

Sylvester J. Stowe was mustered in as a private, re-enlisted as a veteran, was promoted 1st Lieutenant February 15, 1865, and was mustered out with the Regiment.

SECOND LIEUTENANTS.

J. Delta Kerr entered the service as 2d Lieutenant, and died in hospital at Evansville, Ind., March 25, 1862, of disease contracted in the service.

George W. Schell.   See "CAPTAINS."

James Collier.   See "FIRST LIEUTENANTS."

David R. Stopher was mustered in as a Sergeant, promoted 2d Lieutenant July 4, 1863, and attached to the staff of General Vancleve, and died June, 1864.

John E. Casebeer was mustered in as a Corporal, re-enlisted as a veteran, was promoted 2d Lieutenant February 17, 1865, and mustered out with the Regiment.

VETERANS.

Corporal George W. Squier.   See "CAPTAINS."

Corporal Joseph S. Potts.   Kendallville.

Corporal John E. Casebeer.   See "SECOND LIEU-TENANTS."   Defiance, Ohio.

Amos T. Britton.   Corunna, Ind.

John M. Collier.   Michigan.

George Endinger.   Chamberlin, Ind.

Jacob Harreder, Corporal.

Charles H. Higgins, Corporal.   Hall's Corners, Ind.

Joseph Hemmer.   Warsaw, Ind.   Dead.

Andrew J. Johnson.   Missouri.

Jerome A. Kenyon, killed at Chattanooga, by explosion of shell, April 1, 1864.

Henry C. Knepper, transferred to Engineer Corps, August 1, 1864.   Ligonier, Ind.

John Lower, Sergeant.   South Milford, Ind.

Chester Markham, Sergeant.

William J. Opie.   Wolcottville, Ind.

Charles A. Pardee, Hospital Steward.   Wolcottville.
Robert C. Price, Sergeant.   Antwerp, Ohio.
Samuel A. Shanower, 1st Sergeant.   Wawaka, Ind.
Sylvester J. Stowe.   See "FIRST LIEUTENANTS."
Isaiah Smith.   Ligonier, Ind.
Lewis Y. Thompson.   Missouri.
Francis Van Ormin.   Rome City, Ind.

THREE YEARS MEN.

Sergeant Lafayette Perkins.   Hall's Corners, Ind.
Musician Aruna P. Cosgrove.   Warsaw, Ind.
Francis Bartlett.   Dead.
John Farmer.   Harlan, Ind.
Abraham Z. Foot.   Corunna, Ind.
Albert Jackson.   Hall's Corners, Ind.
Martin H. Kessler.   Bureau County, Ill.
Jacob Knepper.   Wawaka, Ind.   .
Samuel W. Reed.   Wolcottville, Ind.
Joseph B. Reed.
Jacob White.   Wawaka, Ind.
Benjamin F. Williamson.   Harlan, Ind.

DISCHARGED ON ACCOUNT OF DISABILITY FROM WOUNDS OR DISEASE.

1st Sergeant Thomas C. Moffett, May 26, 1862.   Dead.

Corporal Philemon Mellington, July 11, 1862.   Antwerp, Ind.

Corporal Thomas J. Stanley, March 20, 1863.   Evansville, Ind.

Corporal Randall Simmons, October 2, 1862.   Hall's Corners, Ind.

Wagoner Joshua Lownsbury, January 3, 1863.   Newville, Ind.

Amandred Anderson, June 23, 1862.   Tullahoma, Tenn.

Joseph Conway, June 20, 1862. Dead.
Alfred Dougherty, Sept. 20, 1862. Fort Wayne, Ind.
Emanuel Detrich, Sept. 6, 1862. Ohio.
Horace Gusten, June 20, 1863. Dead.
Samuel Hartsell, July 31, 1862.
Wm. H. Johnson, Aug. 31, 1862. Fort Wayne, Ind.
Wm. M. Johnson, Aug. 20, 1862. ~~Spencerville, Ind.~~
Henry Markle, Nov. 14, 1862.
Sylvester Miner, July 1, 1863.
Robert D. Rhea, July 31, 1862. Hall's Corners, Ind.
Cyrenus Saunders, March 23, 1863. Michigan.
Joseph Shook, April 29, 1863.
Isaac D. Sockrider, June 23, 1862. Nebraska.
Samuel Stowman, Aug. 29, 1862. Wawaka, Ind.
Adolphus Thompson, Nov. 30, 1862.
Wm. H. Underwood, Sept. 20, 1862. Dead.
Stephen P. Waybill, Jan. 6, 1863. Kansas.
Henry Wentworth, Dec. 31, 1862. Dead.
John Wentworth, Nov. 5, 1862. Hall's Corners, Ind.
Ezra Worden, March 3, 1864. Hall's Corners, Ind.
David Worden, Feb. 23, 1863. Dead.

KILLED.

Corporal Burke D. Shafer, Shiloh, April 6, 1862.
William H. Casebeer, Shiloh, April 6, 1862.
John Haller, Stone River, Dec. 30, 1862.
Jacob H. McClellan, Shiloh, April 6, 1862.
John Poppy, Shiloh, April 6, 1862.
Platt Y. Squiers, Shiloh, April 6, 1862.
Jerome Kenyon, killed (accident) April 1, 1864, at Chattanooga, Tenn.

DIED.

Sergeant Owen T. James, March 29, 1864.
Musician Joseph H. Eckles, Huntsville, Ala., July 12, 1862.

Jacob Baumgardner, Andersonville, June 22, 1864.
Thomas Blackburne, Calhoun, Ky., Feb. 16, 1862.
Frederick Burner, Evansville, March 16, 1862.
George W. Clark, Indianapolis, April 5, 1862.
Henry I. Collier, Lavergne, Tenn., Sept. 28, 1862.
Ebenezer Conway, Evansville, March 25, 1862.
William A. Golden, Evansville, June 9, 1862.
Samuel Hagerman, Pittsburg Landing, April 18, '62.
James Hanan, Maysville, Ind., May 25, 1862.
Barney Knepper, Indianapolis, June 15, 1862.
David McCord, Pittsburg Landing, April 2, 1862.
William Miner, Evansville, Dec. 22, 1861.
Charles Morse, Allen County, Ind., Feb. 23, 1862.
Joseph Murray, Battle Creek, July 20, 1862.
Thomas Parks, Henderson, Ky., Jan. 16, 1862.
William Routsong, Andersonville prison, Oct. 25, '64.
Lewis E. Shook, Jan. 10, 1863.
Ira Worden, Andersonville prison, June 25, 1864.

TRANSFERRED.

Nathan Rex,   to 15th U. S. I., Dec. 24, 1862.
Alfred Wilson,   "   "   "
Cyrus Merriman,   "   "   "

ENLISTED MEN PROMOTED TO COMMISSIONS.

David K. Stopher, George Schell, James Collier,
George W. Squier, John E. Casebeer, Sylvester K.
Stowe.

RECRUITS.

1862.

Nov. 23.   James Dallas, discharged May 2, 1863. Wol-
               cottville, Ind.

1863.

Dec. 23.   James Album,   m. o. Sept. 14, 1865.
 "   23.   Benedict Buckhart,   "   "   "
 "   16.   Robert T. Burris,   "   "   "

Dec. 16. Wesley Burris, m. o. Sept. 14, 1865.
" 23. Samuel J. Folke, " " "
Sept. 16. Alex. W. Lines, Corp'l, " " "
Dec. 21. William Sellers, " " "

1864.

Jan. 6. John O. Adams, " " "
Oct. 19. James Allen, " " "
Jan. 11. William M. Ball, " " "
Feb. 10. John H. Bartholomew, m. o. April, 1865.
    Hall's Corners, Ind.
Feb. 29. Samuel B. Byers, m. o. Sept. 14, 1865.
Nov. 30. William B. Briggs, " " "
Oct. 26. John B. Burch, " " "
Oct. 16. Flavius J. Burnett, " " "
Nov. 16. Robert Cook, " " "
Oct. 20. Ezekiel P. Darling, " " "
Jan. 29. Emanuel Dietrich, Corporal, " "
    Ohio.
" 29. John H. Evans, " " "
Dec. 16. John G. Edwards, " Oct. 12, "
    Fort Wayne, Ind.
Jan. 29. William Farmer, " Sept. 14, "
" 6. Thomas Fleming, " " "
" 8. Tobias M. Grimes, " " "
Feb. 27. John C. Gibson, " " "
" 10. John W. Gusten, died April 26, 1865.
Jan. 6. Harden Gillett, m. o. Sept. 14, 1865. Dead.
Feb. 28. Horace Gusten, " " "
" 28. Oliver Gusten, m. o. July 3, 1865. Harlan, Ind.
Jan. 29. Charles F. Hickman, m. o. Sept. 14, 1865.
    Harlan, Ind.
Mar. 19. Samuel Hartel, killed at Chattanooga, July
    13, 1864. Hall's Corners, Ind.
Jan. 12. Abraham R. Hollingsworth, m. o. Sept. 14,
    1865. Harlan, Ind.

Feb.	10.	William H. Hanan,	m. o. Sept. 14, 1865.
Jan.	12.	William F. Harris,	" " "
"	4.	Joel W. Johnson,	" " "
Dec.	29.	Matthew McKendall,	" " "
April	5.	Norman Luce,	" " "
Jan.	6.	Absalom Lattimore,	" " "
Mar.	5.	Henry Luce,	" " "
Jan.	29.	James McBratney,	" " "
Oct.	26.	Lafayette Mullen,	" " "
Mar.	5.	Richard Morten,	" " "
Feb.	29.	Thomas D. McCortle,	" " "
Jan.	4.	William A. McDaniel,	" " "
"	4.	Joseph A. McDaniel,	" " "
Oct.	24.	John McGowan,	" " "
Mar.	12.	William Matthes,	" " "
Sept.	21.	Wiley M. Mathes,	" July 25, "
Jan.	6.	Astley C. Pomeroy,	" Sept. 14, "

Jan. 27. Lucius C. Palmer, Corporal, m. o. Sept. 14, 1865. Hall's Corners, Ind.

" 3. Charles Quick, m. o. Sept. 14, 1865.

Sept. 26. John M. Rost, died at Chattanooga, July 18, 1865.

Dec.	16.	George M. Riley,	m. o. Sept. 14, 1865.
Mar.	15.	Walter Smith,	" " "
Feb.	29.	Thomas Search,	" " "

July 10. Albert J. Spencer, transferred to V. R. C. March 13, 1865.

Jan. 6. Jesse Swisher, m. o. Sept. 14, 1865.

Mar. 9. Thomas S. Trittapoo, Corporal, m. o. Sept. 14, 1865.

April	24.	Zopher Tyler,	m. o. Sept. 14, 1865.
Dec.	15.	John Teegarden,	" " "
Jan.	27.	John H. Wentworth,	" " "
Mar.	22.	Whitfield Welch,	" " "
"	15.	John Welch,	" " "

Oct. 16. John Westfall, m. o. Sept. 14, 1865.
"   17. John W. Yates, m. o. June 13, 1865.
1865.
Feb. 28. Horace Gusten, m. o. Sept. 14, 1865.
"   21. Israel Hickson, m. o. Sept. 14, 1865.
"   6. Joshua Ballenger, m. o. May 19, 1865.

Forty drafted men and substitutes were added to the Company in November, 1864, and were mustered out in June and July, 1865, except

Halbert McClure, who died at Chattanooga, May 14, 1865.

Whole desertions in Company, 7 ; names omitted.

COMPANY E.

Company E was organized by volunteers from Whitley County, William H. Cuppy taking an active interest in enlisting the men. He was selected by the men as their Captain, Isaac N. Compton as 1st Lieutenant, and Francis McDonald as 2d Lieutenant. These officers were commissioned Sept. 20, 1861, and mustered in with the Company Nov. 22, 1861. The men enlisted mainly in September before.

CAPTAINS.

William H. Cuppy, mustered in as above, led his Company in the battle of Fort Donelson, where he fell seriously wounded while in advance of his Company bravely cheering them on in the conflict. He was entirely disabled, and died from the wound received, July 15, 1862.

William Hildebrand was mustered in as a Sergeant, promoted 2d Lieutenant May 15, 1862, commissioned 1st Lieutenant Nov. 15, 1862, but not mustered ; promoted

Captain January 20, 1863, and was mustered out at expiration of enlistment, Dec. 5, 1864. Residence, Po, Allen County, Ind.

Oliver P. Koontz was mustered in as a private, re-enlisted as a veteran, was promoted Captain January 16, 1865, and was mustered out with the Regiment. Present residence, Bluffton, Ind.

FIRST LIEUTENANTS.

Isaac N. Compton entered the service as 1st Lieutenant at the organization of his Company. Resigned in April, 1862. Residence, South Whitley, Ind.

Francis McDonald was mustered in as 2d Lieutenant at the organization of the Company, received honorable mention at Shiloh ; was promoted 1st Lieutenant April 10, 1862. Resigned Nov. 14, 1862. Residence, Columbia City, Ind.

William Hildebrand. See "CAPTAINS."

Andrew J. Reed was mustered in as a private, was promoted 1st Lieutenant January 20, 1863, and was mustered out at the expiration of term of enlistment, Dec. 21, 1864. Residence, Welt City, Mo.

John D. Spurgeon was mustered in as a private, re-enlisted as a veteran, was promoted 1st Lieutenant March 24, 1865, and was mustered out with the Regiment. Residence, Manchester, Ind.

SECOND LIEUTENANTS.

Francis McDonald. See "FIRST LIEUTENANTS."

William Hildebrand. See "CAPTAINS."

Stephen J. Compton was mustered in as a Sergeant ; was promoted 2d Lieutenant January 20, 1863. Resigned Jan. 10, 1864. Residence, South Whitley, Ind.

William S. Bitner was mustered in as a private, re-enlisted as a veteran, was promoted 2d Lieutenant

March 24, 1865, and was mustered out with the Regiment. Residence, Goshen, Ind.

VETERANS.

Corporal James Collett, Sergeant. Collamer, Ind.

Jay W. Baker, Sergeant.

Hiram F. Biddle, Sergeant. Collamer, Ind.

Harvey W. Bare, Sergeant. Bangor, Mich.

Frederick Banta, Corporal. Georgetown, Eldorado County, Col.

William S. Bitner. See "SECOND LIEUTENANTS."

Samuel A. Baker, killed by railroad accident, January 30, 1865.

Joseph W. Compton, Sergeant. Larwell, Ind.

John Goucher. South Whitley, Ind.

David Hale. Dead.

Oliver P. Koontz. See "CAPTAINS."

Jackson Lippencott, Corporal. Columbia City, Ind.

Barrett Recard. Transferred to U. S. Engineers August 26, 1864. Rochester, Kan.

John D. Spurgeon. See "FIRST LIEUTENANTS."

THREE YEARS MEN.

Corporal Samuel W. Havens. Collamer, Ind.

Corporal John Y. Robbins. Clair, Mich.

Corporal John M. Albright. Dead.

Adam Barsh. Independence, Kansas.

Thomas Combs. Weaver, Dark County, Ohio.

John C. Clapp. South Whitley, Ind.

Martin Hathaway. Allison, Ill.

Samuel Heagy. Goshen, Ind.

Theodore F. Nave. Tracy, Ind.

Cary Pimlot. Wichita, Kansas.

Joseph Ruply. North Manchester, Ind.

Elam Robbins. Liberty Mills, Ind.

Amos Rodearmel. Dead.

Christopher Sonders. Larwell, Ind.
John Shaffner. Roanoke, Ind.
Stephen McCurdy.

DISCHARGED.

1st Sergeant George Sickafoose, April 28, 1862. Buchanan, Mich.

Sergeant Jerome F. Combs, Aug. 8, 1862. Dead.

Corporal Henry Rupley, August 8, 1862; wounds at Shiloh. South Whitley, Ind.

Corporal Stephen Circle, April 28, 1862. Missouri.

Musician William Clapp, July 11, 1862.

Joseph Anderson, Nov. 3, 1862; wounds. Liberty Mills, Ind.

Andrew Arnold, April 28, 1862.

Isaac Byers, April 28, 1862. Van Buren Co., Mich.

Ezra Bushnell, Jan. 23, 1862. South Whitley, Ind.

Christian Burnsworth, April 28, 1862.

Noah Brubaker, Aug. 11, 1864. Dead.

Peter Boblet, Oct. 9, 1863. Collamer, Ind.

Alexander Goff, May 26, 1864. Collamer, Ind.

Nicholas Hapner, April 28, 1862. South Whitley.

Alonzo King, Oct. 26, 1862. Larwell, Ind.

William A. Kelsey, July 23, 1862. Saturn, Ind.

Simeon Oberhaltzer, Jan. 9, 1864.

William Prugh, Jan. 12, 1864. Larwell, Ind.

Henry Rhodes, May 26, 1864; wounds at Chickamauga.

Michael Sickafoose, June 2, '62. Columbia City, Ind.

Albert Snyder, April 28, 1861.

KILLED.

Samuel A. Baker, killed by railroad accident, January 30, 1865.

Corporal Warren Banta, at Shiloh, April 6, 1862.

Nelson Parrett, at Fort Donelson, Feb. 15, 1862.

George Weamer, died of wound at Shiloh, Apr. 6, '62.

James Mullenix, killed at Stone River.

DIED.

John M. Collins, taken prisoner at Chickamauga, Sept. 19, 1863; died in rebel prison.

James Carpenter, taken prisoner at Chickamauga, Sept. 19, 1863; died in rebel prison.

Sergeant Henry Croy, Calhoun, Ky., Feb. 19, 1862.

Corporal Hiram Smith, Evansville, March 1, 1864.

Musician Lafayette Parks, Louisville, June 30, 1863.

Henry Brenneman, May 12, 1862; wounds at Shiloh.

Joseph Carns, Feb. 4, 1862.

Solomon Carpenter, March 15, 1862.

Henry Dilater, Feb. 8, 1862.

John Denny, taken prisoner at Chickamauga, and died at Andersonville prison, June 19, 1864.

Asbury Grobel, Jan. 12, 1863; wounds at Stone River.

George Holloway, in rebel prison, Danville, Va., March 7, 1864.

George G. Hennemyer, Bowling Green, Ky., January 1, 1863.

Nathan Myers, Calhoun, Ky., Feb. 8, 1862.

Henry Parrett, Chattanooga, May 13, 1864.

Joseph Parrett, March 9, 1862.

William Stiver, Dec. 6, 1861.

James W. Samuels, April 11, 1862.

David Werts, Dec. 8, 1861.

TRANSFERRED.

Harrison Sayre, to Company G.

RECRUITS.

1862.

Jan. 5. Henry M. Eagle, died May 15, 1862; wounds at Shiloh.

1863.

Dec. 26. Henry L. Davidson, m. o. Sept. 14, 1865.

"   11. William A. Dawson,   "   "   "

Dec. 11. John Hoon,   m. o. Sept. 14, 1865.
"   23. William McCarty,   "   "   "
"   2. Thomas H. Smith,   "   "   "
"   23. Michael Wade,   "   "   "
1864.
Mar. 5. Alfred Bower,   "   "   "
"   11. Thomas Biddle,   "   "   "
"   11. John H. Biddle,   "   "   "
              as Corporal. Ligonier.
"   19. Samuel Creager,   "   "   "
              as Corporal. Columbia City.
Feb. 27. Henry F. Cannutt, m. o. Aug. 31, 1865.
Jan.· 6. Daniel Etnire,   m. o. Sept. 14, 1865.
"   6. Jacob L. Etnire,   "   "   "
Mar. 19. William Fox,   "   "   "
              Columbia City.
"   19. Elkanah Fletcher,   "   "   "
              as Corporal. South Whitley.
"   19. Noah Fletcher,   "   "   "
              South Whitley.
"   19. William R. Holloway,   "   "   "
"   5. William F. Jackson,   "   "   "
"   5. William T. Livingston, "   "   "
"   6. William Long,   "   "   "
"   11. William McKinney,   "   "   "
Jan. 6. John Malott,   "   "   "
Mar. 19. Samuel Pritchard,   "   "   "
              South Whitley.
Dec. 5. Alonzo M. Porter,   "   "   "
Jan. 4. John W. Parrott, died at Nashville, Aug. 8, '64.
Mar. 11. Israel Rhods, m. o. Sept. 14, 1865, as Corporal. Columbia City.
"   6. Joshua J. Ramy,   m. o. Sept. 14, 1865.
"   5. Lewis Sigars,   "   "   "
"   9. Theodore A. Steward,   "   "   "
              Pawnee, Ill.

Feb.	27.	David Sewall,	m. o. Sept. 14, 1865.		
Mar.	8.	Hiram Sewall,	"	"	"
"	19.	Henry Euric,	"	"	Dead.
Jan.	6.	John T. Weinland,	"	"	1865.
Nov.	30.	William L. Rannson,	"	"	"
Mar.	11.	James L. Cross,	"	"	"
Apr.	20.	George W. Haines,	"	"	"
Mar.	2.	Isaac D. Reed,	"	"	"
1865.					
Jan.	26.	Daniel K. Shelton,	"	"	"
"	26.	Thomas L. Shelton,	"	"	"

Forty-six drafted men and substitutes were added to the Company in the fall of 1864, and mustered out in June and July, 1865, except

Alfred B. Alton, who died at Chattanooga, June 29, 1865;

John Alton, died at Chattanooga, March 4, 1865.

There were 12 deserters from the Company; names omitted.

COMPANY F.

Company F was organized by volunteers from De Kalb County, who elected for their first officers, George W. Merrill, Captain; James Colgrove, 1st Lieutenant; Thomas C. Kinmont, 2d Lieutenant. These officers were commissioned September 20, 1861, and were mustered in with the Company, November 22, 1861. The men mainly enlisted early in September.

CAPTAINS.

George W. Merrill entered the service as above stated. Resigned June 24, 1862. Present residence, Toledo, Ohio.

Thomas C. Kinmont entered the service as 2d Lieutenant, at the organization of the Company; led the Company at Fort Donelson and Shiloh; received a wound breaking the thigh bone; was honorably mentioned in Colonel Reed's report; was promoted Captain June 24, 1862; resigned February 25, 1863. Residence, Hicksville, Ohio.

John Gunsenhouser was mustered in as a Sergeant; promoted 1st Lieutenant May 15, 1862; Captain, July 4, 1863; led his Company at the battle of Chickamauga, where he fell the second day of the battle, September 20, 1863. He was highly praised by Lieutenant-Colonel Aldrich in his official report of the battle.

Irving N. Thomas was mustered in as Corporal, was promoted 2d Lieutenant March 21, 1863, 1st Lieutenant July 4, 1863, and commissioned September 21, 1863, but did not muster, and resigned as 1st Lieutenant January 2, 1864. Gone west.

George H. Cosper was mustered in as a private; was promoted 2d Lieutenant July 4, 1863; 1st Lieutenant, January 8, 1864; Captain, June 3, 1864; and was mustered out with the Regiment. Lives in Kansas.

FIRST LIEUTENANTS.

James Colgrove was mustered in as 1st Lieutenant; was promoted Adjutant, January 10, 1862; was honorably mentioned by Colonel Reed for conduct at Fort Donelson, and at Shiloh. In the latter battle his horse was shot under him. Resigned May 27, 1862. Residence, Chicago, Ill.

John Gunsenhouser. See "CAPTAINS."

Irving N. Thomas. See "CAPTAINS."

George H. Cosper. See "CAPTAINS."

Alexander Kinmont was mustered in as a Corporal; re-enlisted as a veteran; was promoted 1st Lieutenant

June 3, 1864; was promoted Quartermaster January 17, 1865, and was mustered out with the Regiment. Resides at Auburn, Ind.

James M. Thomas entered the service as a private; re-enlisted as a veteran; was promoted 2d Lieutenant March 24, 1865; 1st Lieutenant, June 10, 1865, and was mustered out with the Regiment. Residence, Kearney Junction, Buffalo County, Nebraska.

SECOND LIEUTENANTS.

Thomas C. Kinmont. See "CAPTAINS."

Solomon De Long was mustered in as 1st Sergeant; was promoted 2d Lieutenant March 20, 1862; resigned December 19, 1862, and re-entered the service as Captain of the 129th Regiment Indiana Volunteers. Dead.

Irving N. Thomas. See "CAPTAINS."

George H. Cosper. See "CAPTAINS."

James M. Thomas. See "FIRST LIEUTENANTS."

Alfred Rose was mustered in as a private; re-enlisted as a veteran; was promoted 2d Lieutenant June 24, 1865, and mustered out with the Regiment. Resides at Auburn, Ind.

VETERANS.

Musician Simon Aldrich. Waterloo, Ind.

Isaac Brubaker, Sergeant. Corunna, Ind.

John G. Casebeer, Sergeant. Butler, Ind.

Ludwig Countryman. Newville, Ind.

William Friend. Auburn, Ind.

Samuel Jacques, 1st Sergeant. Lansing, Mich.

Alfred Rose. See "SECOND LIEUTENANTS." Auburn, Ind.

George E. Revette. Dead.

John H. Trauger, Corporal.

Henry L. Wallace, Corporal. Paulding Co., Ohio.

Hiram B. Williams, Sergeant. Gone west.

David N. Yarnell, Sergeant. Quasqueton, Buchanan County, Iowa.

Trusterman B. Totten, Corporal. Kansas.

THREE YEARS MEN.

Sergeant Wilson Nichols. Farmer Centre, Ohio.

Sergeant Nathan T. Fuller. Newville, Ind.

Corporal Marshall Hadsill. Sibba, Osceola Co., Iowa.

David Andrews. Spencerville, DeKalb Co., Ind.

Lewis Beard. Newville, DeKalb Co., Ind.

Joseph Craig. Waterloo, Ind.

Calvin Casebeer. Butler, Ind.

Edward R. Coburn. Isabell, Isabell Co., Mich.

Peter Countryman. Newville, Ind.

Richard Dirrim. Butler, Ind.

George W. Freeby, m. o. April 20, 1865.

Isaac Fireston. Nettle Lake, Ind.

Frederick Ginter. Butler, Ind.

Henry Gunsenhouser. Butler, Ind.

John H. Hart. Gone west.

Harvey Nichols. Dead.

Alexander L. Nichols. Butler, Ind.

George W. Palmer, m. o. Dec. 12, 1864. Hicksville, Ohio.

John Slents. Butler, Ind.

George W. Slents. Butler, Ind.

Robert S. Schamp. Kansas.

Martin B. Turner. Dead.

DISCHARGED.

Sergeant James H. Abell, Sept. 3, 1862. Spencerville, Ind.

Captain James M. Milleman, August, 1862. Spencerville, Ind.

Wagoner Nathan Matthews, March 9, 1863. Auburn, Indiana.

Henry J. Able, May 16, 1863.   Spencerville, Ind.
Hollis B. Aikens, April 28, 1862.   Newville, Ind.
Michael Brubaker, Feb. 11, 1863.   Deerfield, Ind.
William Y. Babcock, April 28, 1862.
Daniel W. Cole, March 11, 1863.   Newville, Ind.
William Cochran, August 11, 1862.
' William Deigh, Sept. 12, 1862.
Ezra Dickinson, April 28, 1862.   Butler, Ind.

Robert R. Dirrim, July 11, 1862; wounds at Shiloh. Butler, Ind.

Isaac Ditmar, Jan. 28, 1862; wounds at Shiloh.   Auburn, Ind.

Francis M. Haughey.
Alexander Hart, April 28, 1862.   Illinois.
David N. Hart, May 7, 1863.   Columbia City, Ind.
Solomon Kinsley, July 5, 1862.
Jacob Myers, Nov. 6, 1862.
Henry Milliman, June, 1862.   Spencerville, Ind.
Robert Matthews, April 28, 1862.
James Revette, June 24, 1862.   Butler, Ind.
George W. Redd, Jan. 10, 1865.
Samuel R. Rickett, Aug. 1, 1862.
Thomas O. Sloan, June 25, 1862.   Dead.
John M. Scott, June 14, 1862.   Dead.
Nathan Stockwell, July 5, 1862.
George B. Weeks, Sept. 21, 1862.
Andrew J. Strole, Feb. 1, 1863.   Dead.
Francis S. Chandler.   Waterloo, Ind.

KILLED.

Henry C. Pryor, Chickamauga, Sept. 19, 1863.
John H. Webster, Stone River, Jan. 2, 1863.
Stephen Turner, Stone River, Dec. 31, 1862.
Nelson Mullenix, Stone River, Dec. 31, 1862.

DIED.

James G. Dirrim, near Corinth, Miss., May 2, 1862.
William Bender, Shiloh, April 6, 1862.
William Collier, Shiloh, April 7, 1862.
Charles S. Beverly, Battle Creek, Tenn., July 20, '62.
William S. Bardon, Huntsville, Ala., Aug. 23, 1862.
Oscar I. Crane, St. Louis, May 21, 1862.
Charles O. Danks, Battle Creek, Tenn., Aug. 1, 1862.
James Flora, Nashville, Nov. 19, 1863.
Hiram Gaff, Evansville, May 3, 1862.
Allen S. Headley, Henderson, Ky., Jan. 4, 1862.
John Hombarger, New Albany, Ind., Oct. 7, 1862.
Leonard Kirby, St. Louis, May 16, 1862.
Warren Milliman, Evansville, April 1, 1862.
Henry I. Monroe, St. Louis, April 23, 1862.
Orlando Oberlin, Pittsburg Landing, March 22, 1862.
Bennett S. Robe, Chattanooga, Dec. 13, 1863.
William M. Smith, Evansville, March 7, 1862.
Louis B. Tiffany, Dec. 21, 1862; w. at Stone River.
Albert P. Totton, Evansville, March 7, 1862.
George W. Wallace, Jan. 7, 1863; w. at Stone River.
Michael McEntaffer, Louisville, Ky., Nov. 28, 1862.
Francis P. Robbins, at Nashville, Feb. 6, 1863.

TRANSFERRED.

Daniel Greenawalt, to Invalid Corps, August, 1863. Auburn, Ind.

Chester B. Greenamyer, to Invalid Corps, May 10, 1863; wounds at Stone River.

Herman P. Colgrove, to Engineer Corps. Allegan, Pierce County, Kansas.

Otis Blood, to Invalid Corps, August, 1863. Newville, Ind.

VOLUNTEER RECRUITS.

1862.

Nov. 12. Roland E. Ford, m. o. Sept. 14, 1865.

Oct. 22. Asaph Harwood, discharged Nov. 2, 1864.

Nov. 12.　Jacob Hicks,　　　　m. o. Sept. 14, 1865.
Dec.　3.　Jarrett W. Hall,　　　"　　　"　　　"
Nov. 12.　Hugh W. Dirrim,　　　"　　　"　　　"
Oct.　7.　Covert Lucas,　　　　"　　　"　　　"
"　22.　Stephen McCurdy, Corporal,　　"　　　"
Nov. 12.　Tempest T. McCurdy, died at Murfreesboro.
Oct.　2.　John Notestine,　　　m. o. Sept. 14, 1865.
"　12.　Samuel Oberlin, Corp'l, "　　"　　　"
Nov. 12.　David G. Robinson,　　"　　　"　　　"
"　12.　Henry S. Reid, drowned at Chattanooga, November 14, 1863.
"　12.　Jacob Slentz,　　　　m. o. Sept. 14, 1865.
"　12.　Henry Slentz,　　　　"　　　"　　　"
Oct. 22.　Frederick Shock,　　　"　　　"　　　"
Nov. 12.　George T. Shick,　　　"　　　"　　　"
Oct.　2.　Jason H. Thurston,　　"　　　"　　　"
Dec.　8.　George W. Townsend,　"　　　"　　　"
"　3.　David Weatherford,　　"　　　"　　　"

1863.

Oct. 23.　Samuel Anderson, discharged March 13, 1865.
April 27.　James Brubaker,　　m. o. Sept. 14, 1865.
Dec. 26.　Henry A. Bailey,　　·"　　　"　　　"
"　2.　William A. Hood,　　"　　　"　　　"
"　15.　John Irwin,　　　　"　　　"　　　"
"　26.　Joseph R. Lough,　　"　　　"　　　"
"　11.　William Morris,　　"　　　"　　　"
April 22.　John H. Smith,　　"　　　"　　　"
Sept. 26.　William C. Spaulding, "　　　"　　　"
Dec. 11.　William F. Stewart,　"　　　"　　　"

1864.

April 12.　John Brown,　　　"　　　"　　　"
　　　　Lagrange, Ind.
Mar.　3.　John C. Baum,　　　"　　　"　　　"
Nov. 12.　Hiram Bright,　　　"　　　"　　　"
April 12.　William A. Diehl,　　"　　　"　　　"

Mar.   3.   Robert W. Ewbanks, m. o. Sept. 14, 1865.
April 2.   William Fisher,   "   "   "
Nov.   3.   John W. Forbes,   "   "   "
April 2.   Samuel Goodman,   "   "   "
  "   12.   David Goff,   "   "   "
            Butler, Ind.
Dec. 31.   Alonzo E. Goff,   "   "   "
April 24.   George W. Goff,   "   "   "
Feb.   3.   William R. Goff,   "   "   "
Oct.   4.   Wilson Hyatt, died, Chattanooga, July 29, '65.
April 12.   Alexander Hoffman, m. o. Sept. 14, 1865.
            Corporal. Butler, Ind.
  "   12.   George D. Hopkins,   "   "   "
Oct.   5.   James W. Hyatt,   "   "   "
Nov. 12.   John Hall,   "   Sept. 7,   "
April 3.   David Jacques,   "   Sept. 14,   "
            Corporal.
Oct. 22.   Chas. Kooster, died, Chattanooga, July 3, '65.
April 2.   Samuel Ludwig,   m. o. May 18, 1865.
  "   2.   Joseph D. K. Lowry,   "   Sept. 14,   "
Nov. 12.   Basil Lamb,   "   "   "
Mar.   9.   Wm. W. McClintock,   "   "   "
Dec. 27.   Geo. Mayers, died, Chattanooga, May 26, '65.
Mar.   3.   John L. Smith,   m. o. Sept. 14, 1865.
Nov.   3.   John Smith,   "   "   "
Dec. 21.   William H. Stoy,   "   June 26,   "
April 18.   William H. Thomas,   "   Sept. 14,   "
Jan.   7.   Isom Tull,   "   "   "
April 2.   Sydney N. Welch,   "   "   "
            Corporal.
Nov.   3.   Henry C. White,   "   "   "
  "   12.   Thomas Wakeman,   "   "   "
Jan.   7.   Caswell York,   "   "   "
  1865.
Feb. 22.   Wesley W. Lowry,   "   June 17,   "

Mar.	3.	Resin Maples,	m. o. Sept. 14, 1865.
"	10.	Adam Oberlin,	" " "
Feb.	22.	Alexander Sloane,	" " "
Mar.	10.	John C. Smith,	" " "
"	1.	George P. Sharp,	" " "
"	6.	Leander Vail,	" " "
"	10.	George W. Groves,	" " "
— · —.		William F. Green, discharged April 6, 1865.	

Thirty-seven drafted men and substitutes were added to the Company in the fall of 1864, and mustered out in June and July, 1865, except

Isaac Rummel, died at Chattanooga, May 6, 1865;

Lorenzo Siphert, died at Chattanooga, Dec. 30, 1865.

COMPANY G.

Company G was organized by volunteers mainly from Noble County. About one half of the Company was recruited by Peter Snyder, of Kendallville, a patriotic citizen too old for service in the field. The balance of the Company was principally recruited by Dr. William C. Williams, of Albion, who was chosen the first Captain, Henry C. Shoemaker, 1st Lieutenant, and David Carey, 2d Lieutenant. These officers were commissioned September 20, 1861, and mustered in with the Company, November 22, 1861.

CAPTAINS.

William C. Williams. See "COLONELS."

Edwin W. Matthews was mustered in as a Corporal, became Orderly Sergeant, and was promoted Captain January 20, 1863, and was mustered out at the expiration of his three years' enlistment, December 5, 1864. Present residence, Green Center, Noble County, Indiana.

Dan S. Johnson was mustered in as a Sergeant; was promoted 1st Lieutenant February 17, 1865; Captain, April 26, 1865, and mustered out with the Regiment. Present residence, Van Wert, Ohio.

FIRST LIEUTENANTS.

Henry J. Shoemaker was mustered in with the Company. For the rest see Adjutant-General's report.

James C. Riddle entered the service as a private, was promoted 1st Lieutenant January 20, 1863, and was mustered out at the expiration of his three years' enlistment, December 5, 1864. Residence, Merriam, Noble County, Ind.

Dan S. Johnson. See " CAPTAINS."

William O. Bidlack entered the service as a private, re-enlisted as a veteran, was promoted 1st Lieutenant April 20, 1865, and was mustered out with the Regiment.

SECOND LIEUTENANTS.

David Carey was mustered in with the Company. For the rest see Adjutant-General's report.

William H. McMurray entered the service as a musician, was promoted 2d Lieutenant January 20, 1863, and was mustered out at the expiration of his three years' enlistment, December 5, 1864.

James Vanness entered service as company wagoner, was promoted 2d Lieutenant July 7, 1865, and was mustered out with the Regiment.

VETERANS.

Sergeant Dan S. Johnson. See " FIRST LIEUTENANTS."

Corporal John G. Burwell, Sergeant. Kendallville.

Henry Aumsbaugh, Sergeant.

William Bidlack. See " FIRST LIEUTENANTS."

Jasper Edsall, 1st Sergeant.

Lucius McGowan.

Job Perkins.

Jacob Pfaff, Sergeant.   Merriam, Noble Co., Ind.

Jefferson Shannon.   Brimfield,   "   "

Emory A. Swemm.

Melvin H. Stoner.

J. Trowbridge, discharged Jan. 7, 1864; disability.

Levi Crume, veteran from the 35th Ohio Regiment. Brimfield, Ind.

THREE YEARS MEN.

Charles Adams, then absent, sick.

DISCHARGED.

[FOR DISABILITY, UNLESS OTHERWISE STATED.]

1st Sergeant B. F. Rawson, September 12, 1862.

Sergeant Lyman Blowers, Jan. 5, 1863.

Corporal O. L. Rawson, Feb. 5, 1863.

Corporal Chauncey Wright, Nov. 25, 1862; wounds at Shiloh.

Corporal Samuel Wright, March 22, 1863.

William Blair, May 7, 1862.

E. E. Hill, Feb. 17, 1862. Wolf Lake, Noble County, Indiana.

Marks Henry, June 25, 1862.

Martin Minard, July 31, 1862; wounds at Shiloh.

Henry Minard, Oct. 8, 1862.

David McDonald. Brimfield, Noble County, Ind.

William McKee, July 31, 1862.

Henry O'Grady, Nov. 17, 1862.

Thomas Pierson, March 27, 1862.

Aaron Pierson, Nov. 1, 1862.

John Prickett, Feb. 7, 1862. Wolf Lake, Noble Co., Indiana.

J. V. Prickett, May 2, 1863. Wolf Lake, Noble Co., Indiana.

Albert Rice, July 1, 1862.

Samuel Wortsbaugh, Nov. 17, 1862.

G. W. Wright, July 31, 1862.

J. Graumlich, unaccounted for. Alma, Noble Co., Indiana.

KILLED.

A. P. Battzell, Shiloh, April 6, 1862.

Jacob Mohn, Shiloh, April 6, 1862.

DIED.

Sergeant Phineas M. Carey, Henderson, Ky., February 22, 1862.

Sergeant Neal Ruthvan, on steamer en route for Paducah, May 10, 1862.

Corporal H. J. Monroe, Andersonville, Aug. 22, 1864.

Corporal Isaac Dukes, Murfreesboro, April 16, 1863.

Corporal Alfred Shields, Murfreesboro, Dec. 5, 1863.

William Adkins, near Nashville.

H. J. Belden, Evansville, April 16, 1862.

Solomon Bean, Nashville, Nov. 2, 1862.

Paul Bean, Glasgow, Ky., Nov. 6, 1862.

Adjuna Bradley, Evansville, April 26, 1862.

George Blowers, near Corinth, June 12, 1862.

Guy Caswell, Kendallville, May 8, 1862.

Henry Ely, May 4, 1862; wounds at Shiloh.

J. Y. Johnson, Corinth, June 11, 1862.

F. Johnson, Newbern, Ind., July 15, 1862.

Henry Leslie, Murfreesboro, Tenn., April 17, 1862.

J. B. Matthews, Murfreesboro, Tenn., Jan. 2, 1863.

L. H. Madison, Hamburg Landing, Tenn., May 1, 1862.

John Minkey, Athens, Ala., July 5, 1862.

J. W. Norton, Evansville, Dec. 18, 1861.

Francis Owen, Tuscumbia, Ala., July 1, 1862.

Andrew Shannon, Murfreesboro, May 26, 1863.

Jacob Zumbran, Murfreesboro, Jan. 21, 1863.

TRANSFERRED.

James Bailey, to 4th U. S. Cavalry, Dec. 15, 1862.
George Carmany, to Engineer Brigade, May, 1864.
Milton Edsall, to Invalid Corps, May 7, 1863.
Ira Fuller, to Invalid Corps, Aug. 1, 1863.
George Weamer, to Co. E, Jan. 2, 1862.

RECRUITS.

1862.

Oct.	31.	John R. Craford, m. o. July 1, 1865.			
Nov.	1.	Lewis Fortune,	m. o. Sept. 14, 1865.		
Nov.	6.	Lafayette Glover,	"	"	"
Sept.	2.	James Lent,	"	June 13,	"
"		Daniel Lent,	"	"	"
Oct.	29.	Joel B. Murphy,	"	Sept. 14,	"
Dec.	1.	J. Q. A. May,	"	"	"
Aug.	9.	Alma L. Matthews,	"	June 13,	"
Sept.	21.	Alphonso Z. Rawson,	"	"	"
Nov.	21.	Alfred P. Short, m. o. Sept. 14, '65. Sergeant.			

1863.

Dec.	29.	George W. Atkins, transferred to V. R. C. Discharged June 2, 1865.			
"	18.	William F. Armstrong, m. o. Sept. 14, 1865.			
"	29.	George W. Bland,	"	"	"
"	9.	Alexander J. Bedall,	"	"	"
"	18.	John L. Coyle, as Corporal.	"	"	"
"	11.	John Carroll,	"	"	"
"	23.	John Chamberlain,	"	Aug. 17,	"
"	6.	John R. Dunlap,	"	Sept. 14,	"
"	25.	James Dailey,	"	"	"
"	2.	John Derby,	"	"	"
"	11.	James Gillespie,	"	"	"
"	13.	Mitchell Gerard,	"	Dec. 13, 1863.	
"	29.	James W. Hall,	"	Sept. 14, 1865.	

Dec.	26.	Jesse Jennings,	m. o. Sept. 14, 1865.
"	9.	George W. Malton,	" " "
"	17.	James McCann,	" " "
"	26.	Moses D. Peacock	" " "
July	14.	Henry C. Reiser,	" July 14, "
Dec.	9.	Jeremiah Smith,	" Sept. 14, "
"	18.	Henry Smith,	" " "
"	18.	Richard M. Swift, died	" " "
"	9.	Charles W. Whitelock,	" " "

1864.

April	6.	Charles B. Allen,	" " "
Mar.	9.	Levi Crume,	" " "
Feb.	11.	John Dunlap,	" " "
April	6.	Elisha J. Ellis,	" " "
Mar.	11.	George D. Flint,	" " "
April	26.	Hymen Howe, Jr.,	" " "
Jan.	7.	Thomas D. Hainey,	" " "
Feb.	5.	Thomas J. Howard,	" " "
Mar.	11.	Jenks P. High,	" " "
Jan.	6.	Thomas E. Hughes,	" " "
Mar.	11.	Charles P. Hubbell,	" " "

        as Corporal.

| " | " | Joseph M. Hathaway, | " " " |
| " | " | Amos Johnson, | " " " |

        as Corporal. Richhill, Ohio.

Jan.	6.	Daniel Kreisher,	m. o. " "
"	7.	John H. Lattimore,	" " "
Sept.	21.	Jacob Loveless, died at Chattanooga, June 11,

        1865.

| April | 6. | Lorin C. Madison, | m. o. Sept. 14, 1865, as |

        Corporal.

Dec.	9.	Manson W. Miles,	" " "
Oct.	4.	Patrick McGraw,	" " "
"	15.	Felix Morgenroth,	" " "
Jan.	7.	Otis Mullen,	" " "

April 6. William Mendham,   m. o. Sept. 14, 1865.

Rome City.

Jan.	9.	Job Perkins,	"	" "
Dec.	9.	Henry Robbins,	"	" "
Mar.	17.	Zachariah Reed,	" Aug. 29,	"
Jan.	9.	Harrison H. Sayre,	" Sept. 14,	"
"	12.	George W. Smith,	"	" "
Mar.	11.	George Tyner,	"	" "
"	11.	James Vanmeter,	"	" "
Oct.	29.	Henry Lawrence,	"	" "

Forty drafted men and substitutes were added to the Company in the fall of 1864, and mustered out in June and July, 1865, except

Andrew J. McGillen, who died April 14, 1865.

There were 15 deserters, names not given here, two of whom were veterans.

COMPANY H.

Company H was organized by volunteers from Lagrange County. William B. Bingham, a soldier of the Mexican war, and who had taken an active part in recruiting in the county, was chosen Captain, Joseph H. Danseur was chosen 1st Lieutenant, and Jacob Newman 2d Lieutenant. These officers were commissioned Sept. 20, 1861, and were mustered in with the Company November 22, 1861.

CAPTAINS.

William B. Bingham. See "MAJORS."

Jacob Newman was mustered in as 2d Lieutenant. He led the Company at the battle of Shiloh, and when color-bearer and guards were shot down and the flag riddled with bullets, "he bore it aloft," as mentioned

JACOB NEWMAN, CAPT. CO. H.

JOSEPH H. DANSEUR, CAPT. CO. H.

by Colonel Reed in his official report, but fell wounded, receiving a gun-shot wound in the bowels, that was at the time supposed to be mortal. He was promoted Captain immediately after, April 15th, but never recovered so as to be able to return to the Company, and resigned Nov. 14, 1862. He has filled the office of county treasurer of Lagrange County two terms since the war. He resides at Lagrange, and is still a sufferer from his wound.

Joseph H. Danseur was mustered in as 1st Lieutenant, and was promoted Captain January 16, 1863. In December, 1863, he was appointed Inspector-General on the staff of Colonel J. P. Fyffe, commanding Second Brigade, in General Vancleve's division, Army of the Cumberland, and while carrying orders of his commander at the battle of Shiloh, was severely wounded in the thigh. The wound disabling him, he resigned June 4, 1863. The injury from the wound finally resulted in permanent and fatal disease of the thigh bone, from which he died in 1866.

Hiram F. King was mustered in as 1st Sergeant, was promoted 1st Lieutenant January 20, 1863, Captain, July 4, 1863, and was mustered out at the expiration of his three years' enlistment, December 5, 1864. He was mentioned by Colonel Aldrich in his official report of the battle of Chickamauga as having " done nobly."

Samuel P. Bradford. See " QUARTERMASTERS."

FIRST LIEUTENANTS.

Joseph H. Danseur. See " CAPTAINS."

Hiram F. King. See " CAPTAINS."

Daniel P. Stricker was mustered in as Corporal, was promoted 2d Lieutenant January 20, 1863, and 1st Lieutenant July 4, 1863, and was mustered out at the expiration of his three years' enlistment, December 5, 1864. Present residence, Fort Scott, Kansas.

Hiram Pontius entered the service as a private, re-enlisted as a veteran, was promoted 1st Lieutenant May 1, 1865, and mustered out with the Regiment.

SECOND LIEUTENANTS.

Jacob Newman. See "CAPTAINS."

John B. Rowe was mustered in as a Sergeant, was wounded at Shiloh, promoted 2d Lieutenant April 15, 1862, and resigned on account of his wound September 1, 1862. Resides at Wolcottville, Ind.

Daniel Stricker. See "FIRST LIEUTENANTS."

Sebastian Shoup entered the service as a private, re-enlisted as a veteran, served some time as Commissary and Quartermaster-Sergeant, was promoted 2d Lieutenant May 1, 1865, and was mustered out with the Regiment. Residence, Coloma, Mich.

VETERANS.

Corporal Seymour B. Preston. Lagrange.
Musician Norman Sessions. Huntington.
Samuel Arnold, transf. to U. S. Eng., Aug. 18, 1864.
Philip Blough, Sergeant.
Charles Beard. Marcy.
Valentine Brown, Corporal.
Joseph Croghan.
George W. Dille, Sergeant. Dead.
Silas K. Freeman, 1st Sergeant. Burlingame, Kan.
John T. Fisher, Corporal.
John Giggy, Sergeant. Lagrange.
Joseph Grice, Corporal. Wolcottville.
Edward Hanslip. Osage City, Kansas.
John C. Hill, Sergeant. Lagrange.
Joseph D. Hill.
Isaiah Newnam. Wolcottville.
John Nelson. North Liberty.
Hiram Pontius. See "FIRST LIEUTENANTS."

David Randall.
William Spearow, Sergeant.
Franklin Strecker. Wolcottville.
Sebastian Shoup. See "SECOND LIEUTENANTS."
James Tuck. Wolcottville.

THREE YEARS MEN.

Sergeant David M. Hart. Lagrange.
Sergeant Daniel Rowe. Dead.
Corporal James Sutton.
Samuel Babb. Dead.
Jacob Deter. Lagrange.
John Gillett. Wolcottville.
George Gregory. Dead.
David D. Moffett. Notre Dame.
John Newman. Flint.
Martin F. Rowe.
Perry Randol.
Charles Wilson. Marcy.
Robert Silbaugh.

DISCHARGED.

[FOR DISABILITY, UNLESS OTHERWISE STATED.]

Corporal George Roy, wounded at Shiloh. Lagrange.
Corporal Charles E. Law. Wolcottville.
Musician John H. Stoner, Aug. 10, 1863. Dead.
Wagoner James H. Hoagland. May 10, 1864.
Peter Alspaugh, Sept. 9, 1863; w. at Stone River.
Daniel Bower, July 23, 1862; wounds at Fort Donelson. Wolcottville.
George Benham, June 25, 1862. Lagrange.
William Crow, wounds at Shiloh. Dead.
John Dawson. Dead.
Samuel Eiman. Lagrange.
Orson Elya.
Carey B. Frisby, July 17, 1862. Lagrange.

Vanburen Fisher, Jan. 2, 1863; wds. at Stone River.
Patrick Foley, Feb. 20, 1863.
Daniel Gindlesparger, July 26, 1862.
David Gindlesparger.
William D. Groves, March 24, 1863. Dead.
Edwin Hulbert, Dec. 31, 1863. Kendallville.
Melancthon Hoff, May 3, 1862. Dead.
Daniel Knight. Brushy Prairie.
William Knight, June 25, 1862. Dead.
James I. Morrison, April 28, 1862. Lagrange.
Matthew W. McDowell, Aug. 21, 1862.
Joseph Opie, Feb. 2, 1863.
Henry Randall, June 13, 1865.
Daniel Spearo, June 18, 1862. Marcy.
John Spearo. Brushy Prairie.
Edward Smith, Dec 27, 1862. Ringgold.
George W. Smith, July 4, 1862.
Charles R. Tyler, July 6, 1862.

KILLED.

Corporal Augustus A. Galloway, Shiloh, April 6, '62.
John V. Curtis, Shiloh, April 6, 1862.
Jerome Wright, Shiloh, April 6, 1862.
Orvin Page, Shiloh, April 7, 1862.

DIED.

Sergeant George M. Fish, Calhoun, Ky., Feb. 24, '62.
Corporal George W. Schermerhorn, Nashville, July 12, 1863.
Corporal James Longear, Evansville, March 10, 1862.
John Burridge, Mound City, Ill., May 20, 1862.
John D. Crist, Nashville, Feb. 2, 1863.
Jacob Coldren, Pittsburg Landing, May 6, 1862.
Henry Croft, Corinth, June 9, 1862.
Vincent C. Dyaman, St. Louis, March 21, 1862.
Andrew J. Hart, Henderson, Ky., Jan. 20, 1862.

David Harris, New Albany, April 26, 1862.
Arthur Haywood, South Carrolton, Ky., Jan. 28, '62.
Elias Holsinger, New Albany, Nov. 8, 1862.
George Holsinger, Pittsburg Landing, March 28, '62.
Victor Ketcham, Nashville, Feb. 28, 1863.
David Nelson, Nashville, Jan. 19, 1863.
Charles H. Nichols, New Albany, April 17, 1862.
Hiram S. Perkins, Evansville, March 17, 1862.

TRANSFERRED.

Henry C. Beam, to Marine Brigade, June 20, 1863.
William Starkey, to 4th U. S. Cavalry, Dec. 1, 1862.
Dead.

RECRUITS.

1862.
Sept. 5. David F. Roe, m. o. June 13, 1865.
1863.
Dec. 31. James M. Caterlin,   m. o. Sept. 14, 1865.
 "   31. Joseph M. Clark,   "   "   "
 "   21. Henry D. Downs,   "   "   "
 "   21. John A. Diehl,   "   "   "
 "   29. Nicholas Foble,   "   "   "
 "   21. Cornelius Gillespie, "   "   "
 "   26. Samuel R. Hutchinson, "   "   "
 "   26. Jacob Hileman,   "   "   "
 "   21. Erastus D. Johnson,   "   "   "
 "   26. James W. Marsh,   "   "   "
 "   26. Jesse Ryan,   "   "   "
1864.
Mar. 7. Isaac Blough, died, Chattanooga, June 21, '64.
 "   7. Eleazer Blough, died at home, Sept. 9, 1864.
 "   5. William S. Clark,   m. o. Sept. 14, 1865.
 "   9. Thomas Cunningham,   "   "   "
Jan. 1. William Cloyd,   "   "   "
Mar. 14. Cornelius Conkling, died at home, April 18,
           1864.

Mar. 11. Ralph P. Clark, died at Indianapolis, March 29, 1864.
"   5. Albert Davis,   m. o. Sept. 14, 1865.
"   18. Patrick Foley, Corporal, "   "   "
April 6. Benjamin Giggy, "   "   "   "
"   6. Abner Gilbert,   "   "   "
Mar. 7. John R. Hickman,   "   "   "
"   7. Henry R. Hickman,   "   "   "
April 2. Jonathan Hinds,   "   "   "
Feb. 2. John Hall,   "   "   "
Jan. 6. John Miller,   "   "   "
"   6. Jacob J. Musgrove,   "   "   "
April 6. Eli Moser, died at Chattanooga, May 22, 1864.
Sept. 4. Benjamin Racine, died, Nashville, July 5, '65.
Jan. 6. Silas Richardson,   m. o. Sept. 14, 1865.
"   6. Francis M. Richardson, "   "   "
"   6. James S. Spaulding,   "   "   "
Mar. 7. George H. Scott,   "   "   "
April 6. John M. Sigler, m. o. Sept. 14, 1865, as Corp'l.
1865.
Feb. 27. Jesse Brandon,   m. o. Sept. 14, 1865.
"   27. Carleton C. Cox,   "   " 23, "
"   27. Scott Hardy,   "   " 14, "

Forty-one drafted men and substitutes were added to the Company in the fall of 1864, and mustered out in June and July, 1865; except

John S. Cannon, died at Chattanooga, Feb. 17, 1865;
John W. Wood, died at Louisville, Dec. 17, 1864.

Deserters, 4; names omitted.

COMPANY I.

Company I was organized by volunteers at Elkhart, the men being mainly recruited by Albert Heath, who was chosen Captain ; Joseph C. Hodges was selected by the Company for 1st Lieutenant, and James F. Curtiss for 2d Lieutenant. The officers were commissioned September 20, 1861, and mustered in with the Company November 22, following.

CAPTAINS.

Albert Heath entered the service as Captain, at date above mentioned, led his Company at the battle of Fort Donelson, and acted as Major for the Regiment at Shiloh, where he was conspicuous for daring bravery. In the afternoon of the first day of the battle, while the Regiment was fighting on the left, and during the momentary absence of the Colonel, who was obeying some order from the Brigade commander, the acting Major ordered a charge, and crying out, "Remember Buena Vista," led on. The men bravely followed, but were slaughtered in the few moments that followed more than during any hour of the day. He received honorable mention by the Colonel in his official report, led his Company on from there to Corinth, Battle Creek, Louisville, and back to Nashville, when he was promoted to Lieutenant-Colonel of the 100th Regiment, and afterward to Colonel. Was wounded under Sherman at Missionary Ridge. Resides now at San Francisco, Cal.

Joseph C. Hodges. See "LIEUTENANT-COLONELS."

James F. Curtiss. See "COLONELS."

David S. Belknap was mustered in as a Sergeant, was promoted 2d Lieutenant January 20, 1863, 1st Lieutenant March 21, 1863, and was mustered out as 1st Lieutenant at the expiration of enlistment.

Onius D. Scoville entered the service as a private of Company A, was promoted 2d Lieutenant of Company A, June 11, 1863, and Captain of Company I, February 17, 1865, and was mustered out with the Regiment.

FIRST LIEUTENANTS.

Joseph C. Hodges.   See "LIEUTENANT-COLONELS."
James F. Curtiss.   See "COLONELS."
David S. Belknap.   See "CAPTAINS."

William H. Hoagland entered the service as a private, re-enlisted as a veteran, was promoted 1st Lieutenant March 20, 1865, and was mustered out with the Regiment.

SECOND LIEUTENANTS.

James F. Curtiss.   See "COLONELS."
David S. Belknap.   See "CAPTAINS."

Frank Baldwin enlisted January 10, 1862, was commissioned 2d Lieutenant October 18, 1862, but was not mustered, served in the battle of Stone River as a Lieutenant, and fell in the line, killed, December 31, 1862.

Charles M. Hinman enlisted January 10, 1862, was promoted 2d Lieutenant March 21, 1863, and died of disease April 27, 1863.

Cullen W. Green was mustered in January 10, 1862, was promoted 2d Lieutenant July 18, 1863, and was mustered out July 23, 1863, under Circular No. 75.

Platt Hoagland entered the service as a private, re-enlisted as a veteran, was promoted 2d Lieutenant July 15, 1865, and was mustered out with the Regiment.

VETERANS.

Corporal Ambrose C. Lamb.
Corporal Joseph B. Stanley.
Corporal Jefferson Bender, 1st Sergeant.   Dead.
Corporal Willis Layton.
Wagoner Samuel F. Miller.
Peter Anderler.
Orlando Axtell.
Joseph Benedict.   Elkhart.

David Burton.
John Bruse. Wolcottville.
Martin C. Danner.
Platt Hoagland. See "SECOND LIEUTENANTS."
William H. Hoagland. See "FIRST LIEUTENANTS."
Peter Hartney, Corporal.
Frederic Johnson. Elkhart.
George W. Keeley. Elkhart.
Allison Knee.
Lorenzo Nolan, Corporal. Niles, Mich.
Adam Schaum.
Charles W. Smith.
Benjamin Stroup, Corporal.
Frederic Stroup, Sergeant.
Simon J. True. Elkhart.
Frederic Tavener, Sergeant.
John Tavener.

The Adjutant-General's report shows very imperfect accounting-for of the original men of this Company. We have been able to make a few corrections, but only a few. Besides the veterans and the killed, the record of the balance of the original men of the Company appears as follows:

Sergeant Levi C. Vensin, died April 28, 1862.
Corporal Ambrose C. Lamb, m. o. Oct. 6, 1865.
    "   Joseph B. Stanley, m. o. Sept. 15, 1865.
    "   Charles L. Fish, unaccounted for.
    "   Charles M. Hinman. See "SECOND LIEU-
        TENANTS."
    "   Alexander S. Devor, missing in action, Sep-
        tember 19, 1863.
    "   Willie Layton, m. o. Sept. 15. 1865.
Musician George W. Keller, discharged Feb. 14, 1863.
    "   William Free, discharged, 1862. Lagrange.
Wagoner Samuel Miller, m. o. Sept. 14, '65. Elkhart.

Hugh Bagley, tranferred to V. R. C.   Dead.

Christian Boss, missing in action, Sept. 18, 1863.

Daniel Brooks, died in Danville, Va., prison, February 14, 1864.

Israel Bolander, unaccounted for.   Elkhart.

Denning Benton, unaccounted for.

Emanuel M. Carpenter, m. o. Nov. 22, '64.   Elkhart.

Isaac Clark, unaccounted for.

William Clark, unaccounted for.

Lemon Clark.

Jacob Clark, unaccounted for.

Cyrus Clapp, discharged April 23, 1863.

Sherman Cordie, discharged Jan. 9, 1863.

Anthony S. Davenport, died at Elkhart, Aug. 4, '62.

James R. Diltz, m. o. Nov. 22, 1864.

Solomon Gruber, unaccounted for.

Martin G. Hurd, transferred to V. R. C.

Wentworth Irwin, unaccounted for.   Niles, Mich.

Marshall Kyle, unaccounted for.

Noah Krieble, m. o. Nov. 22, 1862.

Joseph Layton, unaccounted for.

Benjamin F. Layton, unaccounted for.

George Maybie, discharged Oct. 6, 1862.   Elkhart.

Isaac Marshall, unaccounted for.

Michael McNivy, unaccounted for.

Henry Missler, died March 13, 1863.

Patrick Murt, transferred to 1st U. S. V. Engineers.

Lewis A. Money, transferred to V. R. C. May 8, 1864.

John Martin, discharged June 30, 1862.

Cornelius Millspaugh, unaccounted for.

George Pringle,   "   "

Irvin Robinson,   "   "

William Sluglee,   "   "

James A. Smith,   "   "   Elkhart.

William Smith, m. o. Nov. 22, 1864.

James Smith, transferred to V. R. C.
Samuel E. Smith. See "ADJUTANTS."
Franklin Stone, discharged June 22, 1862. Elkhart.
George Stevens, unaccounted for. Dead.
David R. Spencer,   "   "
Oscar Woodworth,   "   "

KILLED.

Nelson Mansfield, at Shiloh, April 6, 1862.
Giles Drake, at Stone River, Dec. 31, 1862.
Frank Lammers, at Shiloh, April 6, 1862.
John Declute, at Shiloh, April 6, 1862.

RECRUITS.

1862.
Nov. 22. John Hemelin, m. o. Nov. 22, 1864.
  1863.
Jan. 10. N. H. Strong, unaccounted for.
Dec. 11. George Ashby,   m. o. Sept. 14, 1865.
  "   23. James Fisher,   "   "   "
Sept. 23. Barton Lucas,   "   "   "
Dec. 17. Henry Lucas,   "   "   "
  "   26. Jesse Ochel,   "   "   "
  "   23. Silas W. Stotler,   "   "   "
  1864.
Mar. 5. Stephen Aiken, Corp'l, "   "   "
April 14. Samuel Brumer, unaccounted for.
Mar. 7. George B. Beavis,   m. o. Sept. 14, 1865.
April 14. Samuel Bruner,   "   "   "
Mar. 14. Ira D. Batchelder,   "   "   "
Oct. 17. Josiah Best,   "   "   "
Mar. 9. Peter H. Cann,   "   "   "
  "   8. Jackson Clark,   "   "   "
  "   27. William H. Carter,   "   "   "
  "   7. Christopher C. Drake,   "   "   "
Mar. 8. William H. H. Ford,   "   "   "

Mar.	7.	John A. Hooker,	m. o. Sept.	14,	1865.
Oct.	19.	George T. Jackson,	"	"	"
Jan.	9.	Charles O'Neill, Serg't,	"	"	"
April	14.	John Nichols,	"	"	"
Mar.	5.	David Rutter,	"	"	"
"	31.	Daniel J. Smith,	"	"	"
Oct.	12.	William P. Sovereign,	"	"	"
"	5.	Andrew J. Wagner,	"	"	"
Mar.	5.	William Westfall,	"	"	"

1865.

Mar.	8.	George D. Armstrong,	"	"	"
"	14.	James H. Adwell,	"	"	"
"	14.	Horace Andrew,	"	"	"
"	8.	Samuel Fry,	"	"	"
"	29.	Theodore Miller,	"	"	"
"	14.	George Mitchell,	"	"	"
"	14.	Henry A. Parker,	"	"	"
"	8.	William L. Shaw, died at Nashville, Tenn.			
"	7.	John Weldon, m. o. Sept. 14, 1865.			

Forty-two drafted men and substitutes were added to the Company in the fall of 1864, and mustered out in June and July, 1865.

Deserters, 2; names not given.

COMPANY K.

Company K was organized by volunteers from the southern part of Steuben and the northern part of De-Kalb counties. The officers first selected were: Wesley Parks, Captain; Simeon C. Aldrich, 1st Lieutenant; John H. Wilson, 2d Lieutenant. The officers were commissioned September 20, 1861, and mustered in with the Company, November 22, 1861.

CAPTAINS.

Wesley Parks took an active part in recruiting the Company, and was selected by the men as their first Captain, but resigned December 10, 1861, on account of disability. Died in August, 1868.

Simeon C. Aldrich. See "COLONELS."

John H. Wilson was mustered in as 2d Lieutenant, was promoted 1st Lieutenant December 10, 1861, and Captain, January 20, 1863. Was honorably mentioned by Colonel Reed in his report of Shiloh, and by Colonel Aldrich in his report of Chickamauga. Mustered out at the expiration of his three years' service, December 5, 1864. Died a few years after the war.

Moses B. Willis was mustered in as a Sergeant, was commissioned 2d Lieutenant April 17, 1863, but did not muster in, re-enlisted as a veteran, was promoted Captain January 16, 1865, and was mustered out with the Regiment. Resides at Auburn, Ind.

FIRST LIEUTENANTS.

Simeon C. Aldrich. See "COLONELS."

John H. Wilson. See "CAPTAINS."

Norris S. Bennett was mustered in as 1st Sergeant, was promoted 2d Lieutenant December 26, 1861, 1st Lieutenant January 20, 1863, and resigned April 16, 1863, on account of disability. Resides at Orland, Ind.

Eugene S. Aldrich was mustered in as Sergeant, promoted 2d Lieutenant January 20, 1863, 1st Lieutenant November 1, 1863, and was mustered out at the expiration of three years' service, December 5, 1864. Resides at Pleasant Lake, Ind.

John G. Long was mustered in as a Corporal, re-enlisted as a veteran, was promoted 1st Lieutenant March 11, 1865, and was mustered out with the Regiment.

SECOND LIEUTENANTS.

John H. Wilson. See "CAPTAINS."

Norris S. Bennett. See "FIRST LIEUTENANTS."

Eugene S. Aldrich. See "FIRST LIEUTENANTS."

Moses B. Willis. See "CAPTAINS."

Nicholas Ensley entered the service as a private, re-enlisted as a veteran, served several months as chief clerk of courts-martial by order of General Thomas, was promoted Ordnance-Sergeant, Quartermaster-Sergeant, and then promoted 2d Lieutenant, June 24, 1865. Has since served as county treasurer of DeKalb County two terms, overcoming adverse majorities against the party nominating him. Residence, Auburn, Ind.

VETERANS.

Sergeant Moses B. Willis. See "CAPTAINS."

Corporal John G. Long. See "FIRST LIEUTEN-ANTS."

Musician William T. Kimsey, Principal Musician.

Henry Altman, Corporal.

Benjamin F. Cornell, 1st Sergeant.

James M. Chilcoat, Sergeant. Edgerton, Ohio.

Nicholas Ensley. See "SECOND LIEUTENANTS." Auburn, Ind.

Samuel Fair, Sergeant.

Charles Lockwood, Corporal. Auburn, Ind.

George W. McDorman, Corporal.

Orange O. Roe.

Davis Smith, Corporal.

Jeremiah J. Shatto, Quartermaster-Sergeant. Clear Lake, Ind.

James Sloan, Sergeant.

Norman C. Shank. Flint, Ind.

Colfenis Surface, Corporal.

Levi Wallick. Missouri.

NICHOLAS ENSLEY,

LIEUT., CO. K.

Shurban Bullard, mustered in Jan. 9, '62, re-enlisted, and was mustered out with the Regiment.

Martin L. Holcomb, mustered in January 9, 1862, re-enlisted, and was mustered out with the Regiment. Hamilton, Ind.

THREE YEARS MEN.

Sergeant George W. Gordon. Auburn, Ind.

Musician John M. Kimsey. Waterloo, Ind.

Martin V. Hefflefinger. Butler, Ind.

William H. Kynett, m. o. Jan. 11, 1865.

Philip Parnell. Waterloo, Ind.

Madison Rogers. Nebraska.

Sylvester Shank. Hillsdale, Mich.

Franklin W. Willis. Waterloo, Ind.

DISCHARGED.

Sergeant Samuel H. Elliott, March 27, 1863. Pleasant Lake, Ind.

Corporal Malcom Bennett, July 30, 1862. Dead.

Corporal Caleb M. Clark, April 27, 1863. Hudson, Indiana.

Corporal Charles M. Bixler, Feb. 8, 1862. Middleville, Mich.

Corporal Thomas O. Leslie, June 17, 1863; wounds at Shiloh. Albion, Ind.

Wagoner Henry Eldridge, Oct. 3, 1862. Dead.

John Cook, Jan. 20, 1833. Dead.

Jacob G. Casebeer, March 23, 1863. Dead.

James Gaylord, Oct. 3, 1862. Dead.

William A. Greenamyer, March 19, 1863. Hudson, Indiana.

John Guice, April 11, 1864.

Gerard F. Housel, Dec. 11, 1862. Auburn, Ind.

Robert Hall, Dec. 20, 1862. Dead.

John H. C. Hoffman, July 15, 1862. Ligonier, Ind.

Henry H. Hawley, Nov. 10, 1862.

Albert Higgins, March 23, 1863.

Leonard Hoodlemeyer, Sept. 20, 1863. Auburn, Ind.

Reuben Lockwood, April 28, 1862. Auburn, Ind.

Henry C. Lemon, Sept. 21, 1862.

Jacob Link, Oct. 1, 1862. Auburn, Ind.

James Miller, Aug. 18, 1862.

William Mid lleton, Jan. 27, 1863. Dead.

George Morley, Oct. 1, 1862. Angola, Ind.

Lanson Munday.

James E. Pearse, Aug. 7, 1862; wounds at Shiloh. Auburn, Ind.

Lemuel Richey, July 5, 1862. Cherubusco, Ind.

Daniel W. Squires, Aug. 55, 1862. Dead.

Charles M. Thomas, Aug. 29, 1862; wounds at Shiloh. Fort Wayne, Ind.

James G. Wiseman, April 12, 1864. Dead.

KILLED.

John M. Chillcoat, Chickamauga, Sept. 20, 1863.

Harrison Harwood, Stone River, Dec. 31, 1862.

George F. Wilson, Chickamauga, Sept. 20, 1863.

DIED.

Corporal Hiram L. Smith, London, Tenn., April 25, 1864.

Elias Baylor, Nashville, Jan. 2, 1863.

Simon M. Cutler, Battle Creek, July 20, 1862.

Charles Creiger, supposed to have died at Louisville.

Robert Douglas, died, place not known.

Abram Depuy, St. Louis, May 19, 1862.

Samuel Ensley, Henderson, Ky., Dec. 25, 1861.

Cornelius Hinton,   "   "   Jan. 1, 1862.

Andrew Hollopeter, Murfreesboro, April 17, 1863.

Elijah Lock, Corinth, June 1, 1862.

Samuel E. Mease, St. Louis, June 15, 1862.

John O. McMillen, New Albany, Oct. 10, 1862.
William Melandy, Nashville, Nov. 10, 1863.
Edward Musser, Henderson, Ky., April 11, 1862.
Henry Severence,   "   "   Feb. 26, 1862.
George Sanderson, May 14, 1862; wounds at Shiloh.
John L. Shotto, Evansville, Dec. 11, 1861, of wounds received at Shiloh.
Orlo A. Whipple, Nashville, Feb. 21, 1863, of wounds received at Stone River.
Solomon E. Watros, Keokuk, July 4, 1862.
George W. Swain, died at New Albany, Ind.

TRANSFERRED.

Corporal W. H. H. Cornell, to V. R. C., Aug. 1, 1863. Auburn, Ind.
John J. Frampton, to Marine service, Sept. 21, 1862.
Joseph P. Sisson, to 4th U. S. Cavalry, Dec. 7, 1862.
Samuel E. Squires, to V. R. C., Oct. 21, 1863.
Joseph Thompson, to 4th U. S. Cavalry, Dec. 25, '62.
Isaac M. Wood,   "   "   "   "   "
Hiram M. Fanning, wounded at Shiloh; detached to Pioneer Corps.
William T. Hinkle, promoted to 2d Lieutenant of Company A, 74th Indiana Volunteer Infantry.

VOLUNTEER RECRUITS.

1861.
Nov. 22. William H. Kynett, m. o. Jan. 11, 1865.
1862.
Aug. 19. James Arnold,   m. o. Sept. 14, 1865.
  "   19. Fearless Arnold,   "   "   "
Jan. 20. Hiram L. Fanning, m. o. Jan. 26, 1865. Dead.
Aug. 19. James Jones,   m. o. Sept. 14, 1865.
  "   9. Jediah Killum,   "   "   "
Dec. 5. William H. Malott,   "   "   "
            as Sergeant.

14

Nov. 21. Emanuel Rex,   m. o. Sept. 14, 1865.
              as Corporal.

Aug. 2. Adam Stutsman,   "   "   "
1863.

Dec. 23. Samuel E. Anderson,   "   "   "
   "   23. James C. Benson,   "   Sept. 2,   "
   "   23. Daniel C. Cook,   "   Sept. 14,   "
   "   23. William H. Clark,   "   "   "
   "   23. William Clark,   captured, June 9, 1864.
   "   23. Richard Foster,   m. o. August 22, 1865.
   "   26. Victor D. Hodshier, m. o. Sept. 14, 1865.
   "   23. John A. J. Mitchell,   "   "   "
   "   23. James Montgomery,   "   "   "
   "   26. Francis M. Rust,   "   "   "
   "   23. John M. Ryan,   "   "   "
1864.

April 4. William H. Boran,   "   May 15,   "
Mar.   9. John Chillcoat,   "   Sept. 14,   "
Feb. 20. Joseph Connell,   "   "   "
Jan.   9. Archibald Curry,   "   "   "
   "   13. Francis M. Chamberlain,   "   "
Sept. 24. William Cannon,   "   "   "
Feb. 24. Andrew F. Dull,   "   "   "
   "   20. Isaac Dinwiddie,   "   Aug. 24,   "
Jan. 23. John D. Elliott,   "   Sept. 14,   "
Mar. 11. Isaac Ebert, died June 4, 1865.
   "   15. James E. Fair, m. o. Sept. 14, 1865. Carson
              City, Nevada. Sheriff.
Jan. 16. David Frazer, m. o. July 29, 1865.
Mar. 17. Levi Guthrie, m. o. Sept. 14, 1865. Hudson,
              Indiana.
Mar. 15. Jas. H. Harkrader, m. o. Sept. 14, '65. Dead.
April 14. Leonard Hoodlemeyer, m. o. Sept. 14, 1865.
              Auburn, Ind.
Jan. 13. Albert Heusler,   m. o. Sept. 14, 1865.
Mar. 17. Charles Hickson,   "   "   "

GEORGE W GORDON,

COMPANY K.

June 16. Abraham W. Hooker, m. o. Aug. 16, 1865.
April 2. Lyman Lockwood, m. o. Sept. 14, 1865. Auburn, Ind.
Jan. 13. August Koehler, m. o. July 2, 1865.
Mar. 11. Jerome Morse,   m. o. Sept. 6, 1865.
Feb. 20. Joab Moffatt,   "   Sept. 14,   "
Jan. 13. George F. O'Byrne,   "   "   "
Mar. 15. Albert Pepple,   "   "   " '
              Patten Station, Ind.
Jan. 7. DeForrest Parker,   "   "   "
Feb. 20. Zachariah Rozell,   "   "   "
Mar. 15. Joel Smith, discharged June 2, 1865.
April 2. Ambrose Smith,   m. o. Sept. 14, 1865.
   "   2. Isaiah Smith,   "   "   "
Mar. 15. Christopher C. Simon,   "   "   "
              Swan, Ind.
Oct. 7. Isaac Snyder, died, Chattanooga, April 8, '65.
Mar. 5. John L. Stacy, m. o. Sept. 14, 1865.
Jan. 31. William F. Smart, m. o. Sept. 14, 1865.
Feb. 20. Samuel Thomas, m. o. Sept. 14, 1865.
Jan. 7. Martin Whittig, tr. to V. R. C. May 11, 1865.
   "   14. David Williams, m. o. Sept. 14, 1865.
Mar. 17. James E. Washington, m. o. Sept. 14, 1865.
   "   17. Isaac Washington,   "   "   "
Feb. 26. Moses B. Willis, promoted.
1865.
Jan. 27. John W. Chance,   m. o. Sept. 14, 1865.
Feb. 21. Silas Morehouse,   "   "   "

Thirty-four drafted men and substitutes were added
to the Company in the fall of 1864, and were mustered
out in June and July, 1865, except

Henry I. Barckman, who died at Chattanooga, June
28, 1865.

Deserters, 4; names not given here.

UNASSIGNED.

James R. Devor, mustered in Oct. 3, 1864; served in Camp Carrington, Indianapolis, in command of Guards, Guard Quarters, and Prison; mustered out May 2, 1865.

George Cassel, mustered in Jan. 10, 1862; unaccounted for.

Noble Cherry, mustered in Jan. 10, 1862; discharged.

Henry O. Cole, mustered in April 28, 1864; unaccounted for.

John Dickerhoof, died at Nashville, Tenn., September, 1863.

Edward Durgar, mustered in October 26, 1864; unaccounted for.

Charles Fike, mustered in Jan. 10, 1862; unaccounted for.

Almon Gray, mustered in Sept. 17, 1862; unaccounted for.

Isaiah Gardner, mustered in Dec. 27, 1864; unaccounted for.

William P. Hodges, mustered in January 16, 1862; unaccounted for.

Thomas Hall, mustered in Jan. 10, 1862; discharged July 16, 1862, on account of wounds.

John A. Haughey, mustered in Oct. 2, 1862; unaccounted for.

Samuel Hartle, mustered in March 3, 1864; unaccounted for.

Francis A. Johnson, mustered in November 12, 1862; unaccounted for.

John Lent, mustered in Sept. 12, 1862; unaccounted for.

Michael McEntoffer, mustered in Oct. 2, 1862; died Nov. 20, 1862.

William N. Morrison, mustered in Oct. 2, 1862; unaccounted for.

John Mustard, mustered in Oct. 26, 1864; unaccounted for.

Marion W. Mills, mustered in Dec. 9, 1864; unaccounted for.

Ransom B. Miller, mustered in Feb. 10, 1865; m. o. May 13, 1865.

Francis P. Robbins, mustered in Nov. 19, 1862; died at Nashville, Tenn., Feb. 6, 1863.

Jeremiah Woolford, mustered in January 10, 1862; unaccounted for.

THE SUTLERS.

The Forty-fourth Indiana Regiment was well favored in respect to Sutlers. Wesley Parks, after his resignation as Captain of Company K, was appointed Sutler, and filled the place until April 22, 1862, when he resigned on account of ill health. His son, A. B. Parks, succeeded him, and assisted by his brother Henry, served the Regiment with sutler supplies until the day of its muster out. Their dealings with the officers and men were honorable and generous. In several financial emergencies they rendered important and needful aid. They are both living now at Kendallville, Indiana, and at the first reunion of the Regiment, April 6, 1880, manifested their old war-time generosity and kindness by taking charge of all the arrangements for the meeting, and providing a free supper for the soldiers present.

Personal Recollections.

BY

Colonel Hugh B. Reed.

APPENDIX.

PERSONAL RECOLLECTIONS.

—BY—

COLONEL H. B. REED.

CHAPTER I.

At the suggestion of our friend, the Author of this History, I will attempt to give some personal recollections that may at least interest those who took part in the stirring times to which they refer.

As Major Rerick has well said of our Regiment, it was composed of the better class of citizens, many of its members occupying independent positions in life. They left their farms, shops, stores and homes, at their country's call, from no other than patriotic motives. There was no thought of drafting or bounty at that day. They gave up home, family, friends, to fight their country's battles, from love for these—that their children might retain the blessings which had thus far been theirs. This alone prompted them to cast aside every comfort and all that had heretofore made life desirable, to face the dangers of the battle-field, death in hospital, starvation and inhumanity in rebel prisons; to give up their own liberty to the will, and too often the caprice, of men no better nor wiser than themselves. As our Chaplain, Dr. Beeks, said in a sermon he preached while we were at Evansville, Ind., where he had formerly resided: "The men of my Regiment are of the salt of the earth, every man of the 1.000 being the equal of the highest and best in your midst."

After leaving Indianapolis for the front, and while at Evansville, Ind., awaiting orders, the Colonel received a letter from General T. L. Crittenden, to whose Division the 44th Indiana had been assigned, welcoming us to the tented field. About the same time a committee from the loyal citizens of Henderson, Ky., visited our camp, urging the importance of our Regiment going to that point for their protection from rebels that beset their town. When this was represented at headquarters by the Colonel, the 44th was ordered to Henderson, Ky., where it was most hospitably received by many Union-loving citizens, and as heartily cursed by those of rebel proclivities.

While here, "my nigger" was the main topic of interest with all—Union and rebel. The slaves thought the year of jubilee had come, and were marching for the land of Canaan, and naturally came to the Regiment for help across the river. Nor were they disappointed, in so far as members of the Regiment could help them "over the river," notwithstanding the "strict orders" to the contrary. The Colonel could only wink at it and abuse the Adjutant, who was a full blooded

Abolitionist and an ex Congressman to boot. They must not be seen, but they were hid in all parts of the camp.

Even in this year of grace 1880 very few people but those that were in the army have any conception of the intense interest manifested by the people of the Slave States for their "institution." Intelligent, well-to-do planters would ride for days with the Regiment on its marches, to try to capture a slave of whose escape they had heard, or even from thinking it probable there might be one with us—not their own, but a *slave*, no matter whose. They gave up their time, labor and money to *that*, under all circumstances. To help catch "a runaway nigger" was more exciting than a fox hunt; a pair of hand-cuffs was a toy carried in the coat pocket, to be slipped on the wrists—representing the brush stuck in the cap of the victor.

The slaves were hunted like hares, and were covered up, the pursuers foiled, thrown off the scent, with equal zest. When just about ready to leave Henderson for Green River, they pounced down upon and drove two "likely boys" to cover, in an old cabin in our camp. While the captors were getting out their manacles, one of the "boys" as quick as a flash was past them, out the door and away. His shadow was often seen afterwards, flitting from wagon to tent. The other, slower witted, gave up mournfully, and without a word submitted to be carried off. On another occasion, at Calhoun, Ky., a "boy" hotly pursued was boxed up, a canteen of water and his rations added, and shipped to Evansville, Ind., to a *sure* friend. Major Stoughton, Surgeon

Martin—both Democrats of the strictest sect, the former
having been candidate for Elector on the Breckenridge
ticket, and Surgeon Martin a man of as much weight in
the councils of his party at home as any other—and Sergeant Sol. DeLong (afterwards Lieutenant-Colonel of
another Indiana regiment), stood godfathers to this de-
liverance from bonds to freedom. This is but an illustration of the spirit with which the game was played—
one intent on capture, the other on defeating the wily
slave-catcher—as it also illustrates theory *versus* practice. Both Stoughton and Martin were pro-slavery at
home, and the members of the 44th Indiana, generally,
indignantly spurned the imputation of going out to free
the slaves of our "Southern brethren," as was charged
by rebel sympathizers.

And yet these same men were the most hospitable,
kind and companionable to be found anywhere. Should
you visit their house, if nothing was on their table but
"coon, pone," you would be pressed to partake with
the same cordiality as if a feast had been prepared.
Their *bonhommie* and geniality were irresistible. With
a bottle of peach, apple or Bourbon at their elbow to
cheer, all care was given to the dogs, enjoyment reigned
supreme.

The following letter from an ex Governor of Kentucky is in point :

JANUARY 18, 1862.

COLONEL REED :

DEAR SIR.—A boy of mine by the name of Newton,
as I am informed, followed your Regiment from this
place to Calhoun. I have reason to believe that he is
now in camp, and I will be under great obligations to
you for any facilities you may afford Mr. —— in taking

possession of him and returning him to me at this place. The boy is about 22 years old, 5 ft. 10 or 11 inches high, copper colored, a blacksmith by trade, and a large mark down his forehead of lighter color than the rest of his face. Mr. —— is fully authorized by me to take the said boy and bring him to me.

Very truly, etc.,		*_*

The goods were *not* delivered to the ex Governor's order.

———

CHAPTER II.

AFTER some weeks the Regiment became weary of inactivity, the men longed to be doing something—to push on, and help put down these rebels in arms; this done, to go home to their legitimate callings. We took up our line of march for Calhoun, Ky., where we joined our Division, under command of General Crittenden. Here we spent some time in drilling, and marching up and down Green River in the mud and slush of that malarious region, and passed through the fiery ordeal of acclimation to camp life. The hospital was soon filled with those that had been used to a far different life.

After marching to South Carrolton and back without meeting the enemy, the order for our brigade alone to prepare for a campaign against Fort Henry and Fort Donelson was hailed with the liveliest anticipations by all. To go where some fighting was to be done delighted every one but the unfortunate sick in the hospital. After the mud, slush, drill, bad fare, malaria, and Buell's slow movements, it was glorious to be booming down the Ohio by steamer. When we arrived at Fort Henry we found General Grant preparing his forces for a march to Fort Donelson. Our brigade was ordered to return by steamer down the Tennessee and up the Cumberland River to Fort Donelson. The whole army was jubilant. Speeches of the spread-eagle order were made from the decks of our steamers, in tones that made the welkin ring—doubtless (?) making the hearts of the secesh quake, as they rang from the river banks to the wooded hills and valleys between. While still under this patriotic fervor, it was proposed and carried *nem. con.* that the Colonels of the brigade should in a body call upon and offer our congratulations to the commanding General, and take his dimensions. We found General Grant in the cabin of his steamer, deeply immersed in the plans of his campaign, and apparently weighed down with his responsibilities, great drops of sweat standing on his brow. But a few months previously I had met *Captain* Grant on board the cars of the Illinois Central railroad, acting as mustering-in officer. Myself and friend were on our way to Cairo, to take a look at the military at that important post, hoping we might see a fight. We were well provided with good cigars and Cognac, and being interested in all that pertained to military affairs, we soon made acquaintance with Captain Grant. He informed us that he had been elected Captain of a company raised at his town, and had refused to accept; that having been a Captain in the regular army, he felt that he was entitled to a higher position ; but proffered to drill and go with them to the rendezvous at Springfield, where he hoped to find a better opening. He had been disappointed, and was about to return home, when a friend had interested himself in his behalf with the Governor, who had thereupon sent for him, and offered him a position on his staff until opportunity presented for something better; and he was then engaged in mustering in recruits along the line of that road. The something better soon came, and here we find him at the head of an army invading the " sacred soil " of Kentucky and Tennessee.

On the following day we steamed down the river to Paducah, where we were joined by other steamers bearing troops for the same destination, the whole making a grand procession, with banners, music and cheers, perhaps the most impressive sight that had there been seen, witnessed from the river banks on either shore with bounding hearts or gnashing teeth, as the beholder's sympathies inclined North or South in the coming conflict.

The boat on which the 44th Indiana was embarked was the fastest of the fleet. There were no " orders " on the subject of procedure, and we were in no way averse to taking the benefit of our speed. The Colonel of a regiment of Kansas "jay-hawkers," whose steamer had started from Paducah first, bellowed himself hoarse in protest and threats, making much merriment by his efforts to drown the whistle of our steamer, standing on a stool, gesticulating and perspiring. His regiment had the reputation of cleaning a *green* regiment out of all their possessions. When they passed through a camp it was left as bare as a field of grain by the army-worm. This made " old soldiers " of *that* regiment when they awoke to a realizing sense of their condition, in the morning. The next *green* regiment had to pay the penalty.

When our imposing and brilliant array had reached the vicinity of Dover, the 44th Indiana was disembarked, and at once marched forward to the battle-field. Knowing little what awaited us, we made small preparation for creature comfort. When night found us in front of the enemy's entrenchments, not permitted a fire to cook our coffee, most of our blankets left with a guard at the landing, and no means of getting them, without rations, our first introduction to the enemy was not made under the most favorable circumstances. We were compelled to " bundle " as best we could to protect ourselves from the cold of the most inclement night of the year. The snow that fell during the night covered us like a garment. On our beds of dry sticks we slept the sleep of the just. In the morning we drank our coffee, munched our " hard-tack," which had now reached us, fell in, and marched forward to the attack. The 44th Indiana's first position was taken, by request of General McClernand, in support of a battery. Here the enemy's shot were aimed too high. passing over our heads. After a time, the enemy not assaulting as expected, we moved further in advance, and formed our line of battle on the left of the 17th Kentucky (being part of our brigade—the 1st Brigade of Lew. Wallace's Division). As we moved forward we received a heavy fire, wounding a number of our men. When our line of battle was formed, Colonel John A. Logan, of the 32d Illinois, came to me and asked that I withhold our fire for a time. I complied with his request, which I found a much more difficult matter than he, probably, and I most certainly, anticipated, as we were exposed to the enemy's fire for what seemed an interminable time—the bullets whistling about our ears and the men being wounded, thus making our position a very trying one in this our first baptism of fire. The enemy's fire slackening, to make sure there were no others than the enemy in our front (the brush and small timber obstructing our view), that we might get at them without further delay, Captain Bingham, Co H, carried our flag forward to a prominent position and waved it in the air as a gage of battle. This was at once responded to by a volley, and answered with great zest by the men, who had hitherto served only as targets. General McClernand's troops had fallen back. A portion of our brigade alone was left. The enemy being repulsed in our immediate front, an attempt was now made to turn our left flank with cavalry and infantry. Three companies of our left wing were wheeled to the right, and opened fire upon and repulsed their attempt to get to our rear. The Colonel's attention was now called to a fact which we had been too much occupied to notice, that the 44th was entirely alone, and the other regiments of our brigade had withdrawn. Having repulsed the enemy and thwarted their attempt to surround us, we slowly withdrew, in perfect order. After going some distance we were met by the Colonel commanding the brigade, who informed me that our forces were at a certain point, where we joined them. While occupying this position we could see the enemy reforming his lines, on a steep wooded hill, not far from the battle-field of the morning. After some delay our brigade was ordered, in conjunction with Colonel Morgan L. Smith's brigade, to storm the very strong position held by the enemy. The 8th Missouri had the advance. When the 44th Indiana arrived at the scene of action, the 8th Missouri was hotly engaged in by far the fiercest contest of the day. We at once pressed forward to their aid, and formed our line of battle amid a hurricane of bullets. Finding that we were in rear of the 8th Missouri, we were compelled to perform the difficult feat of changing our position to the left of that regiment under the heavy fire of the enemy, which was done. We then charged up the hill in the most gallant style, at double quick, cheering loudly. Without intending thereby to detract from Colonel Morgan L. Smith and the 8th Missouri, who fought gloriously, it was the charge of the 44th Indiana that started the rebels from their position. We pursued them some distance, and were then joined by other regiments of the brigade which had passed further to the left. While consulting as to whether we should pursue them into their works, they opened fire upon us with artillery, the shot and shell falling in our midst. An order was now received from General Grant, recalling us. We returned to the foot of the hill from whence we had routed the enemy, and bivouacked for the night.

We were ordered to attack their works early next morning. We were all ready to march forward, when news reached us of the surrender. This not being official, we continued our march. The 44th Indiana, at the head of the column, passed over their entrenchments and through the ranks of the enemy, drawn up in line of battle. We marched to the landing at Dover, and took possession of the immense stores of captured property.

From some cause the 44th Indiana failed to receive, in the reports of the brigade and division commanders, the credit to which it was justly entitled for the part performed by it in the battles of the morning and afternoon of February 15th. With no intention to lessen or in any way detract from other regiments engaged, I will here say that to the 8th Missouri and the 44th Indiana belong the honor of storming the position held by the enemy on the hill, and their defeat here induced the surrender of the Fort next morning. The part of the 44th in this most important engagement attending the capture, was as conspicuous and brilliant as that of any regiment engaged. We were exposed to the same bullets as were the 8th Missouri, which had the advance. The 44th formed in line of battle under a heavy fire, moved to the immediate left of that regiment, and made the brilliant charge which decided the battle. In my official report I say :

" My regiment advanced to the foot of the hill occupied by the enemy, formed in line of battle in the face of a storm of bullets. Finding the ground in our front occupied by the 8th Missouri regiment, I advanced my regiment one hundred yards, faced to the front, and charged up the hill at double quick—our men loudly cheering."

And yet General Lew Wallace, by a shuffle, manages to give to the 11th Indiana the position occupied by the 44th Indiana, in his official report, without reason or

15

justice, unless it may have been that the 11th Indiana was his former regiment.

As has been said elsewhere, the 44th Indiana fought its own battles of the morning and afternoon, without seeing or receiving an order from any other officer than its own Colonel commanding, after taking up its line of march for the battle-field. Had either brigade or division commander been with us, we could hardly have failed receiving the justice denied us in their official reports.

Immediately after the surrender our brigade received marching orders, and we returned to Fort Henry, where we remained for a time, while the Army was reorganized. Our 1st Brigade, 3d Division, was transformed into 3d Brigade, 4th Division, General S. A. Hurlbut commanding.

The reorganization of the Army completed, we were now ready for a forward movement into the heart of rebeldom. Early in March, 1862, the Army was embarked at Fort Henry on steamers and transports, with attendant gunboats, for Pittsburg Landing, making altogether the grandest spectacle ever seen by the inhabitants of that wild region. All were warriors of tried metal now. Each Hector and Achilles wore his honors thick upon his brow, to whom all must homage pay. Had not Fort Henry and Fort Donelson succumbed to the prowess of these mighty men? Why should we not feel that " No pent up Utica contracts our powers—that all the boundless continent was ours " ?

Our fleet was composed of the largest Mississippi River steamers (whose occupation was gone), loaded

down with victorious troops; our banners proudly floating in the Southern breeze, as we boldly steamed up the
Tennessee; bands playing the most martial and inspiring airs; a sight long to be remembered by all—every
heart swelling with "the pride, pomp and circumstance
of glorious war." And yet there was an under-current
of more subdued feeling, that Donelson had taught,
which contrasted with the joyous abandon that attended
our voyage to Fort Henry and thence to Fort Donelson.
Then the realities of "the siege, the fight, the disastrous
chances of the deadly breach," were before us only in
imagination, while now we understood the full signifi-
cance of "soldiers slain, and all the currents of a heady
fight."

On the way up the river many conflicts as to seniority occurred, each division and brigade commander
claiming to outrank all others.

The 44th Indiana embarked on a steamer on which
was part of a regiment belonging to General McClernand's division, in command of a Lieutenant-Colonel,
who informed me in the most kindly manner that his
orders were to retain command of the boat. I replied,
in the same spirit, that that was out of the question, I
being senior officer. He yielded the point personally,
saying he was well aware of the fact, but that his orders
(which he exhibited) were imperative. I explained that
there was no probability of a conflict of authority, but
that I could not yield my right to act, if there should
be. He felt called upon to report the facts to his brigade commander, whereupon General McClernand's
steamer came alongside and was made fast to ours. His

brigade commander came on board our boat, and wanted to know, "You know," and after some wordy demonstrations on his part, without effect, retired and reported to his chief, and I received an extremely polite note requesting that I would call upon him, with which I complied. I found General McClernand an exceedingly urbane and suave gentleman. He used all his power of persuasion to convince me that the boat was his, having first been occupied by his troops. I explained that I had no personal feeling in the matter; that there was very little probability of a conflict of authority, but that he had failed to give any sufficient reason why the king should take the ace in this game. Whereupon he very peremptorily called for his clerk, and dictated a written order that I should relinquish command; to which I replied that I was not aware that I was subject to his orders; that I represented my division commander, and should feel compelled to disregard his order, unless it came through my commanding officer. Thereupon he asked that I would show my division commander the order. When opportunity offered, I did so. General Hurlbut wrote across the face of it : "Countermanded by superior officer." When shown to the inferior officer, he swore a blue streak, and at once sat down without his clerk and wrote—well, what tended towards "pistols and coffee for two." By this time, however, we were at Savannah, and would in a few hours be at our destination. The matter was not further pressed, and we landed without bloodshed.

When the war broke out, General McClernand was in Congress. A brigadier's commission was at his acceptance. He was an Illinois man ; and did not Illinois own the President, together with all that that implied ? No braver men or more capable officers were found in the armies. Of course they were justly proud. General McClernand was as fiery and impetuous as Hotspur, and was a commander of much ability; and he merited far greater credit for our success at Donelson than was awarded him. On his part, he failed in giving credit due to troops of other divisions that aided him at a critical time. General McClernand was a gallant soldier nevertheless. He was the only officer seen at that day dressed in splendid regimentals—epauletted—Wellington boots, gold spurs, gauntleted hands, and equipments to match. He sat his war horse—a blooded stallion—like a Centaur, and managed his charger with the ease and grace of a Bayard ; with his commanding presence, "the observed of all observers," while the General commanding the Army might have been mistaken for a slovenly-dressed Major of an Illinois regiment. I rode to him, and saluted profoundly. "General, are we to have a fight here ?" "A fight here ! Yes, the greatest battle ever fought on this continent ; they will fight us like h—l." A true prophet.

CHAPTER III.

SHILOH.

Upon disembarking, our fourth division, General Hurlbut commanding, moved out about two miles from the Landing, and went into camp.   Here we spent some weeks, enjoying the beautiful March weather, warm and balmy as May, giving little thought to the enemy. General Grant held a grand review of his troops, thus breaking the monotony of camp life.   On Friday eve, April 4th, we were aroused from our quiet repose, and pushed rapidly to the front to meet the enemy.   This proved a reconnoisance in force.   They drove in our pickets, learned our position, and after some skirmishing withdrew.   Our division returned to camp, to .resume our lazy life, little dreaming we were to be awakened to the feast of horrors preparing for us by this same enemy who had just knocked at our door.

Early on Sunday morning following, April 6th, the "long roll" called us to arms.   We were soon in rank, ready for "forward to meet the enemy."   General Hurlbut sent part of our 4th division to General Sherman's aid.   With the 1st and 3d brigades we moved forward at about 7:30 A. M., and had gone but a little distance before meeting General Prentiss's regiments rushing back from the front pell-mell, holding up their gory hands, shouting: "You'll catch it !—we are all cut to pieces—the rebels are coming."   Passing by these panic-stricken wretches without a reply—except the one incident related by Major Rerick of Lieutenant Hodges —or with muttered curses at their cowardice, we marched on, the men setting their teeth hard and grasping their guns more firmly, feeling for their cartridge-boxes, to be sure they were prepared to meet this victorious enemy and welcome him "with bloody hands to hospitable graves."

It is past finding out why, but it is a fact well understood, that soldiers once panic-stricken are worthless—they do not recover during that battle at least, if ever entirely, from their fright. Some of these men of Prentiss's division were brought back to where we were fighting the enemy, but they acted like a flock of frightened sheep, ready to start in any direction. At first one of them crept up to a large tree standing near our line of battle. Gradually others followed, until a line like the tail of a kite extended back some thirty or forty feet, each clutching the one in front in an agony of fear. Their Captain walked hurriedly up and down near them, unable to control himself, much less them. I talked with him quietly; asked him if he could not get his men to use their muskets on the enemy; that if they became engaged they would forget their fear. To no purpose. These men were not "native to the manor born." They soon after left us—perhaps to swell the crowd at the Landing, of which so much was made by Buell and his army.

These men were not really greater cowards than others. The fault was not theirs. It belonged higher up—in placing raw troops where they could be pounced down upon, as were these, without a shovelful of earth or a tree felled for protection. Donelson should have taught us better. All were green alike, from private in the ranks to General-in-Chief of all the Armies, and had to learn the art of war from actual experience in the field. I saw General Prentiss in rear of our line, clamoring for he knew not what—the line to be pushed forward to his former position, etc. He was as demoralized as his troops. He rode off to the front with his staff, to be captured—and was.

I have been led off, and left my Regiment on the way to the battle-field. We went forward about a mile, and formed our line of battle a short distance in rear of General Prentiss's camp, the left wing of the 44th reaching to "Peach Orchard." Our line was formed along a country road. In our front were bushes and saplings, with a few trees of large size scattered here and there. We were soon fiercely attacked with musketry. The enemy charged up to within a few rods of our line, and were repulsed with heavy loss. After some delay they again renewed the attack, and charged up to within a few yards, and were again driven off. The musketry firing here was as fierce and continuous as any during the battle; the brush and small saplings were cut off by bullets, giving it somewhat the appearance of a Southern corn-field that had been topped, as is the custom there. Our men fought as coolly and effectively as if it had always been their occupation. They required no urging. I found it irksome enough sitting on my horse with nothing to do but be shot at. It was a curious study to note the manners of the different officers.

Lieutenant-Colonel Stoughton sat his horse like a statue, neither swerving right nor left, keeping his face to the front, as if his only thought was to be shot with his face to the enemy.

Captain Heath (acting Major) was all movement. He could not be still. He rode up and down the line, at times, as fast as his horse would carry him. If an order was to be repeated, it did him much good to cry it along the line.

Captain Williams kept up his martial bearing, moving with a more stately step than was his wont, trim and erect, grasping his sword with a firm hand. If he was to be killed, he wanted it done "with his martial cloak around him." This was his first battle-field, and he displayed great gallantry.

Captain Cosgrove looked as if devising some plan to get at the enemy to better advantage, as he stood near his men, ready for an emergency.

Captain Tannehill wore a stolid, bull-dog expression. He was going to see that out.

Captain Aldrich moved about from place to place in a quick, nervous way, to be sure that his men were doing their very best.

Lieutenant Hodges, commanding Company I, looked on at his men with a cool, calculating manner which evinced that being shot did not enter into his calculations; it was the enemy he was after.

Lieutenant Newman, commanding Company H, was active and energetic, wanted to be doing more, and would like to know what the enemy were about.

Acting Captain Weamer had probably a premonition of his fate Every nerve quivered, but he never flinched. His moral courage was equal to the occasion. He stood to his post bravely to the end.

Captain Murray was amongst his men, and looked as if he would have preferred a musket to his sword. His manner was more subdued. He may have been pre-monished also, as are very many men. He did his whole duty manfully to the last.

Lieutenant Kinmont, commanding Company F, showed by his steady bearing that he could be relied on for determined action under all circumstances. He might have said "Git ep" instead of "Forward," but would have gone to the right place all the same.

Second-Lieutenant Burge Smith, commanding Company A, looked as if he just wished he had something to do, as he towered over his Company like Saul among his brethren.

All of these, as well as other commissioned officers, were too proud to follow the example of their men, who had been ordered to "fall and fire," but stood erect, facing the enemy.

The men being fully occupied with their fighting, had no time for other thoughts. When one was hit he would quietly crawl back, or be helped to the rear by a comrade, into the hands of our Surgeons, who were at hand, exposed to the same bullets and as much inter-ested as any in the fight.

Surgeon Martin, excited and fiery, moved about in his quick, impetuous way, wanting his horse to be shot in battle; while Assistant Surgeon Rerick was as cool and collected as if in his hospital. The only doubt he felt was whether he had not mistaken his calling. If he could have had his choice then, it would have been a sword or a musket, and in line with the foremost. There could not well be a greater contrast than these men presented. Dr. Martin was genial, demonstrative, full of sympathy. He would take off his coat, and go at the sick in such a way as to make them feel it a comfort to be in condition to have his help. He would give them a teaspoonful of calomel, to "respond the liver,"—a tablespoonful of jalap, "to respond the bowels;" if that did not fetch them, a pint of blood, to "respond the circulation." By this time, perhaps, they would fall into Dr. Rerick's hands, who would build them up, and tend upon them in his careful, considerate way, without any demonstration. That took longer to impress itself on the men; when done, it remained. But they let nothing interfere with their duty, and soon had their hands full.

The enemy had enough at this point. After some delay they form in column and march forward over cleared ground called the Peach Orchard, on which our left wing rested. On they come with a quick step, in gallant style, without firing a gun, the stars and bars flaunting jauntily in the breeze—and I must admit it to be as bold and defiant a battle-flag as one could wish to meet in battle's stern array. I at once wheeled two companies of the left wing to the right, and when they had come within point-blank range, opened fire. Their ranks were mowed down as with a scythe. Yet on they come. It seemed almost barbarous to fire on brave men pressing forward so heroically to the mouth of hell. But human nature could not longer endure it. They wavered, faced about at the word of command, and retired as if on parade. Bravely fought, my gallant foe, worthy of a better cause—my misguided countrymen! They had enough of the 1st and 3d brigades of the 4th division. We had fought them from 8:30 A. M. to 2 P. M., and beaten them in fair fight, gloriously.

But now a pressing call for help comes from the left wing of our Army. Colonel Stuart's brigade had been driven in, thus leaving our flank exposed. Our 3d brigade, consisting of the 44th and 31st Indiana, the 17th Kentucky, with a small number of the 25th Kentucky, and Willard's battery, were rapidly pushed half a mile to our left. We found the enemy marching to our rear. I here quote from General Hurlbut's official report:

"In a few moments two Texan regiments crossed the ridge separating my line from Stuart's former one, while other troops also advanced. Willard's battery was thrown into position, under command of Lieutenant Wood, and opened fire with great effect on the two Lone Star flags, until his line of fire was obstructed by the charge of the 3d brigade, which, after delivering its fire with great steadiness, charged full up the hill, and drove the enemy three or four hundred yards."

We then took position on the brow of the hill, this being on open ground, with here and there a large tree scattered over the field. The 44th Indiana and the 17th Kentucky, in all not to exceed a thousand men, (the 31st Indiana being in reserve,) fought the enemy for nearly three hours; this being by far the fiercest contest of the day. The enemy outnumbered us at least three to one. Their tactics were altogether different from ours. While we stood in line of battle, they were marched about hither and yon at a lively step, in column, by companies. Their flags flaunting defiance, they would move forward as if to make a charge, wheel to right or left, march obliquely, or to the rear, face about, move forward, again form in line, and open fire. At no time were all deployed in line of battle, and yet some of their regiments were firing away at us almost continuously. Our flag was a target at which they fired persistently, and it was riddled with balls. Never was flag more heroically defended. Our color-bearer, A. P. Waterhouse, was soon wounded. It was borne by Michael Harrison, William Woodford, William Underwood, Augustus A. Galloway, William McNeal, John Keifer, Samuel B. Sweet (a boy of 17), James Riddle, James Nicodemus, Frank Baldwin, Sergt. I. N. Thomas, N. P. Lewis, Sergt. Samuel Havens, John Engle, Sergt. M. B. Willis, Joseph Anderson, George Roy, Sergt. O. Z. Rawson, Sergt. Alexander Kinmont, C. M. Thomas, Lewis Griffith, H. A. Lords, Sergt. John Ulam, Edwin Matthews, James M. Flutter, Ralph Goodrich, Owen Shaw, Joseph Reed, Marion McGinnis, Sergt. George W. Schell, Samuel Hartzell, Nicholas Ensley, Owen Shaw, Peter Stahl, Sergt. Nelson Mansfield, Randall Simmons, Henry Twitchel, J. B. Rowe, and Lieutenant Jacob Newman, all of whom were either killed or wounded.

But I feel that I am doing injustice to other brave men in giving the names of any where all fought with equal valor. Never was greater bravery exhibited on a battle field. We lost fully one-third of our number in killed and wounded, in this battle. Officers and men "rallied round the flag" not only "once again" but again and again, well knowing it to be almost certain death or wounds they faced. At the bridge of Lodi, where Napoleon led his troops and carried the flag, to insure their passage to victory, was no greater act of heroism than was here displayed by these men.

It may not be considered in good taste for me to say it—yet it is the truth, nevertheless—that our little brigade saved the day by their heroism on this battle-field. There were no other troops but these between the enemy and the Landing, which, had they reached, General Sherman and General McClernand would have had the enemy both in front and rear. Beauregard's boast, that he would water his horse in the Tennessee River at Pittsburg Landing that night, would have been fulfilled.

This same enemy had driven Colonel Stuart's brigade from the field. We met them, flushed with success, drove back and held at bay thrice our numbers for nearly three hours, and when compelled to fall back, from lack of ammunition, we had taught them discretion. Their advance was slow and cautious, thereby giving the needed time for their reception.

I will here quote from General Hurlbut's General Order No. 20, which is of course addressed to the 4th division—most of which, however, fought elsewhere—and it should be understood to apply more particularly to our 3d brigade of the 4th division, who held the position on the left referred to :

HEADQUARTERS OF THE 4TH DIVISION,
Pittsburg, April 9th, 1862.

The General commanding tenders his heartfelt congratulations to the surviving officers and men of this division for their *magnificent services* during the two days of struggle, which, under the blessing of God, has resulted in victory. Let this division remember that for five hours on Sunday was held, under the most terrific fire, the *key point* of the left of the Army, and only fell back when outflanked by overwhelming masses pressing through points abandoned by our supports.

Let them remember that when they fell back, it was *in order*, and that the last line of resistance, in rear of heavy guns, was formed by this division.

Let them remember that on the morning of Monday, without food and without sleep, they were ordered to reinforce the right, and that whenever a brigade of this division appeared on the field of action, they were *in time to support broken flanks and hold the line.* * * *

S. A. HURLBUT,
Brig. Gen. Commanding 4th Division.

Official:
F. C. SCHOFIELD, A. A. A. G.

To return to our fighting. As Generals Hurlbut, Lauman, and myself were talking together about how we could get a supply of ammunition, the enemy's sharpshooters sent a volley about our ears. We looked in each other's eyes to note the effect, and moved each to his post.

After the first opening of the battle here—from what cause I do not now remember—Willard's battery was silent. Neither did the enemy use artillery. It was a fair open-field fight, each force in plain view of the other; the enemy's movements giving interest to the scene. Our men lost all sense of danger, as they stood and deliberately fired. There was no disposition to get down out of the way of bullets; and had we been amply supplied with them, we should have driven the enemy from the field. They were only held by consummate handling.

I had, during a lull in the firing, ridden over to the left of our line, and found Colonel ———, as brave and efficient an officer as any in the Army, sitting with his back to a tree, just in rear of his line of battle, holding his horse by the bridle. He jocularly exclaimed: "What in h—l are you riding about in that way for? Do you want to be shot? Get down. You can see my men are all right." While I sat on my horse talking with him, he leaned over on his elbow— whiz!—a shot passed through the fleshy part of his arm. He sprang up, exclaiming: "There, you have got me shot." As his wound was being tied up with his handkerchief: "I will keep my face to the enemy hereafter. I thought those fellows were going to let me have time to rest a little." He was very proud of that "hit," after the battle was over.

The 44th Indiana had already twice filled their cartridge boxes here, and had emptied them at the enemy; but now, our last cartridge gone, the 31st Indiana was ordered up from where it had been held in reserve up to this time, to take our place. We withdrew a short distance, to where the ammunition wagon stood. In hunting over the empty boxes the men found a few cartridges scattered about, giving to each man a few rounds. We were now ordered by General Hurlbut to a position further to the left—the enemy moving part of his force to his right, with the evident intention of outflanking us, at the same time moving forward on our front. General Hurlbut, concluding his position no longer tenable, ordered the line to retire to a new position to our left and rear. The 44th acted as rear guard. After going a short distance our brigade commander, General Lauman, came to me and suggested that I form a line across the road by which the enemy were advancing; which was done, thus demonstrating to them that it was not a rout, and delayed their advance, giving our brigade time to reach their new position, when we again resumed our retrograde movement. The enemy advanced very slowly and cautiously, and when they made their attack we were fully prepared for them. Had they pushed forward rapidly it would undoubtedly have been disastrous, as there were no other troops than our small brigade between them and the Landing. This last stand therefore proved of the utmost importance. When they made their final attack they were not only repulsed, but driven back to where they started from in the morning, three miles distant, the shot and shell of the gunboats hurrying them on their way; and this is where General Nelson's division found them next morning about ten o'clock.

Upon reaching our new position, where a battery of large guns was in position, our first thought was ammunition. Seeing an officer with stars on his shoulders moving slowly about, looking "grand, gloomy and peculiar," sitting on his horse instead of a "throne," I rode to him, touched my visor reverently, and inquired if he were able to direct me to where I could find ammunition. "No, sir," he replied, fiercely, "nor do I believe you want ammunition, sir." I looked at him in astonishment, doubting his sanity, but made no reply, further than to ask his name. In the same angry tones: "It makes no difference, sir, but I am General Buell." Turning my horse about, I rode to where I now saw my men had found ammunition and were engaged in filling their cartridge-boxes. I joined them. There may have been an expression on my face that did not please General Buell. He again presents himself, apparently in a frenzy of wrath, and demands to know who I am and where I come from. My answer was as fierce and insulting as I could make it, in my anger. After many threats of what I had to expect, and retorts in no measured terms, intermixed with some strong Anglo-Saxon adjectives, he rode off, furious. Surgeon Martin, standing near, his eyes glaring with sympathetic indignation, exclaimed: "Who is that?—who is he?" When told: "General Buell! My God, he will have you shot. How could you talk to him in that way?" In a little time Buell returned with General Grant. Both of them sat on their horses looking at us while completing our task, forming our ranks and moving forward into line of battle. But nothing further was said then or afterwards.

I will here quote from General Hurlbut's official report giving the final repulse of the enemy:

"Perceiving that a heavy force was closing on the left between my left and the river, while heavy fire continued on the right and front, I ordered the line to fall back. The retreat was made quietly and steadily, and in good order. I had hoped to make a stand on the line of my camp, but masses of the enemy were pressing rapidly on each flank, while their light artillery was closing up rapidly in the rear. On reaching the twenty-four pounder siege-guns in battery near the river, I again succeeded in forming line of battle in rear of the guns, and by direction of Major-General Grant I assumed command of all troops that came up. Broken regiments and disordered battalions came into line gradually upon my division." (It should be "part of my division," as stated elsewhere in his official report; the 2d brigade did not join us till 4:30 A. M.)

"Major Cavender posted six of his twenty-pound pieces on my right, and I sent my Aid to establish the light artillery—all that could be found—on my left." * * * "Many gallant soldiers and brave officers rallied steadily on the new line. I passed to the right, and found myself in communication with General Sherman, and received his instructions. In a short time the enemy appeared on the crest of the ridge, led by the 18th Louisiana, but were cut to pieces by the steady and murderous fire of the artillery." * * * * "General Sherman also was rapidly engaged, and after an artillery contest of some duration the enemy fell back." * * * * "I advanced my division one hundred yards to the front, threw out pickets, and officers and men bivouacked in a heavy storm of rain. About 12 P. M. [should be about 3 A. M.], General Nelson's leading columns passed my line and went to the front, and I called in my advanced guard. The remnant of my division was reunited, Colonel Veatch with the second brigade having joined me about half-past 4 A. M."

This shows clearly that there were none of Buell's fresh troops engaged in this last defeat of the enemy on Sunday eve, as is claimed by General Buell in his official report. The 44th Indiana were in line of battle where they must have seen them had any come to our aid. None of his troops had crossed the river at the

close of the contest, which lasted but a short time.   It
was yet daylight when we moved to the front and took
up our position for the night, placed our pickets, gathered brush on which we spread our horse-blankets, with
our saddles for pillows, we made the best disposition possible under the circumstances, to rest—sleep being out
of the question in the pouring rain-storm.   General
Hurlbut and General Lauman spent the night with us.
Many of the officers of the 44th Indiana were present.
The events of the day were discussed.   Our decisive
defeat of the enemy was a subject for congratulation
with all.   The anticipated arrival of Buell's forces in
the morning was a matter of interest talked over.   No
one dreamed that such a claim could be made.   General
Buell "lost his head."   He could see nothing but
"stragglers."

About 3 o'clock A. M. General Nelson, with his staff,
at the head of his column, advanced without giving a
very definite account of himself, and the guards did
not make a very intelligible report at headquarters.
The tramp of horses being heard, General Hurlbut
sprang up, went forward a short distance, and demanded
"Who is invading my lines?" in very angry and em-
phatic tones, using some profane expletives at the same
time.   General Nelson, in much milder tones than
was his habit, replied: "Be a little civil, General; I
am General Nelson, with my division; I wish to establish my line on your right, and throw forward my
pickets."   This was the first appearance of General
Buell's fresh troops on the battle-field of Shiloh, or any
other, for that matter.

With daylight our stomachs reminded us that we had eaten nothing for twenty-four hours. How vividly my memory retains the taste of a drink of cold coffee taken from the canteen of General Lauman on this Monday morning (which his orderly had in some way procured). The traditional drink of hard cider that could not be bitten off, was nothing to biting that off. We now moved a short distance to the rear, and about 8 A. M. succeeded in getting some crackers, which, with coffee, was our preparation for a renewal of the conflict, after nearly twelve hours' fighting, and without sleep. With this moiety of food, the 44th Indiana was again on the march for the battle-field. The effort of will necessary to move men to such a task dwells in my memory as fresh and green as any superhuman effort is impressed on the mind ever after.

The 44th Indiana and 17th Kentucky alone of our brigade responded to this call. With nearly one-half our number left dead on the battle-fields of the preceding day, or in hospital, both regiments did not exceed, all told, more than five hundred, worn, weary men. We resolutely turned our faces forward and took up our line of march for the front, to meet the enemy.

We were led by a guide over a very rough country, for two or three miles, when we suddenly came upon the enemy charging upon and driving some of General McClernand's troops over a level, cleared field. The enemy were again in column by companies. The 44th being in advance, were immediately deployed in line, and opened fire on their flank. They were taken by surprise, but returned our fire. Colonel McHenry gallantly brought his men into line and opened fire. The enemy's battery opened upon us. After some time they began to fall back. Our men having lost all sense of fatigue, pushed them vigorously, and after pursuing them half a mile they disappeared in the woods, where their main force was posted. As our men had become much scattered, I called a halt and collected our force. General Lauman having been unhorsed at the first fire by a rebel bullet, was not with us. I soon saw General Sherman at a distance, and rode to him and reported. He ordered me to form line of battle in his immediate front and await further orders.

General Hurlbut was engaged elsewhere, but I will quote what he says in his official report of our part here: " The third brigade was deeply and fiercely engaged on the right of General McClernand, successfully stopping a movement to flank his right, and holding their ground until the firing ceased."

The position held by the enemy was in our front, in the woods, but a few hundred yards from Shiloh chapel, which has given name to the battle; with the Corinth road in their rear. This was the same position held by General Sherman when the battle opened on Sunday morning, and from which he was compelled to fall back. A cleared field intervened between the enemy and the position assigned us by General Sherman, which was in open ground, with the exception of a few large trees here and there, giving us a good view of our troops as they marched across the open field and into the dreaded woods, and also of the vicissitudes attending the fight.

A portion of Buell's fresh troops had now arrived on the field, and moved forward to the attack, and we opened ranks for the 30th Indiana to march in. After a fierce and continuous musketry fight of about thirty minutes' duration, the enemy were driven from their position, and fell back on the Corinth road about a mile. Their main force had already been in full retreat for some hours—in fact since about ten o'clock in the morning; this, their last stand, being made to cover their retreat, ended the struggle. General Buell did not pursue the retreating foe, but at once ordered his fresh troops into camp.

General Lauman now rejoined us. He had been unable to find a remount, and was thus detained until after the final withdrawal of the enemy.

General Grant was soon seen riding along the lines, being loudly cheered by the troops, and we rode forward and added our congratulations; all of which was received by him with his usual taciturn, uncertain manner, without showing the least appearance of exultation.

We now led our weary men back to our camps, for rest and refreshment, and never had men more richly earned this boon. We found them unmolested. My tent was in all respects as when I issued from it to meet the enemy on Sunday morning. The enemy had not occupied our camps, as has been erroneously stated, but after their final defeat on Sunday eve they were driven by the fire of the gunboats back to where they started from Sunday morning.

CHAPTER IV.

NEVER was battle so misunderstood by the public at large; never battle so systematically misrepresented, as was the battle of Shiloh. For many months General Buell, like his great prototype, the King of France, with his ten thousand men, had marched up the hill, and then marched down again, on Nolan's fork of Green River, Ky., patiently waiting for the rebels to get ready to evacuate Bowling Green, Ky. At last General Mitchell and Colonel Turchin, becoming impatient and restless, insisted upon giving them a push in the rear to hurry them out. When they arrived, however, it was too late. What could not be carried off, was smouldering piles that had once been army stores. After spending further time, General Buell leisurely marched his army within sound of our victorious guns at Fort Donelson, and then marched back again and took possession of Nashville, Tenn., which was evacuated by the enemy because of our victory at Donelson. Marching in on the heels of this bloodless victory, General Buell at once embraced the occasion to read his troops a lecture on "my policy," reiterating and enforcing what had. long since become nauseous to the stomachs of his troops—that their chief duty was to protect rebel property, so that those of them who were absent in the rebel army fighting us might feel the comforting assurance that their property, families and friends at home were in good hands, and would be free from molestation from the hated Yankees. A whole division has been known to be placed under arrest for burning a few rails to cook their coffee, while on the march to meet these same rebels in arms, to enforce this " policy." Details were ordered from regiments, after marching all day, to stand guard all night over rebels' houses, that the inmates should not have their slumbers disturbed by the weary, foot-sore soldiers getting a drink of water from the well at the door.

This was the Colossus that came with his army the day after the battle, and boasted, " I came, I saw, I conquered." This man, who had never seen a battle—whose time and mind were wholly given to the care and protection of rebels, their slave property being in his eyes more inviolable than the sanctuary—could find nothing on his arrival but " fugitives, panic-stricken stragglers; the banks swarmed with a confused mass of men of various regiments; there could not have been less than four or five thousand." Yes, there was somewhere about that number of our wounded sent to the Landing. That there were " panic stricken stragglers" congregated at this point, is not denied. But this, as is well known, is an attendant on all great battles.

The enemy had been defeated, as I have shown, on Sunday evening, and were driven back to General Prentiss's position, from whence they started Sunday morning. Here General Buell's fresh troops found this beaten, worn-out enemy, who had fought us for twelve hours the previous day, without food or rest.

Let any soldier who was there on both days, or in any similar battle elsewhere, say what the difference is between meeting this enemy in their then condition, and in fighting these same troops fresh, organized and equipped especially for this great battle, which they had bravely fought and lost on the preceding day. I repeat, let any one—soldier or citizen—judge.

Beauregard commenced to withdraw his forces when he found Buell's army had arrived. The positions he held had this end in view.

That Buell's army did help to drive the enemy off the field is true, but what can be said in extenuation of only driving him off? A competent commander would have pursued and captured five thousand prisoners of this beaten, demoralized, fleeing enemy, and all his artillery.

The time has long since come when the truth of the history of this battle should be vindicated. General Grant was in no position to demand justice for his army that fought and won the battle of Shiloh. He was soon in disgrace—deprived of his command—all his thoughts given to extricating himself from the consequences of his blunders. General Grant had this merit, and a most important one: he profited by his blunders, and in contradistinction from Don Carlos Buell, he did place his troops where they would have to fight.

General Sherman has somewhere said that this was a rough and tumble fight, that tested the muscle of the raw troops there engaged, and was useful in developing their pluck. (I mean only to give the substance, from memory.) I think this might also be applied to general officers, as it is well known that General Sherman was tumbled about some—but his pluck always brought him out uppermost. I will ask if he found any such tussle on his pleasure trip "to the sea," of which so much is boasted in song and story? It is true he left "Pap" Thomas in his rear to take care of the rebel army, and General Grant in his front to keep them fully occupied. This trip had this merit, if no other: it was a "bummers'" paradise, and differed in this respect from Buell's "policy." I join in the chorus of praise.

With the help of Lew. Wallace's loitering division, which arrived on the field Sunday night, we could have dispensed with General Buell's army altogether. But I have no intention or wish to deny them all the credit due for their part on Monday.

Of course all of Buell's army had to fight their way through "the horde of panic-stricken stragglers" that beset them at the Landing, and this might have misled s)me of them into the belief that it was the rebels who were there Sunday evening; but this could hardly be. And yet the pertinacity with which they cling to the "stragglers" is wonderful. Even to this day the first utterance of any of these men, if Shiloh is but mentioned, is "stragglers." But now one of them says he sternly invited them out to see *men* fight, as he fought them off from clinging to his skirts for protection. I don't know how many were drowned; but I can't tell how these "stragglers" could swim in the condition he describes them, when forced into the river, they so assailed him with their dismal cries for help.

It may be asked, were there no "panic-stricken stragglers" among all these gallant regiments of Buell's?

No, not one,—if you are to believe the official reports of his regimental, brigade and division commanders.

I will yet venture upon giving a little incident that happened immediately under my own eye. A very gallant regiment, that wanted to make a bayonet charge, moved forward in splendid style; but it "got a little squeezed," and came out at the first fire. No men in Sunday's battle were ever half so utterly panic-stricken. The agony of fear exhibited is beyond description. A perfect Babel of tongues—cries, groans—throwing themselves upon the ground in desperation of fear. The bugler was beset to make the calls to drown their cries, but he could not make a toot. In his vain endeavor he fell over against the root of a tree, exhausted by his effort. With contortions and cries that would have shamed the geese whose squall saved Rome, they were only recalled to consciousness by the peal of derisive laughter from our line that greeted this grotesque exhibition. Never was such a shout of boisterous mirth before heard on a battle-field. This ridicule alone enabled their Colonel to lead them off the field and away from danger, and hide them in the thick woods. They saw the enemy no more. You will say they were in disgrace, of course. No such thing. This regiment was as highly commended as were all others in official reports of the commanding officers.

I happened upon this same regiment next morning, in passing. It was drawn up as on dress parade. Its length of line would have excited the envy of any Colonel in the armies, and it was composed of good, rugged, soldierly looking men too, and they were evidently well drilled. Probably most of them had been accustomed to military drill from their youth, and may have seen service. As I passed by, their Colonel, with tears in his voice, was talking to them "like a Dutch uncle." From the hasty glance I cast along his line, I judged his reproaches had little effect. All the posthumous glory in the world was as nothing to being where they were—in capital condition, equal to their rations any day. Contrition? No. Indeed I rather expected to hear them shout in chorus: "He that fights and runs away, lives to fight another day."

The Colonel of this regiment was a brave man, a brilliant officer, and a genial, kind-hearted gentleman, but I could not altogether suppress a smile when my appearance, like Banquo's ghost, suddenly interrupted the recital of "hair-breadth 'scapes by flood and field" that was being poured into the ears of the loyal governor's representatives, who had come from home with congratulations and good cheer. He looked "Thou canst not say I did it." He had his reward. These men fought well and faithfully afterwards, and the incident is given here simply to show that "the panic-stricken stragglers" belonged to both armies alike, and was the exception, as were the panic-stricken men of Grant's army, who had far greater cause.

Apropos to nothing, the hero of the Franco-German war, Baron von Moltke, scorned making a comparison between the fighting qualities of his finely-drilled troops and "the undisciplined mob" that fought four years for the preservation of their country—and conquered a peace. Query: Did Louis Napoleon's malign influence so utterly demoralize the French nation, or were his generals subsidized by influences similar to those which governed an exceedingly small number of ours?

Buell's army was composed of.as brave men and gallant soldiers as wore the uniform. But the malign influence at their head overshadowed and crushed them. General Buell, with his arrogance, could no more comprehend what was due to brave men who had voluntarily come out to fight their country's battles, prompted by patriotism alone, than he comprehended what true loyalty to his government meant. His troops had been marched up hill and down so long, that the first fight, —like the first baby, always wonderful,—human nature could not be expected to resist blazoning their achievements to the world in all the splendor of the newly risen sun.

The battle over, the immense number of wounded required an army of surgeons. Many young doctors, among others, were sent from home to help care for them, and, with the best intentions, their want of practical knowledge left much to wish for. One was reminded of a synod, conference or other gathering of church dignitaries, where the wise old heads performed the work, and left the fledglings to put on airs—to be petted by, and amuse themselves with the ladies.

A day or two after the battle, I went on board a steamer filled with wounded men. Very many of them were wandering aimlessly about over the boat, presenting ing a most ghastly appearance, their wounds having been tied up hurriedly, the blood and grime of battle being left to be removed at a more convenient season.

It had been the understanding that the boat was to leave with its living freight at an earlier date. I do not now remember why it was detained. The floor of the cabin was filled with those most dangerously wounded, lying on pallets. Among these I found my friend and fellow townsman, Colonel S. S. Bass, of the 30th Indiana, who told me that his wound had not as yet been examined by a surgeon. He was cheerful, and felt confident that in a few weeks he would again be fit to return to his regiment. I questioned him particularly, and examined his wound. He pointed out where he thought he could feel the ball, and said if the surgeon would cut in there it could be easily extracted; that done, he would soon be well again. While not sharing his hopes fully, I talked cheerfully, telling him he could take a furlough of some months for a less hurt. Our last meeting had been on the battle-field, on Monday afternoon, when he, at the head of his regiment, passed through our ranks to engage in the final struggle of the day. He now told me that he had received his wound very soon after entering the fight, had ridden off the field, and had been taken by ambulance to the boat where he then was. After some time spent with him, I left him, with the promise that if it were possible to find a head to the boat, he should have a state-room, where he would be more comfortable. He did not share my hopes of success in this endeavor. I hunted over the boat in vain for one in authority. The invariable answer from subordinates and others attached to the boat was: "The state-rooms are all filled; there is no room for more; we are doing all we can." "Where are the surgeons?"   "I can't tell; you will find them somewhere about."   I returned to my friend, who smiled at my heat and indignation, and silently pointed to his fellow-sufferers.   After a little while a young doctor came into the cabin, looked along the rows of prostrate forms, moved down the space between them, occasionally stopped, removed a cloth from a wound, replaced it, and moved on.   When he came to Colonel Bass he made a more decided stop.   Daintily removing a cloth as large as my hand, he looked at the wound a moment, and replaced it without a word.   To my inquiries he replied that he was not in charge—that some one else (giving the name) would give the needed attention soon—thought it impossible that a state-room could be had—and passed on.   After doing all that was possible to supply his wants in every way, I left Colonel Bass, telling him I would bring one of our surgeons to examine his wound and *demand* a state-room.   He thought it hardly worth while—that he would get along all right when he got to Paducah.   After some unavoidable delay I found our surgeon, Dr. Martin.   When we got back to the Landing the boat was gone.   But a few days after, I heard of his death at Paducah.

Our surgeons devoted themselves to the care of the wounded day and night, without thought of self, the consciousness of doing their duty alone supporting them through their labors.   Soon after, Surgeon Rerick's health gave way.   When I saw him in an ambulance, completely broken down, being conveyed to a steamer, I said to myself: "That is the last I shall see of our brave surgeon."   But no.   He returns, a mere skeleton in appearance. I could not greet him as cordially as he so richly merited, for thinking: "Why *did* you come back here to die!" In this I was mistaken, however. There are yet, I hope, many years of work left for him to do.

I feel inclined to give here some extracts from a few of the many letters of prominent citizens of Fort Wayne, giving the estimate held at that time of the services of the Forty-fourth.

"APRIL 22, 1862.

COLONEL REED,—I feel like tendering to the 44th my hearty thanks for the glorious part taken by it in this battle (Shiloh) and the Donelson fight, by which every citizen of the county and the district has been honored. When I think of the peril of our cause and our Government, indeed, at Pittsburg Landing, and the narrow escape we made only through the bravery of our troops, I am almost overcome with emotion. It may be unmanly, but I confess to you that I have shed tears of joy * * * my heart melts with gratitude to the brave men * * * and with gratitude to God, who overrules all, for the heroism with which they received and withstood the shock of the traitorous hosts. I can understand now better than ever before why it is that military heroes are so honored by the majority of men. It is right. It is honorable to our human nature that men who leave their quiet homes * * * and place themselves in the breach, and save their country by exposing themselves to such danger as this, should be honored."

Another:

" Indiana soldiers generally have a proud reputation throughout the country, and I think it is no exaggeration to say the 44th now stands No. 1 of the list. With pride I recall all their unprecedented deeds of heroism in the late battle. With tears I mourn the sacrifice of so many heroes. All honor to the living and dead."

Yet one more :

" * * * I will embrace it, to return to the noble 44th. My most sincere thanks for the distinguished service rendered in the terrible battle of Pittsburg Landing. It was a terrible ordeal that you were called to pass through; but, thank God, the officers and men showed themselves equal to the emergency. The praise of the regiment is in the mouth and upon the tongue of every man, woman and child in the county. * * * The 44th ought to be recruited, * * * but all seem fully impressed * * * that going into the service means something more than being dressed in uniform, drawing rations, and living in a tent. * * * The return of quite a number of your wounded men serves to give an inkling of the stern realities of war."

Enough. " Those scraps are good deeds past—forgotten as soon as done." *Ita est.*

I shall have to leave the other side of the medal covered until a more fitting opportunity for singing the praises of " the martyred General " Milligan and his ghostly heroes, drilling by starlight, with traitorous thoughts intent—nor fife nor drum to quicken their steps and aid their fast-oozing courage while marching to the music of the wind—start in alarm at the watchdog's honest bark. Hist ! What's that ? Away ! The moon is up ! Scatter ! Where are these heroes now ?

I would gladly, if time and space permitted, dwell at more length upon the scenes that cling to memory with a halo, from contrast with excitement of a different kind. Pittsburg Landing presented the most stirring appearance. The eyes of the Nation were directed to this one point. Immense crowds flocked hither from all over the broad land. Steamers loaded with all that our army craved, from our long abstinence from civilized comforts, were pushing their way through those already there, crowding the river fuller with shipping than New York harbor at the busiest season. When a fresh arrival was sighted there was a rush to be the first to board her, to secure the longed-for prize, either eatable or drinkable. What a scramble I made over the decks of a score of intervening boats, accompanied by Major Stoughton, Captains Williams, Heath, and others, to be the first to reach the deck of a steamer just arrived on the outer line of boats—the objective point a barrel of lager ! The "charge of the light brigade " was tame in comparison. *We* had the advance, and our charge successful,—and it cost dear—in cash. We bore off in triumph two half-barrels, which were on tap as soon as the bank was reached, and drunk to the health of all good fellows by the men of the Forty-fourth fortunate enough to be present. A toast to our wounded recalled us in time. The second cask was at once hurried off, and reserved for their benefit. Whose pen can describe the difference in taste of *that* lager and the glass you deliberately walk up to the counter—drink—and lay down five cents ?

I have failed to relate at the right time an incident which has a place in my recollection, and I will give it here. One day, while we were yet at Camp Allen, a splendid war-horse, caparisoned to correspond, was led into camp. My courage, like Bob Acres', oozed out at the palms of my hands as I looked upon him, but I had to face the music. The charger was presented in due form, as a fitting testimonial, etc., etc., from my friends, Hon. Samuel Hanna and Samuel H. Shoaff, Esq., of Fort Wayne. How I ever got through the trying ordeal is more than I can tell; but to mount and display him to the gaze of the admiring on-lookers was the feather that broke the camel's back—impossible.

When at Donelson, my friend Surgeon Martin had a fine large black horse, that he very much wished to have wounded in battle. As I did not want my horse shot, I yielded to his solicitation, and exchanged horses with him for the time being. His horse was not shot; while mine, in the excitement attending our first battle, was ridden about so furiously that my orderly, Andrew Jackson Strohl "Dad," "resigned" on the spot, when the horse was delivered to his care. With tears he swore the horse might go to the devil,—and he did.

In giving my recollections as I have, without definite plan, or giving to them other consideration than I do while writing, I find that many incidents long forgotten come back to memory, which I should like to relate if space permitted. As we go forward in life, our earliest impressions grow brighter as we recede from them.

Just now, what transpired while we were yet at Camp Allen stands out as on printed page. Our lamented Lieutenant-Colonel, Baldwin J. Crossthwaite, to whom the regiment owed the proficiency it acquired in drill, returns to life, and is before me in plain view while he marshals his regiment in the intricate evolutions so imposing to the uninitiated. He had served as officer of cavalry in the Mexican war, and was an able tactician, whose knowledge of the details of army life was of the greatest benefit to us. He had brought with him from Mexico a disease that would have prevented most men from attempting service again, but his patriotism led him to disregard his own comfort and health; he chose rather to sacrifice his life in his country's cause. He died at his home in Angola, while our guns were thundering at the gates of Donelson—a fit requiem for so true a soldier and patriot. His memory is cherished in the hearts of the brave men who honored him for his many virtues.

The Hon. Charles Case had represented our district two terms in Congress. He used all his large influence and ability in the furtherance of his country's cause. He took the position of Adjutant of the 44th, to fit himself, by actual service in the field, for higher and more important duties. In pursuance of this, he soon accepted a position on the brigade staff. His health gave way, from exposure at Donelson; and while at his home on sick leave he was commissioned Major of a cavalry regiment, and soon after was commissioned Colonel of the 129th Indiana.

Our Chaplain, Dr. Green C. Beeks, at the time of his acceptance of the chaplaincy, was presiding elder of Fort Wayne circuit. As an eloquent preacher his prominence gave him much influence, which he used in the enlistment of men for the regiment. Having been formerly a practicing physician, his knowledge and skill rendered his services valuable at all times. He was with us at Donelson, and devoted himself energetically to the care of our wounded. He accompanied the regiment to Pittsburg Landing, was taken sick on the way up the river, and sent to the hospital, thence to his home, where he lay at death's door for many months. His health was so much impaired that upon his return to his regiment he found himself unequal to the duties of his position, and resigned his commission and returned to his home at Fort Wayne.

George W. McConnell, Esq., of Angola, Steuben County, was a gentleman of high standing, who accepted the position of Quartermaster of the 44th, and used his best efforts for the good of his country by devoting himself to the health and comfort of the men of the regiment with untiring zeal. Upon our getting fairly under way in the field, he resigned his commission, in February, 1862. He is remembered with the kindliest feelings of regard by all.

But I must hurry on. I find that I have more than filled the space allotted me, and I much fear that, in traveling over the same ground as our Historian, I have been repeating what has already been far better rendered. I wish much to add a short chapter on the "Siege of Corinth," and then bid a long farewell to the "Iron Men" of the 44th Indiana.

CHAPTER V.

General Buell had not forgotten us, and did not fail to reclaim the regiments of our brigade. I was ordered to report to him, which I at once did in person. I found him a solidly-built, soldierly-looking martinet of about 5 feet 7; shoulders well back, breast thrown out, head erect—in feeling, an embryo Napoleon. I was referred to his chief of staff, and by him directed to report to our former division commander. General Thomas L. Crittenden was a true Kentucky gentleman, every inch a soldier—plain, straightforward and unpretending, his only thought being to do his whole duty to his country. He esteemed every brave man as a friend and comrade. I have known of his telling his chief of staff that he deserved to be shot, for marching his troops an unnecessary long distance on a blistering day, the hot southern sun heating our rifles so as to be almost unbearable to the touch. His sympathies were with the men, to whose care and comfort he devoted himself without stint. Himself and family were looked upon with the warmest feelings of regard by all his soldiers. They moved amongst us like the patriarchs of old, their presence giving a home and kindred feeling to all. In battle he was a Saladin,—with his only child—a boy of some seven years—on his horse behind him, he would have cut his way with his good sword through a host.

General Buell took exceeding good care to provide for us a brigade commander after his own heart. General Von Blank was a West Pointer. A man of sedate and sober aspect, exceeding tall and gaunt; his length of leg greatly out of proportion to the trunk—dangling about, when mounted, in a supple-jack fashion. His face was small and sharp, his lower jaw receding; but his prominent, peaked chin made amends for this evidence of indecision. To be soldierly, he chewed tobacco in a feeble way. His eyes were small and faded, gray in color, and covered with large, gleaming spectacles. When he looked at you while speaking, your mind was so distracted by trying to decide to what to compare him, it was difficult to understand what he was saying. As he ambled around on his fat horse, he was as a whole an object fearfully and wonderfully made up. The "boys" very irreverently called him "Old Double Eye."

He had, from some sort of conscientious scruples about fighting, as he said, resigned his commission in the army rather than take part in the Mexican war. Afterwards his conscience had given him so many twinges for dishonoring his country's draft for the debt he owed it, that he had resolved to wipe it out now,—and here he was, in all his glory. It goes without saying, that he was an immense tactician, but his specialty was "orders."

He soon set himself about organizing a school for the instruction of his Colonels in all the lore he had imbibed. An order was promulgated that each and every Colonel appear at brigade headquarters at 7 P. M.

sharp. This, as a matter of imminent peril, was discussed in committee of the whole. One of the Colonels had in other days commanded a brigade. He felt the indignity deeply. To be called upon to attend school—and night school at that—and be put through his paces by this "slab-sided dotard." was a little too much. Another of the Colonels had for years "taught the young idea how to shoot." To be thrust back into a pupil,—would see him d— hanged, first ! The other two, being of more pliable natures, and not having had the same advantages, reported as directed. The General, with imposing deliberation, opened school by placing himself at his camp desk with book in hand, and demanded what we knew of the recusants. We smoothed down his ruffled mane with assurances of their presenting themselves on a future evening. We soon got in accord when we found the General relied upon his tactics entirely, and was easily led to read the whole question and answer to us. Our report led the other Colonels to reconsider their determination, and we presented ourselves in a body. The General's digestion was at fault, probably,—after a time he propounded a difficult problem that we professed our inability to demonstrate, and asked that he would expound for us. The General looked wise, adjusted his glasses, read, but could not find the right place—commenced again, got confused, blundered. School closed. Other duties prevented a re-opening.

On April 22, 1862, we left our camp, where we had so long remained, and around which so many memories clustered, and moved forward three miles and reported to General Crittenden. From this time forward we were almost constantly in front and on picket duty, and skirmishing with the enemy, changing camp almost daily, constructing roads, cutting down timber, building bridges, throwing up entrenchments, etc., had but a tithe of which been done while we were doing nothing but waiting for the enemy to attack us at Pittsburg Landing, our position would have been impregnable, while now there was as little use of all this wasted labor, our heavy picket line being three to four miles in advance, and almost continuously fighting as the enemy were slowly driven back. When we had arrived within six miles of Corinth there was immense artillery firing ; heavy siege guns were got into position on eminences, and thundered away at space. The black-bearded, short and stout General P. would climb a tree or some other elevation, and with a field-glass at his eye scan the enemy's earthworks, six miles away, to decide whether a breach was made. This booming of big guns came to be á lullaby to which the men would fall asleep as quietly as a babe on its mother's lap. At other times we were called into line of battle half a dozen times a day, during which time there would perhaps be fierce skirmishing, as the enemy were gradually, inch by inch, driven back ; and at no time was there any good reason why we should not have moved forward to within point blank range of our siege guns and opened fire upon their works and at the town of Corinth, unless it might have been in deference to the wish of General Buell that the rebels should not be hurried too much. Almost every day afforded us the amusement of throwing up breastworks and skirmishing, while the rebels were making up their minds which way they should go.

May 30th we were on picket at an old log meeting-house on the main Corinth road, when explosions and dense clouds of smoke and dust within the enemy's fortifications indicated evacuation. I rode forward within plain view, could see no guns or troops, and returned and informed General Crittenden. Next day we occupied the camp of the 19th Louisiana, in Corinth.

June 4th we marched, with three days' rations in our haversacks, following the rebels' line of retreat as far as Booneville, Mississippi. We returned by way of Iuka, stopping here until June 14th, when we took up our line of march for Florence. We went into camp on the Tennessee River near Tuscumbia, where we spent some time, while our army was building block-houses and other fortifications, from Mississippi to Georgia ; thence to Athens, Huntsville, and to the Tennessee River at the corner of the three States of Alabama, Georgia and Tennessee, and went into camp at the junction of a little stream called Battle Creek with the Tennessee River, a few miles west of Chattanooga.

While on this long, weary march under the scorching rays of the southern sun—a cloud of dust following us by day, and all manner of creeping things to annoy us at night—the men would manage to pick up some crumbs of comfort, in spite of the surveillance of " Double Eye " or Don Carlos, who rode from rear to front with his staff, and did not fail to note any irregularities as he passed. One day : " Colonel, I see many

of your sergeants without their guns. Why is this?"
"They are in command of their companies." "Where
are the company officers?" "Killed or wounded in
battle." "They should carry their guns instead of a
sword." "Am I to consider that an order?" After
evading a direct reply for a time, he finally said "No,"
and passed on.

Among the hills and in the hollows, all over the
South, are ragged nooks where the scouts and "bummers" knew by instinct apple-jack, peach and bourbon
must grow, in the nature of things, and of course must
somehow be unearthed from its caché. Canteens were
very handy. If one was thirsting for a drink of water,
and asked one of the men for his canteen, he would
say, "Haven't any," and would call out for a canteen
of water to be sent to the front. After some delay
some one in the rear would pass forward his canteen.
When put to your lips for a good long drink, you would
sputter, cough, and grunt "Whisky!" If good, you
would finally become reconciled.

An army passing through an enemy's country *will*
have some of the good things, eatable or drinkable, if
there are any within five miles on either side of the line
of march. The unhappy man with a well-stocked cellar
on the line of march will go thirsty for the balance of
that year. I have seen men rush to a stagnant, swampy
mud-hole, get down on their stomachs, and drink water
that the horses would not touch.

One day, while halting, one of the men spied a baby
in a house near by. He was off like a shot, secured it,
and brought it out, and it was passed from one to an-

other, was caressed and kissed as never was babe before. The poor mother stood trembling, in an agony of fear lest it never reach her arms again.   On another occasion the sight of a baby raised a shout that caused its frightened mother to clutch it and run off and hide out of reach, and no persuasion could induce her to return with it.

On one occasion, when away down in Mississippi, Alabama, or some other God-forsaken place, when on half rations, fresh meat had grown to be one of the things that memory dwelt upon with longing.   A little party found a slab-sided land shark roaming the woods, and soon brought it down to fresh pork.   While in the very act, red-handed, the General pounced down upon them.   In passing I was hailed by his Adjutant, and taken to the spot.   The General stood aghast at the enormity of this breach of "orders," and went on lecturing the men upon the heinousness of the crime. I did not interrupt him, wanting time to think of some way out of the dilemma, but could find none, other than to charge back upon him the folly of expecting men with guns in their hands to resist such temptation, when living on half rations of "sow-belly and hard-tack." When ordered to prefer charges against the men, I bluntly refused, telling him that if he wanted it done he must do it himself—that I considered it an act worthy of commendation.   Whether the boys sent him a roast, and thus mollified him, I do not remember.   I heard no more of it, at all events.

Another time, after marching all day, a detail was ordered for guard duty.   Upon inquiry I learned that

it was to guard the house of a prominent rebel. I
directed the Adjutant to pay no attention to it. Some
hours after, the brigade Adjutant rode over to learn why
it was not furnished. I told him we came out to fight
rebels, not to guard their property. Of course the 44th
stood badly at court. Its Colonel was looked upon as
most insubordinate, and a good opportunity awaited for
his overthrow. I attended this same " court " on occasion, and saw richly-appareled secesh ladies drive up in
grand style—their coachman and courier in livery—
alight, present themselves to the commander of a Union
army, who bowed himself to the very ground—the
slightest intimation of their wishes a command to be
obeyed.

We remained for some weeks in camp at Battle
Creek, guarding the river—the rebel pickets on the
opposite shore.

Many incidents of interest, happening here, time
and space will not permit my dwelling upon ; but one
incident I will give. General Buell was by instinct, if
not by birth, possessed of all the *chivalry* of the true
Southerner. Within our camp was the residence of an
an officer in the rebel army. His family, living in our
very midst, were on intimate terms with the officers and
men of our army, and were fully informed of all going
on about them. Their slaves, cattle, horses, sheep and
all other property were guarded with scrupulous care.
The wife of this rebel officer, desiring to visit her husband, was, after some weeks, passed over the river
within the enemy's lines, by order of General Buell.
This lady was escorted by myself and others to the

river. She was undoubtedly expected by her friends on the other side. This took place while General Bragg was getting ready for his invasion of Kentucky ; and when fully prepared he marched his army north, leaving Buell to follow at his leisure—which he did, abandoning all of his immense line of fortifications and railroad bridges, for the benefit of our Southern brethren. Then commenced the great foot-race for Louisville, which was won by Buell, while Bragg was bagging the game on the way and capturing many thousands of federal troops.

After waiting at Louisville to reorganize, and for the large reinforcements the loyal North hurried to his aid— while Bragg and his army overran Kentucky—at length Buell leisurely moved his army into the neighborhood of the enemy, but carefully avoided giving battle.

When we reached Perryville, Bragg forced a fight with a portion of our army, and a whole hecatomb of lives of brave men was sacrificed—for what ? Let Don Carlos Buell answer. He was not even aware, for some hours, that there was a battle in progress; which might possibly indicate that Bragg ungenerously failed to give due notice of his intentions. Our division was within easy reach, and for hours in line of battle, awaiting orders to move forward into the fight. At last they came.

Away down in memory's depths I can see that chivalric Kentuckian, Colonel H——, move to the front of his brigade,—his face newly shaven, his long hair smoothly combed back from his martial brow, mustachios freshly waxed, and twisted into rat-tails on each side his face ; his chapeau-bras in hand, and with it gently beckoning forward his brave knights to the charge as he backed his caracoling steed with the skill and grace of a knight of old in list of tournament,—when lo ! the enemy were on their winding way in full retreat —the cravens.

We arrived only to find the battle-field strewn with the slain. Never was such a ghastly sight as was here presented—in cold blood to be called to look upon the slaughtered thousands—the enemy gone.

This was Buell's first and only battle. To him alone belongs the credit of this massacre. He was displaced from command, and compelled to render an account before a tribunal presided over by—*General Lew. Wallace.*

After some days wasted, we were ordered in pursuit of Bragg's retreating army, which was loaded down with the rich spoils gathered in his Kentucky raid. When we had overtaken him we could only skirmish with his rear guard as he was driven out of the State.

Here I must bid a final adieu to the 44th Indiana. My recollections have carried me far beyond what I intended or was expected, and I owe an apology for the delay caused thereby. I will close with a sentiment.

Here's to the men of the glorious old 44th Indiana. May their memory be ever green in the hearts of their countrymen—" May they live a thousand years, and their shadow never be less."

A LETTER

FROM COLONEL HUGH B REED TO HON. F. P. RANDALL, FORT WAYNE.

————•—•—————

HEADQUARTERS FORTY-FOURTH INDIANA VOLS.,
Pittsburg Landing, Tenn., April 1st, 1862.

Hon. F. P. Randall, Mayor, Fort Wayne, Ind.:

MY DEAR SIR,—Your very kind and welcome letter of the 20th inst. was handed me yesterday. Your commendations and congratulations, if applied to the regiment, are merited. It is certainly very gratifying to me to know that our efforts are appreciated by our friends at home.

We have not had full justice from the press—nor yet in official reports of commanding officers; neither does my own official report, gotten up under a constant demand for it every half hour, give a fair understanding of what we accomplished in this our first battle. I do not know how it was done, but another regiment is given the position the 44th Indiana occupied in the battle of the afternoon. We were in *advance* of the 11th Indiana when the 44th made its brilliant charge up the hill. As to the "supporting part," I never heard of it until I saw it in the published reports. The 8th Missouri being in advance of us, engaged the enemy first. We were exposed to the same bullets, however, and to get at the enemy I was compelled to change our position to the left of that regiment—one of the things, I can assure you, both difficult and dangerous to do in the face of a perfect hailstorm of bullets. It was successfully accomplished, however, and we charged up the hill in gallant style, cheering lustily.

Our charge was what started the rebels back to their entrenchments. At this time the 11th Indiana was yet in our rear and passing to our left. I do not mean by what I say to detract from other regiments, but to make plain our part and to claim what is justly our due. I very freely acknowledge that Morgan L. Smith

18

and the 8th Missouri deserve greater credit than any, as they had the advance, engaged the enemy first, and fought gloriously. To him and his regiment I give the full meed of praise. The 41th fought its own battles of the morning and afternoon, neither seeing nor receiving an order from any other than its own Colonel. Had either division or brigade commander been with us during the battle, we might not have been denied the justice we failed to get in their official reports.

It would afford me great pleasure to be able to comply with your suggestion to send you a fine secesh flag. I would most gladly do this, as a very slight return for the "old glory" you and the ladies presented us. I will bear it in mind, and make a dash for .the finest looking one when opportunity offers. Had we not been hurried off with such cruel haste from Donelson, after the surrender—scarcely given time to bury our dead or care properly for our wounded—I might have sent you the mementoes of interest you request; others carried them off. You will ask why we were thus hurried away. Well, perhaps because our brigade was first to march in and take possession of the Fort. The 41th, at the head of the column, marched through the ranks of the enemy to the river, and took possession of the immense stores of property captured. Whether we were too fast in doing this or not, I won't say. We had been ordered to make an attack that morning on the rebel works, and were all ready to march forward for this purpose, when news reached us of the surrender,—it was not official, and we marched on and took possession.

It looked very much for a time as if we would have to fight our way in. The enemy were drawn up in line of battle on each side of the road, with their guns ready to bring to their shoulders. Had any officer given the command, "Ready—fire," we should not have gone in without a fight.

While we were marching over the battle-field of the preceding day, and over the rebel entrenchments, I for the first time fully realized all the horrors of war. The ground was in many places strewn with the dead, many of them horribly mangled by cannon-balls. But this is the dark side of the picture; it had best be left covered.

I have already written a long letter, but have not yet done what I started out to do. I wish to give some account of the battle of the morning, this being the first time we were under fire—especially the part performed by company officers and men —so that should I not return to tell, they may have some little portion of the credit due them. I wish this, because of not having given it in my official report, for reasons already stated.

Captain Murray, Co. B, of Pierceton, left wing, fought gallantly. His fire was well directed, and did much execution when repulsing cavalry and infantry attacks. Co. B deserves high praise. Captain Murray is an old soldier—was in the Mexican War and in the regular army. He says he has been in a number of battles, and never saw a better fought one. This company was much exposed, and lost heavily.

Captain Cuppy, Co. E, of Whitley County, was very dangerously wounded in the early part of the action, while in advance of his company. He is as dauntless as a lion. Nothing but a bullet could put him *hors de combat*. He is yet unable to return to his regiment. His 2d Lieutenant, McDonald, was in command of his company the balance of the day, and did well. Co. E lost a number of brave men in killed and wounded.

Captain Bingham, Co. H, Lagrange County, was cool and intrepid. While we were waiting our chance at the enemy, and yet uncertain whether Colonel Logan's 31st Illinois regiment was out of range of our guns, he took our flag from where it had been placed in front of our centre, and carried it forward ten or twelve paces, to a prominent position, and waved it in the air. He was saluted with a volley. I expected each moment to see him fall, but he walked back unharmed. Both his Lieutenants were absent, sick. Co. H fought bravely and well.

Captain Tannehill, Co. C, of Fort Wayne, did his duty fearlessly. Prompt and decided, always kind and considerate, he looks to the welfare of his men first, his own last. This, our color company, occupied an exposed position and fought bravely. 1st Lieutenant Wm. Story was the first to place our colors ten paces in front of our line, that the enemy might know we were ready and our friends that we were there. 2d Lieutenant Philip Grund is as valiant as Hercules. He was detailed on other duty, but was not to be cheated out of the fight. He performed his part manfully, as did Sergeants Carman and Livingston. You will probably remember a freckled-faced boy of 16—Sam. Sweet, Co. C, son of Francis Sweet, and Tom Stanley, Co. D, son of Chauncey Stanley, who I thought, when they came into camp, had far better be at school; both of them stood their ground and fought like heroes—blazed away at the rebels as coolly as the bravest. They won their spurs, and are fairly entitled to a " well done, good and faithful soldiers," for present reward. A. P. Waterhouse, John Strong, Michael Harrison, William Woodford, Owen Shaw, John Keefer,

Fred. Stine, Wm. Hedges, Wm. Nodding, John Elzie, James M. Flutter, Wm. Henderson, Peter Stahl, Robert Stewart, Jos. Nicodemus, Frank Baldwin, Milton Sites, Marion McGinnis, Jacob Kress, Aug. Travener, Jos. Harsh—a little dumpling of a boy of 18, with a fresh, chubby face, (called "Chub,") a general favorite. John C. Dee was the very first to fall, while fighting like a hero, giving up his young life in defense of his country. All deserve honorable mention, as do many others, if time and space permitted.

Company I, of Elkhart County: Captain Heath is a Trojan, brave as a lion, prompt and wary, ever ready for an emergency, active and decided in fight or counsel. There is no better soldier than Captain Albert Heath. The more you know him, the better you like him; and his company partake of his qualities. 1st Lieutenant Hodges, though sick, was at his post, and did his whole duty nobly. 2d Lieutenant Curtiss is as steady and brave as one of the Old Guard; and Sergeant Mansfield, D. Belknap, B. F. Layton, and very many others, are of the same sort.

Captain Cosgrove, Co. D, of Allen County, is an intrepid soldier, cool and prudent, of much experience, having served in the Mexican War. In strategy he is an adept, and fought with valor and judgment. "You can tie to him." His 1st Lieutenant Wayne is as spirited and brave as his namesake, Mad Anthony. He will quibble over the ninth part of a hair in a bargain, and will give his last dollar to a friend in need. He is a good officer and a brave man. 2d Lieutenant, the lamented J. Delta Kerr, who died at Evansville, of typhoid fever contracted at Donelson—the bravest of the brave. Ever foremost in all that was valiant, his chivalric bearing won the hearts of all. Alas, no more shall he be with us on the march, or his kindly beaming face cheer our bivouac.

> "He sleeps his last sleep, he has fought his last battle,
> No more shall he waken to glory again."

Sergeant Geo. W. Schell, James Reed, Platt Squires, William Underwood, William Casebeer, D. McCord, J. McClellan, John Poppy, and John Trauger, deserve honorable mention, as do many others.

Captain Merrill, Co. F, of DeKalb County, was sick and unable to take much part. 2d Lieutenant Kinmont had command. He is a brave, determined soldier, did his whole duty, and is deserving of high praise. Sergeant Sol. DeLong is entitled to especial commendation for his coolness and intrepidity. He preferred to pick his man as a sharpshooter, and did execution. Alexander Kinmont, Sol. Kinsley, Thos. Sloan, Samuel Jacques, and others, did well. Adjutant Colgrove, first lieutenant of this company, performed his duty bravely during the entire day.

Acting Captain Sowers, Co. A, of Steuben County, is a good officer, cautious and "full of cunning fence," a dangerous foe, a great tactician. He has won his spurs,—may he wear them to the end. 2d Lieutenant Smith is a brave man and a good soldier. He fought valiantly, as did also Lewis Griffith, Samuel Tinsley, John Gilbert, Oliver Throop, John Ryan, and many others. Captain Kinney and 1st Lieutenant Rose, of this company, were both absent, sick.

Co. G, Captain Williams, and Co. K, Captain Aldrich, were unfortunately separated from the regiment, having been left at Henderson, Ky., to guard that post. They were highly indignant at being left behind, when the 11th stopped on its way down the Ohio, *en route* for Fort Henry.

Our Surgeon, Dr. Martin, deserves much praise. No man ever devoted himself more faithfully to his duties. His whole time was given, day and night, to the care of the wounded and sick.

Surgeon Rerick was in charge of the sick at Henderson and in hospital at Calhoun. The important duties of his position were never more faithfully and conscientiously performed. His whole soul is in his work.

Our Chaplain, Dr. Beeks, was detailed to take charge of the wounded and sick on board of the steamer to Paducah. He now suffers from the effects of his arduous labors in their behalf. He was taken sick upon his return to the regiment at Fort Henry, and refusing to go where he could have proper care, he came with us to Pittsburg Landing, but was unable to leave the boat. He returned to Evansville, and from thence was sent to his home at Fort Wayne.

If I could but give to each man of the regiment his due! This thing of being drawn up in line to be shot at—fizz—fizz—about your ears,—to look at the men while they stand waiting, waiting for the word *Fire!*—bowing with a most subdued air to the enemy's salutations—well, it was not comfortable. The Illinois regiment did get away (if they ever were in our front), and we did blaze away, and soon became so intent upon doing it that we were not aware that we had been left entirely alone, and the enemy attempting to surround us. We gave them a very warm reception, repulsed their cavalry and infantry attack, and withdrew slowly and in good order to where our other forces had taken up their position. The 11th was the last regiment engaged during the morning, and the very last to leave the field. I have already said we engaged the enemy in the afternoon, and drove him inside his entrenchments.

Now all this may not seem of sufficient importance to you, at this late day after the battle, to justify my leaving many matters you refer to unanswered. Nevertheless, I shall have to defer them for another occasion.

We are, as you say, pretty well down into Dixie, and I suppose we shall have a fight before going much further. But I will spare you. With kindest regards to Mrs. Randall and all the other ladies who helped with our flag,

I am very truly yours,

HUGH B. REED.

JOHN H RERICK,

SURGEON.

FIRST RE-UNION

—OF—

THE 44TH INDIANA VOLUNTEERS

AT KENDALLVILLE, IND.,

TUESDAY, APRIL 6, A. D. 1880.

On the 19th day of September, 1879, at a soldiers' reunion at Auburn, Indiana, the members of the 44th Indiana Volunteer Infantry, then present, met and formed a temporary organization, with Major W. B. Bingham as President, S. B. Sweet as Secretary, and Major J. H. Rerick as Biographer; and set April 6th, 1880, the eighteenth anniversary of the battle of Shiloh, and Kendallville the place, to hold the first reunion and perfect a permanent organization of the regiment.

On the early trains on that day members of the regiment began to arrive, and by mid-day upwards of one hundred had congregated. Now was witnessed a scene never to be forgotten by the participants. Comrades true, and brave men, long since parted, once more clasped each other by the hand with a spirit that betokened a friendship as lasting as life, heartfelt greetings were heard on every side, familiar faces brought to memory scenes and incidents long since forgotten, battle scenes were re-enacted, incidents on the march and in the camp were rehearsed. The enjoyment was at its height when the long roll was beat and the regiment fell in line under the old regimental flag they had so often followed to victory.

Under command of Major Bingham, the regiment, headed by martial music, marched to the depot to meet expected comrades on the east and west trains. On the arrival of the trains, the regiment, with augmented ranks, took up the line of march for the city. Arriving in front of the Hall, a halt was made, when Captain Cosgrove advanced to the front and center of the line with the old 44th flag, and proposed for it three cheers, which were given with a will that only old soldiers can appreciate.

Once more in the Hall, the meeting was called to order by Major Bingham, President of the temporary organization, after which S. H. Pierce delivered an address of welcome in behalf of the citizens of Kendallville.

The President then announced that Colonel H. B. Reed would not be present, being detained at his home in New Jersey on account of sickness.

The Secretary, S. B. Sweet, then stepped on the stage and read the address the Colonel had prepared to deliver in person. The address was listened to with marked attention, and at its conclusion the boys arose to their feet and gave three rousing cheers for Colonel Reed.

Colonel W. C. Williams offered the following resolution, which was adopted unanimously:

"That the Secretary, in behalf of the society, prepare and send to Colonel Reed a letter appreciative of their deep feeling of regard for him, his gallantry and devotion to the interest of the regiment while connected with it. Also their sympathy for him in his illness, which had prevented him meeting with them this day."

Several letters were read from absent members of the regiment, including a telegram from Colonel Philip Grund, all regretting their absence, and expressing a wish to be remembered by their comrades; each of which was applauded by the boys.

Captain S. P. Bradford moved that the regiment at once proceed to effect a permanent organization, which motion was adopted with cheers.

Major Rerick then presented a constitution for the consideration of the society. Several amendments were offered and added. After remarks on the merits of the constitution and for the best interest of the society, by Captain S. P. Bradford, E. O. Rose, Captain Newman, F. W. Willis, Nick Ensley, R. Lockwood, and others, the constitution was adopted as a whole, and reads as follows:

Constitution of the Forty-fourth Indiana Soldiers' Association.

We the undersigned ex-members of the 44th Regiment Indiana Volunteer Infantry, hereby organize ourselves into an association, and adopt for our government the following Constitution:

Article I.—Name.

Section 1. The name of this society shall be known as the 44th Indiana Soldiers' Association.

Article II.—Object.

Sec. 1. The object of the association shall be the holding of reunions of the members of the regiment, the renewal of acquaintance and friendship, also the preservation of the memory of the services of the regiment and the names of its faithful members.

Article III.—Officers.

Sec. 1. The officers of the society shall consist of a President, a Vice-President, a Secretary, and a Treasurer; also an Executive Committee consisting of one from each company of the regiment.

Sec. 2. Each officer shall perform the usual duties of his office, except the Secretary, who, in addition to the usual duties of Secretary, shall keep a record of the members of the society, also a record of all living members of the regiment so far as he may be able to obtain them, together with the post-office address of each.

Sec. 3. The President, Vice-President and Secretary shall also be members of the Executive Committee.

Sec. 4. The officers shall be elected at each regular meeting, and serve until their successors are duly elected.

Article IV.—Membership.

Sec. 1. Any honorably discharged member of the 44th Indiana Volunteer Infantry may become a member of this association upon signing the Constitution in person or by authorizing his name to be attached.

Article V.—Revenue.

Sec. 1. The President, Vice-President and Secretary shall constitute a Committee on Finance, and shall credit all bills and accounts presented to the association for payment.

Sec. 2. Each member of the association will be expected to contribute to the payment of the expenses according to the amount required and his ability.

ARTICLE VI.—TIME AND PLACE OF REUNIONS.

SEC. 1. The time and place of reunions shall be determined by the Executive Committee, and shall require the vote of five members exclusive of the member living at the place where the reunion is to be held.

ARTICLE VII.—DUTIES OF MEMBERS.

SEC. I. Each member of the association will be expected to inform the Secretary of all changes in his address; also of the decease of brother members of the society and of the regiment, not likely to be known by the Secretary.

ARTICLE VIII.—AMENDMENTS.

SEC. 1. This Constitution may be amended by a majority vote at any regular meeting.

____

After the adoption of the Constitution, the following officers were elected to serve the ensuing year:

President—W. B. BINGHAM.
Vice-President—J. H. RERICK.
Secretary—G. W. GORDON.
Treasurer—F. W. WILLIS.

Executive Committee—Company A.—LEWIS GRIFFITH.
                                        " B.—JOHN B. WALDO.
                                        " C.—SAMUEL B. SWEET.
                                        " D.—F. K. COSGROVE.
                                        " E.—SAMUEL HAVENS.
                                        " F.—ALEXANDER KINMONT.
                                        " G.—DAN F. JOHNSON.
                                        " H.—SAMUEL P. BRADFORD.
                                        " I. —D. L. BELKNAP.
                                        " K.—NICHOLAS ENSLEY.

Moved by E. O. Rose, that a contribution be raised to defray the expenses of this reunion and for the publication of the proceedings in pamphlet form, for distribution to the members; which motion was adopted unanimously.

Announcement was now made, by Amos B. Parks, that a free supper by the citizens of Kendallville was in readiness for the boys as soon as adjournment took place. The announcement was received with cheers.

After remarks by Major Rerick with reference to the forthcoming history of the regiment, the meeting adjourned to meet at 7 o'clock.

MEETING OF EXECUTIVE COMMITTEE.

During the adjournment the Executive Committee met and organized, when Major Rerick moved that the next meeting of the 44th Indiana Soldiers' Association be held at Fort Wayne, on Wednesday, February 16th, 1881, the nineteenth anniversary of the battle of Fort Donelson, being the first battle of any importance the regiment was engaged in. The motion was adopted unanimously, and so reported to the association.

EVENING SESSION.

Promptly at 7 o'clock the meeting was called to order by the President, and the following programme carried out :

1. Music by the martial band.
2. Historical record of the movements and marches of the regiment, by Major J. H. Rerick.
3. Song by the Glee Club—" John Brown,"—which was encored.
4. Address by Colonel W. C. Williams.
5. Address by Lieutenant E. O. Rose.
6. Song by the Glee Club—" The Red, White and Blue."
7. Remarks by Captain F. K. Cosgrove.

On motion, a vote of thanks was tendered the citizens of Kendallville for their hospitality; also to the Glee Club, and to Mr. Mitchell for the free use of his hall.

The proceedings of the day and evening were enlivened by martial music by three members of the old 44th band—W. T. Kimsey, John Kimsey, and W. H. Free—assisted by Messrs. Odell and Levi Hays, of Lagrange. Billy Free played on the same snare drum used at Shiloh.

Three cheers were then given the Mexican veterans, of whom four were on the stage, namely: Major W. B. Bingham, Sergeant N. T. Fuller, Captain F. K. Cosgrove, and J. Riddle—all members, also, of the 44th Indiana.

Much credit is due comrades Amos Park and Henry Park, who arranged the programme and superintended throughout, and by their kindness made the boys feel at home.

REPORT OF TREASURER, F. W. WILLIS.

Total Receipts of the Association ______________________________$22 25
Total Expenses of Reunion _____________________________________ 11 38
　　　　　Balance in Treasury _________________________________$10 87

On motion, adjourned to meet in Fort Wayne on Wednesday, February 16th, 1881.

F. W. GORDON,
SECRETARY.

MEMORIAL

TO THE

STATE LEGISLATURE OF INDIANA

ADOPTED

JANUARY 25, 1863.

THE undersigned, officers and soldiers of the Indiana Volunteer Regiments, submitting with patriotic self-denial to the policy which denied us a voice in the late elections, and approving the wisdom of that feature of our government which secures the civil from the influence of the military power, nevertheless desire to participate in the preliminary councils which are to shape the popular ideas of the State, and consequently to control the action of its representatives in the General Assembly.

We speak as soldiers, because our lives are staked upon the issues of the present struggle as citizens, because at no distant day those of us who survive are to share with you the responsibilities of citizenship, and to experience in common with the people at home the results of your present deliberations. Whatever prejudices may exist against any interference of the military in the affairs of State, certainly even the most vigilant guardians of the public interest could not expect the army to await with indifference the result of deliberations which involve not only the common interests of the people, but also the lives and fortunes of those who have taken up arms to defend the integrity of the Union in a contest with our common foe in the field.

Defeat strips the citizen of his fortune and his political enjoyment, the soldier of both these and his honor, and, it may be, his life. It requires no argument to convince an intelligent mind that a war sustained by a united people, and urged with that energy and determination which proceed only from undivided councils, presents a less fearful array of casualties, with a better hope of success, than a sluggish contest waged by a party and merely sustained by a wrangling of factions at home. In other words, it requires more lives to sustain a government hampered and restricted by the jealousy of a political party, than to sustain one supported by the voice of a united people. As well might you expect a fettered victim to struggle successfully with his untrammeled oppressor, as to hope for a nation to subdue its enemies when its energies are cramped by the unwise restrictions of a doubting majority. To live in spite of disease, every function must be characterized by the utmost vigor, and all unite against the common enemy, who seeks in the destruction of one the certain ruin of all. Believing, then, that as soldiers we have a deeper interest in the great struggle than you can possibly have as citizens, and, further, that the influences of military life have not unfitted us for the high duties of citizenship, we present ourselves before your honorable body as petitioners without apology.

We come boldly, asking only what we have a right to expect, either as citizens or soldiers, battling for the integrity of the Union.

We ask simply that you will give this war a cheerful and hearty support; that you will strengthen and energize every department of government; that this unhappy struggle may be pressed to a successful termination; that you will pour out the treasure of the State as your soldiers have poured out their blood on the field of battle, to aid in the holy cause of restoring the Union of our fathers; that you will abstain from heated political discussions and violent party wranglings, until the authority of our government is once more established; that you will resist the infernal spirit which would waste victory in humiliating compromise, or render temporary reverses a pretext for the alienating of an offending community; that you will sacrifice every thing except liberty and political equality, to national integrity; that you will sustain all the officers of the State and general government in their efforts to subdue this unholy rebellion; and especially that you will sustain our worthy Governor, whose every energy during the past two years has been so entirely devoted to the cause of the government and its supporters. We appeal to you especially to sustain him for the reason that it is chiefly to his unceasing care and labor, exhibited in arming and supporting the troops of Indiana, that we have to attribute our present proud position among the loyal States of the Union; and for the further reason, that he has demonstrated by his acts that he is an earnest and zealous patriot, devoting his time with untiring energy to the glorious cause for which we are battling.

We appeal to you as our Representatives, to encourage him in the good work of ministering to the wants of our unfortunate comrades, who have been stricken down in the strife of the battle-field, and by the cruelty of relentless disease; that you will confer on him all the necessary authority and place in his hands the requisite means to carry on the good work which he has begun, remembering that one human life is worth all the treasure of the proudest State.

In conclusion, we propose the following resolutions be adopted by the Legislature of Indiana, and to constitute the basis of all their acts bearing upon the interests involved in the foregoing address.

1. *Resolved,* That we are unconditionally and determinedly in favor of the preservation of the Union.

2. *Resolved,* That in order to the preservation of the Union, we are in favor of a vigorous prosecution of the war.

3. *Resolved*, That we will sustain our State and federal authorities with money and supplies in all their efforts to sustain the Union and prosecute the war.

4. *Resolved*, That we discountenance every faction and influence tending to create animosities at home, or to afford consolation to our enemies in arms, and that we will co-operate only with those who will stand by the Union, and by those who are fighting the battles of the Union.

5. *Resolved*, That we tender to his Excellency, Gov. O. P. Morton, the thanks of his grateful friends in the army, for his extraordinary efforts in their behalf, and assure him that neither time nor the corrupting influence of party spirit shall ever estrange the soldier from the soldier's friend.

———

HEADQUARTERS 44TH REGIMENT INDIANA VOLS.,
Camp at Murfreesboro, Tenn., Jan. 25, 1863.

This is to certify that the members of the 44th Regiment Indiana Volunteers, on dress parade, being formed into hollow square, and the above preamble and resolutions being read in their hearing, and the question put that those in favor of them would shoulder their arms, every gun was raised. Upon calling upon those who were opposed, to shoulder arms, no gun was raised. There were then proposed three cheers for our *glorious* State and State officers, which were given in a manner indicative of Indiana soldiers.

S. C. ALDRICH,
Lieut. Col. Com'd'g 44th Ind. Regt.
W. W. MARTIN,
Surgeon 44th Regt. and
Brig. Surgeon, 2d Brig., 3d Div.
JOHN H. RERICK,
Assistant Surgeon.
GEORGE W. CARR,
Assistant Surgeon.
J. C. HODGES,
Adjutant.
NELSON A. SOWERS,
Commanding Company A.
MARVIN B. BUTLER,
Acting 1st Lieutenant.

JOSEPH BURCH,
> Acting 2d Lieutenant, Company A.

JOHN GUNSENHOUSE,
> 1st Lieutenant, Company F.

I. N. THOMAS,
> Acting 2d Lieutenant, Company F.

JAMES COLLIER,
> Acting 1st Lieutenant, Company D.

G. W. SHELL,
> Lieutenant Comm'd'g Company D.

DAVID K. STOPHER,
> Acting 2d Lieutenant, Company D.

JAMES CURTISS,
> 2d Lieutenant, Company I.

WILLIAM S. STORY,
> 1st Lieutenant, Company C.

PHILIP GRUND,
> 2d Lieutenant, Company C.

HIRAM F. KING,
> Acting 1st Lieutenant, Company H.

DANIEL P. STRECKER,
> Acting Lieutenant.

WILLIAM HILDEBRAND,
> 2d Lieutenant, Company E.

S. J. COMPTON,
> Company E.

JOHN S. WILSON,
> 1st Lieutenant, Company K.

N. S. BENNETT,
> 2d Lieutenant, Company K.

JAMES C. RIDDLE,
> Acting 1st Lieutenant.

M. W. McMURRAY,
> Acting 2d Lieutenant, Company G.

JAMES S. GETTY,
> 1st Lieutenant, Company B.

WILLIAM SHERBURN,
> Acting 2d Lieutenant.

These are all the officers present of the 44th Regiment Indiana Volunteers, Colonel Williams being taken prisoner in the late battle.

> SIMEON C. ALDRICH,
> Lieut. Col. Com'd'g 44th Regt. Ind. Vols.

NOTE.

As the kind assistance rendered in the preparation of the preceding pages was rendered mostly after the Preface was in print, it is due that I should here make expression of sincere gratitude to Colonel Hugh B. Reed for his very interesting contribution under the title of "Personal Recollections," for the Shiloh battle scene, and much other valuable assistance; to all who contributed plates for the personal illustrations; to Sergeant George W. Gordon for the use of his published letters, "Life in the Ranks of the Forty-fourth Indiana"; to Samuel B. Sweet, and others, for aid on the Company records: and to R. H. Rerick for the map. Thanks to all.

I could find no record of the names of the killed and wounded at Chickamauga, which accounts for this omission.

The following errata are noticed: On page 193, in the record of Captain Danseur, for "Shiloh" read *Stone River*; on page 138, in the record of Surgeon Martin, for "Indiana" read *Maryland*; on page 137, for "Rev. George W. Beeks" read *Rev. Green C. Beeks*; on page 43, for "4th brigade" read *3d brigade.*

Two typographical errors are noticed on page 43, where *preceded* is made to read "proceeded," and *probably* to read "probable." There may be other like errors, but these and all other imperfections I must now submit to, and trust to the charitable consideration of my old comrades.

THE AUTHOR.

CONTENTS.

CHAPTER XIII.

CHAPTER XIV.

CHAPTER XV.

CHAPTER XVI.

CHAPTER XVII.

PERSONAL MENTION.

PERSONAL RECOLLECTIONS.

By Colonel Hugh B. Reed.

CHAPTER I.

CHAPTER II.

CHAPTER III.

CHAPTER IV.

CHAPTER V.

LETTER FROM COL. REED TO F. P. RANDALL.

FIRST RE-UNION OF THE FORTY-FOURTH.

MEMORIAL TO THE INDIANA LEGISLATURE.

ILLUSTRATIONS.

9 783337 118778